The Judas Field

The Judas Field

A NOVEL OF THE CIVIL WAR

———◆———

Howard Bahr

HENRY HOLT AND COMPANY
NEW YORK

Henry Holt and Company, LLC
Publishers since 1866
175 Fifth Avenue
New York, New York 10010
www.henryholt.com

Henry Holt® and 🅷® are registered trademarks of
Henry Holt and Company, LLC.

Copyright © 2006 by Howard Bahr
All rights reserved.
Distributed in Canada by H. B. Fenn and Company Ltd.

Library of Congress Cataloging-in-Publication Data

Bahr, Howard, 1946–
    The Judas Field : a novel of the Civil War / Howard Bahr.—1st ed.
        p.   cm.
    ISBN-13: 978-0-8050-6739-2
    ISBN-10: 0-8050-6739-6
    1. United States—History—Civil War, 1861–1865—Fiction.   2. Southern
States—Fiction.   I. Title.

PS3552.A3613J83   2006
813'.54—dc22

                                                        2005055011

Henry Holt books are available for special promotions and premiums.
For details contact: Director, Special Markets.

First Edition 2006

Designed by Meryl Sussman Levavi

Printed in the United States of America

1   3   5   7   9   10   8   6   4   2

For Patti and Joseph

Now this man purchased a field with the reward of iniquity. . . . And it was known unto all the dwellers at Jerusalem; insomuch as that field is called in their proper tongue, Aceldama, that is to say, The field of blood.

ACTS 1:18–19

The New Country

C ASS WAKEFIELD WAS BORN IN A DOUBLE-PEN LOG cabin just at break of day, and before he was twenty minutes old, he was almost thrown out with the bedclothes. The midwife, Queenolia Divine, heard him squalling, however, and so it was that Cass, blue-faced and complaining, was untangled from the wad of bloody sheets and saved for further adventures.

The first light he saw fell on the northeast corner of Yalobusha County, Mississippi, in a cleared place among ancient oaks and hickories and sweetgums called Lost Camp. By the time Cass was born, the frontier had passed the village by, and the westerly road was busy with travelers. Ox-drawn wagons filled with bewildered women and children groaned and creaked through the settlement, the men riding beside with long rifles laid across their saddle bows. Soon Texas beckoned with the Possibility that always burns so bright over a revolution. Captain David Sansing—he was not a real captain, but he *seemed* like one, so that is what they called him—left early, invited by Sam Houston himself to join the fray. The balance of the Lost Camp men—including Cass's daddy, John, and his uncle Estes Burke, and the elder Wakefield brothers, Augustus and Rome—formed a company, twenty-three men, which they called the Yalobusha Yellow Jackets. With a retinue of Negroes for the camp chores, they rode away to fight for Texas independence, promising to return in glory with land grants that would make them rich. As it turned out, they never returned at all. They got lost on the way, and six of them died of fever before they got out of Arkansas. The rest found Texas finally, but before they could lift a hand in its defense, the Mexicans captured them and shot every one, even the Negroes, at Goliad in '36.

Months later, the Memphis post-rider appeared in Lost Camp accompanied by a wagon. In the bed was a wooden crate bound with tin straps and tight as a cedar skiff, lettered "General Delivery, Lost Camp, Yalobusha County, Mississippi." The post-rider was in a bad humor, for the box swarmed with flies and sugar-bees and had a musky smell about it. The women and children and old men gathered about under the oaks, and it was decided to let the post-rider open the box in the presence of them all. The man's crowbar grated as he prized at the lid.

All his life to come, Cass could remember the smell that

burst from the opened box when the lid fell off. The people lurched back, and some of them ran away. The women set up a keening, grabbing at one another, at their children. One went mad on the spot—they were never far from madness anyhow. The old men, after a while, laid them out in the sun: twenty-two yellow roundabouts trimmed in red, smeared with blood, and punctured with ragged, smoke-rimmed holes where the musket balls had entered, then left again on the other side.

Cass's mother, Prudence, recognized the stitching in the jackets she had made. She sat in the dust, took one up, and pressed it to her face while Cass stood by, trying to understand what it all meant. Prudence, her eyes dry, her voice steady, made it plain to him. She said, "Your father is dead, and your uncle Estes, and Rome, and Augustus." Cass knelt beside her, in the hot dust that swarmed with fleas, and spoke in the language he had learned early from the men. "I will see to it, Ma," he said. "I will find them who did this, and you will have your—" But he never finished, for Prudence slapped him hard across the mouth, another lesson learned, then drew him to her hard and held him and the jacket both so close that Cass lost his breath and could not have cried had he wanted to.

At first, no one could imagine who had done this thing, and all wondered what happened to the twenty-third jacket. Certain ones began to look to Estes Burke.

Cousin Sally Mae Burke was the first girl Cass ever fell in love with, and the first, but not the last, to discourage him. Sally Mae's mother, Diana Maria Velez, was a Spanish woman who gave her daughter eyes and hair and skin that might have suggested Mediterranean twilights to the Lost Camp lads, had they known of such. Sally Mae Burke strode among her pale

Anglo-Saxon neighbors, tossing her black hair, scorning the boys, especially Cass, and igniting the girls with jealousy— teaching them all (and quick they learned, and early, for life was often short) what it meant to be beautiful. Many were the miniature fights Cass Wakefield fought to defend his cousin against boys who loved her, were rejected, and thus grew bitter in their learning. "Nigger girl" they called her, and "Greaser," and other things, while the girls, learning their own ways, shut her out with cold silence.

On the hot afternoon when the jackets came, the people of Lost Camp forgot, if they ever knew, the distinction between Spanish and Mexican. A single thought, born of whispers by night, ran through the settlement.

Next morning, just after daylight, a crowd of women stormed up the road to the Burke cabin. It was a mob of despair, all the women red-eyed from crying, their hair in disarray, some with suckling babes, intent to revenge themselves on the Mexican. The madwoman came tottering behind, tearing at her hair, her mouth a dark oval. Prudence Wakefield counseled reason and was shouted down. Annie Frye counseled reason, but she had lost no one and so was scorned to shame. Cass Wakefield ran beside the column, among the packs of barking dogs; he cried for his cousin, pulled at the women's faded dresses, at last was cuffed into the roadside ditch by a hand that might have petted him once. Young Alison Sansing, toting her baby brother, discovered Cass there. They held tight to one another and wept while Perry squalled for milk.

The women found voice in the yard. Prudence and Annie moved among them, pleading, touching hands and faces, all futile, for someone had to carry the blame. The women shook their fists, held up their infants in accusation, cried terrible things from throats grown raw with weeping. They cried foolishness, how Burke was spared because he had married a Greaser. His was the lost jacket, they cried. He was a coward and betrayed the rest, they cried, for this was what had come to their minds as reason. They shouted until their voices were harsh, but received only silence in return. The cabin was empty; Diana Maria Velez, with the foresight common to those who are different, had vanished with her daughter in the night. The women burned the cabin anyway.

No glory or riches, then, for the widows and orphans of Old Yalobusha, nor even anyone to bury among the cedars. They learned months later, by home-traveling men, that the Mexicans had burned all the bodies, including Estes Burke's, way out yonder in the Land of Promise.

Cass's mother went to work at Frye's Tavern, cooking and cleaning and serving meals to the people filling up the new country, who came with slaves and cottonseed to make riches in the Leaf River bottoms. Times were flush then, and Lost Camp became a Land of Promise all its own. Meanwhile, the widows married again, and new ground was cleared at such a rate that, in a few years, a tree was hard to find anywhere but along Leaf River or in the cemetery.

Prudence Wakefield did not marry. She scorned her few suitors, who were tubercular or crippled anyhow and could find no prospects among the more robust women. In any event, Prudence and all her suitors, and a good many wormy children and broken-down old people, were struck by the scarlet fever of

'44, as if Providence had decided to tidy up the place once and for all.

The fever came in a warm November, a season of drizzling rain, low clouds, deep mud, when the sun, the moon, the stars seemed to have deserted the heavens. The prosperous holed up on their farms, where they died just the same, or fled north into Tennessee. Smudge fires burned day and night on the square, blanketing the town in a dingy gray pall meant to drive the miasma away. The Presbyterians owned the only bell, and it tolled constantly to keep the atmospheres stirred. Every day, droves of blackbirds came from their roosts along Leaf River, and more crows than anyone could remember. Dogs roamed the deserted streets, licking at the mud, and the wheels of the dead-cart creaked through the nights.

Cass's mother lay dying in a room above the tavern. All the boarders had fled, and the place groaned with emptiness. Only Mister Frye and his wife remained, and their black girl, Queenolia Divine, who changed the sheets and emptied the bedpan until only gravelly vomit was left to empty. Miz Annie Frye did the cooking right on the hearth, spooning broth between Prudence Wakefield's cracked lips, around her swollen tongue.

Once, Prudence said, "Leave. It will come on you, too, if you don't. Take the lad and go."

"Why, Prudy," said Mister Frye, "you don't really want that, do you?"

"No," she said. Her eyes were hot and glittering. "I can't stand the thought of bein' alone."

"Then don't think it," said Mister Frye.

So they stayed, all of them, in the close loft smelling of bile and wood smoke, and of their own bodies, while the rain hammered at the shutters. The clocks had long since wound down, and Mister Frye did not bother to wind his watch, so time was only light and dark, passing almost imperceptibly, one to another. By night, Miz Frye read Psalms aloud by candlelight, but only the pretty ones, and over and over again the story of the woman at Jacob's well, for Prudence loved to hear about the living water and the dauncy girl with all her husbands.

Meanwhile, Cass sat by his mother's bed, bathing her face or listening to her voice ramble through other times, among people he did not know. Now and then, she clutched his hand tight, her eyes moving, watching some shadow pass before her. "I am so sorry," she would say to someone in the shadow. "I am so sorry." At such times she wept.

Sometimes, when she was sleeping, Cass left the tavern and wandered along Town Creek, going down to where it joined the little river Leaf. The living water went its way, slow and indifferent; only the birds seemed interested in his passage. He felt aloneness like a physical pain, and now and then he would call on God to see if He was anywhere around. No answer ever came that he could tell.

On the last day of Prudence Wakefield's life, a minister came by: a little round man with half-spectacles who rode the Hardshell Baptist circuit. The regular Baptist man was gone off somewhere, the Methodist and Presbyterian shepherds were dead, and the mission priest had yielded up the ghost among his scattered flock down on the Natchez Trace. So here was the circuit rider in his muddy boots and clothes, come to ease the soul of the dying woman.

Evening was coming on, and the gloom in the loft was

thick, even with a candle burning. The minister took the dying woman's hand. "Sister," he said kindly, "what's on your heart?"

"I am grievin'," said Prudence, her voice no louder than the hissing of the fire. "I am afeard. I have not done well in most things. I want to . . . make confession."

"Open your heart to the Lord Jesus Christ," said the minister. "Bring your sins to Him."

"I done that," said Prudence.

"And what did He tell ye?" asked the minister.

The dying woman thought a moment. "I . . . well, never nothin' in words. But *you* can say 'em. I want to hear *you* say 'em."

"I can't speak for the Lord," said the man.

"Yes, you can," said Prudence. "I want . . . I want you to tell me I am goin' to heaven."

The minister leaned forward in his chair. "Well, Sister, have ye been . . . bip-*tized?*"

"A long time ago," said Prudence. "By the old church in Albemarle."

"Ah," said the minister. He laid her hand back on the counterpane and leaned back in his chair. "Romish?" he said.

"English," said Prudence.

"The same," said the minister. "*Sprinkled,* I reckon?"

"That was our custom," said Prudence.

The minister leaned forward in his chair once more. "Well, that is the custom of false teachers," he said. "Ye must be bip-*tized* in the way of Jesus. Ye must be buried and raised agin."

Cass began, "She told you once already—" but Mister Frye laid a hand on his shoulder.

The minister said, "Woman, will ye be bip-tized in the way?"

Prudence Wakefield's eyes were bright with fever, and a little flame of her fear leaped up in them. "It says once is enough," she whispered.

"It says true," answered the minister.

"I fear goin' down in the cold river."

"Then I can make no promises," said the minister. He stood up then, scraping the chair back. "Hit's a narrow gate," he said.

"Now, wait a minute," said Prudence. She held out her hand; it trembled in the space between them. "You promise me I'll go to heaven. You *say* it!"

"I won't say it. I *can't* say it. 'Less you be bip-tized in the way of the Lord Jesus Christ—"

Cass shook off Mister Frye's hand and moved against the minister. He closed his hand on the man's sleeve. "My ma is afeared," he said. "You *tell* her."

The man shook his head sadly. He looked at Prudence. "You best get your heart right," he said. "You best get ready. Hit's a long time in hell."

"Get out, sir," said Mister Frye.

The minister shook his head again and looked at them all. Then he was gone, clumping downstairs in his muddy boots.

"Don't you be worryin', Prudy," said Annie Frye. She took the dying woman's hand. "We'll all meet by the river one day and listen to the angels sing."

"Well, I don't know," said Prudence. "I don't know."

Cass left the tavern and walked blindly through the foul, smoky afternoon until he came to the river. He could hear the trees rattling and the soft chuckle of the water as it moved over a tangle of fallen logs. He looked up at the yellow sky smeared by a ribbon of smoke or cloud. "Is that the best You can do?" the boy said. "Ain't it enough You are takin' her? You had to send that man to punish her too? What did she ever do to You?" He listened, but of course no answer came. "What did she ever do to You!" he cried, but heard only his own voice echoing off the clay bluff.

⁜

That night, Cass woke from a troublesome dream. He had been among some trees by a dark shore, where a great bird visited him. He could hear it coming a long way off, then all at once it lit high in a spindly oak. There it stirred, restless, a black shape among the branches. Cass woke with the rustling of the bird in his ears. The room was hot, the window a pale square of starlit clouds. The fire was licking at a new log and made a dancing light on the walls.

"Ma?" said Cass. He listened, but no sound came from the bed. He understood then. He could not imagine God, but Death was another matter. Death was always in evidence among them; he had a smell, a substance, that followed him. Cass knew he had been here, had passed his wing over Prudence Wakefield and taken her soul away. He was about to rise when something fluttered on his chest. It had no weight, but he could feel it resting over his heart. He thought it might be a chimney sweep—the little birds got inside sometimes. Cass raised his head and saw, on his bare chest, a moth, wings outspread, eyes glittering in the firelight. The warm weather had brought it out, or the heat of the room, perhaps. When Cass moved, the moth fluttered aloft and batted against the pale square of the window. Cass could see the dust from its wings floating in the firelight.

"Ma," he said again, and rose from his pallet and peered into the low bed. At that moment, the moth flew again from somewhere, straight into the flames on the hearth. Cass heard it sizzle and pop, though he could not see it. He touched his mother's hand and found it cold. He took it anyway and held it until dawn, when Mister Frye arose and prized their fingers apart.

"Let her go, lad," said Mister Frye. "Let her cross."

"Do you think she was afeard?" said Cass.

Queenolia was there then, and enfolded the boy in her strong black arms. "Yo' mama won't afeard," said the woman. "She was all right when she heard the angels come."

But Cass knew it was no angels that took her away. He looked to the hearth and the glowing coals; they moved and glittered, but the shell of the moth was nowhere among them. Then he went to the window where the dawn was growing and put his hand against the cold glass. He pushed the palm of his hand against the glass until it broke, drawing blood. Annie Frye came to him, wrapped him in her arms, told him that his mother was peaceful now, in a better place. Cass wasn't listening. He watched the blood drip from his hand and cursed God—silently, for he had not the words.

They lit candles at his mother's head and feet, and Queenolia washed the body. Cass and Mister Frye dug her grave among the cedars. They had no coffin, so Miz Annie fixed a winding sheet of her good table linens, and in this way Prudence Wakefield went into the earth. It was cold now, and their breathing made wisps of fog in the air. In a drizzling rain, they struggled

with the heavy spadefuls of mud until the grave was a low sodden mound, the rain already cutting rivulets in the mud. The
fresh-turned earth seemed to have a light of its own, so that it
glowed among the gloom of the cedars.

"We'll plant some periwinkles in the spring," said Annie.
"It'll look some better then."

Mister Frye, splattered and caked with mud, squinted at
the sky. A big flock of blackbirds was streaming over, going to
roost, and the sight filled Cass's heart with a new measure of
sorrow, until his cup runneth over, as the Psalm said. Then he
looked over Mister Frye's shoulder. Huddled in the branches of
a big cedar was a redbird, bright against the green. It was the
only one Cass had seen all winter, and it watched him now
with its quick black eyes.

"Pray, Annie," said Mister Frye. "Pray for her, if you
would."

Miz Annie nodded and folded back her shawl. Queenolia
did the same, and the two women stood with the rain streaming down their upturned faces. When Miz Annie lifted her
voice, it was steady, mostly. Forever afterward, Cass wished he
could remember what she said. But he did remember this:
when she was done, he looked at the cedar again. The redbird
had flown.

The Citadel

❖ 1 ❖

THE CITADEL OF DJIBOUTI STOOD ON THE OLD SITE OF Frye's Tavern, in a yard barren of grass even in deep summer. This Christmas eve, cigar smoke swirled in wraiths around the blackened lamp chimneys. A wood fireplace blazed and crackled at one end, and a stove burned red-hot at the other, but the drafts were numerous, and the few patrons sat around with their coats and hats on. Not even the drafts, however, could clear the place of a generation's tobacco smoke and the smells of fried meat and spilled beer. Under the floor, a dead tomcat smoldered in decay; the patrons knew it was a cat, for L. W. Thomas had told them so. Other, more subtle smells lingered: the residue of hard times, of tired and sweated men, some of them gone forever, some of them here now.

L. W. Thomas himself leaned on the bar, a toothpick in the corner of his mouth, reading the *Police Gazette*. Two country men discussed in whispers the recent murders along Yellow Leaf Creek, where a family were butchered in their sleep. A pale, malarial man wrapped in a greatcoat paced before the hot stove, shivering, arguing with a woman who was not there; who, in fact, had been dead since the previous summer.

In a corner, Cass Wakefield, trifling drunk, leaned back in his chair, fingers laced across his waistcoat, feet propped on Thomas's old black dog, which lay beneath the table. In the chair opposite, Lucian Wakefield, his head cradled on his arms, slept his restless, dreamful sleep.

Cass would like to be someplace else, but there was no place else. Certainly the house on Algiers Street where he and Lucian lived would be no improvement. Still, they had to go home sooner or later. Cass said, "Lucian," and poked at the boy. (Lucian was thirty-three, but Cass still thought of him as a boy.) Lucian made no response, but the dog stirred resentfully under the table. Thomas folded his magazine and slapped at a fat winter fly, of which there were a good many in the tavern due to the cat down below. This was Christmas, then, in the Year of Grace 1884. In most details, it resembled last Christmas, and, in fact, every one since 1865. Cass leaned back in his chair again and thought of the shepherds who watched in the fields of Bethlehem on the first night of Our Lord. They were lonesome, dirty, homesick, trifling drunk maybe, with no idea that soon they would be at the center of a holy hour, witnesses to time in its shifting. Then the angels came from on high and changed everything. Cass wished some angels would show up at the Citadel of Djibouti, but he considered that unlikely.

"Lucian," he said again, and this time the boy looked up. "Merry Christmas," said Cass.

Lucian blinked and rubbed his eyes. He was thin of face and body, and his hair was shot with gray, and his clothes seemed to hang off him.

"It's a fresh new day," said Cass.

Lucian peered groggily about. "I do not see that it is so God damned fresh."

Cass had to agree. He could remember little of the year behind, only a blur of filthy railway coaches, tired hotel rooms, dim saloons, worry, emptiness—and the year ahead seemed to offer no other prospects. In this sacred hour, he could remember no single good thing that had happened: not to him, not to Lucian, not to L. W. Thomas, not to anyone else he knew. It was a God damned sacrilege, he decided, to be unable to remember any single good thing. Something was bound to happen, some change that would set them right. Cass pushed his chair back and walked to the bar.

L. W. Thomas said, "What's the matter with you?"

Cass propped his foot on the rail. The smoke burned his eyes, and he rubbed at them, feeling the grit. "I'm damned if I know," he said.

Thomas said, "Well, I will tell you. It's Christmas eve. On Christmas eve, a man feels real good, or he feels like owl shit, and there is no in-between, and the choice is not yours to make. There you have it."

"Right," said Cass. All at once, the smoke and heat and whiskey—and the various smells of the tavern—began to dizzy him. He felt sick, felt as if he were falling into a deep black hole. "Right," he said again. He lifted his hand to Thomas and turned, moving quickly. Lucian was asleep again, but Cass dared not stop for him. He stumbled through the door, shut it behind, and made it to the porch railing before he lost his supper.

Cass waited until the cold air cleared his head before he risked movement. A lantern hung smoking and guttering on the doorjamb, the globe blackened so that it offered no light at all. Cass turned the wick down until the flame went out, then looked around at the windless night. The world was illumined by starlight, shrouded in the moon. He went down the steps and for a moment stood dazzled in the middle of the barren yard. All across heaven were the strewn stars burning. Across the road, a grove of cedars huddled like fat mourners. If you stared long enough, they seemed to move, one of the tricks of night.

He set off down the road, trying not to look at the cedars, for they always reminded him of the Stones River battle, where the field was full of cedars, brittle with ice. At Stones River, the cedars had broken up the line, and the blood on the grass was frozen like some strange confection. At last, he came to the first street lamp on the square and stood under it for a moment to consider the scene before him. He had forgotten the Christmas tree on the courthouse yard; it was ablaze with candles now, and people were gathered around it singing, their voices rising to the stars. Others were coming from church, walking by families, the children glad to be up so late—for some, this was the first midnight they had ever seen abroad—and glad for Christmas. Presently the courthouse bell began to toll, and all the bells in all the churches, and the bells of all the switch engines in the yard, and the sawmill whistle blew.

Cass did not care to join these revelers. Their easy joy was oddly repulsive to him, the thought of idle conversation unbearable. He slipped behind the buildings on the east side, where it was dark and quiet. The alley was full of rats, busy among ash bins and garbage, but they paid him little notice. Orion was climbing over the cotton gin, the icehouse, the ramshackle houses of Negroes—over the dark buildings behind which Cass moved in shadow. Finally the buildings ran out, and the mud of the alley flowed into the deeper mud of the Pontotoc Road.

He stopped and waited while a dray horse and a slide went by. The driver stood on the slide with his reins, and around him sat a dozen children bundled to the eyes, singing of Good King Wenceslas. One of the children saw him and waved; Cass slipped back into the darkness and perched on a barrel of ashes and let them pass, and watched others pass homeward, and listened as the bells died away one by one. Finally the streets were empty, quiet, the street lamps burning for no one—but still he did not cross the Pontotoc Road.

He fell asleep presently and was a little on his way to freezing to death when Lucian appeared out of the shadows. Lucian, too, had come through the alley, though no one was left on the square to see him stumbling drunk, muttering to himself: a thin, angular man with a drawn face, scarf thrown over his shoulder, hat askew, with ragged gloves and muddy breeches like some minor character in Dickens. Cass woke shivering to the sound of breaking glass—Lucian had thrown a bottle at the rats—and saw the boy lurch past, then stop at the edge of the road, where he stood swaying, moving his hands.

"What are you doing?" said Cass.

"*Jesus* H. Christ," said Lucian, and turned so quickly that he fell backward into the mud. He sat up and fumbled at his coat pockets a moment, then looked at Cass. "What you mean, scaring me half to death?"

Cass climbed down from the barrel, slowly, for the cold had stiffened him. He found a bottle and smashed it against the bricks. "Go ahead," he said. "Cross the road, chicken shit."

"Fuck you," said Lucian. "I don't want to cross it."

Cass threw another bottle. He found he liked the sound of the breaking glass and the way the rats scurried. "You are God damned pitiful," he said.

Lucian wiped at the mud on his black frock coat. He rose to his knees and pointed up the road. "Something is coming," he said.

"All that is over with," said Cass. "Now, get up." Cass put out his hand, but Lucian knocked it away. "Lemme 'lone," he said, and scooted behind the ash barrel.

"What are you doin'?"

"Lemme alone," said Lucian. "I am stayin' here till daylight."

"You are not," said Cass.

"My brain hurts," Lucian said. "My brain is going to explode." He pressed his hands to his head. "Stand back 'less you want to get splattered."

"Lucian—"

"I won't cross that road till daylight, by God," said the other. He drew his pistol and cradled it in his lap. Lucian always carried a pistol, as Cass did, and most of the men in Cumberland.

"Suit yourself," said Cass. He went down the alley and collected an armful of old rags, scrap lumber, a half-filled can of kerosene. He built a fire in an old coal scuttle, a good, hot blaze. The boy had fallen asleep. "You are a God damned idiot," Cass told him. Cass dragged the boy close to the fire, then sat down against the wall to wait the coming of day. In a little while, he grew bored and began to shoot at rats with his own pistol, which woke up Lucian, who also began to blaze away at the rats. Presently, they shot a possum that wandered by. The noise was deafening in the closed space of the alley. As they were reloading, Lucian said, "Cass, something has got to happen."

"You mean like angels descending from on high?"

"I don't know what I mean," said Lucian. "Only, something has got to happen." He thought for a moment. "I got to feel something, or I will die."

Cass said, "It is better not to feel anything." He aimed and fired and missed his rat. The creatures did not seem to mind being fired upon, but went on as usual.

"That is only the whiskey talking," said Lucian.

Presently Mister Will Casper, the constable, appeared with orders to cease and desist. Cass argued that everybody fired pistols on Christmas eve.

"Well, it's Christmas morn now," Casper said, "and all decent people are abed, and we will have no more shooting." Casper had a jug, however, and the three of them used it to pass the time until the sky began to lighten. They talked about frying up the possum for breakfast. It wouldn't be the first time.

✢

The bells woke her. The courthouse bell, church bells, locomotive bells, all tolled midnight, heralding the Christ child. She thought of what the old ones said about the cattle; how, at this hour, they would kneel in reverence in their pens and stables. She thought of the railroad men stopping their work to listen; children abed, sleepless, listening; birds bowing their heads; the scattered stars for an instant winking brighter. The bells pealed across the cold, vast night, brushing the rooftops, the fields, and the barren woods beyond; she could believe, in that moment, there was no meanness anywhere, except that she was dying.

The bells ceased after a time, and the silence closed around her. She held to it, and to the darkness, as sacred things. She burrowed under the featherbed, drew her legs up, and floated in the darkness, counting back from the hour. Fourteen hours since Doctor Culver Craddock said, "I will offer no vain hope. I reckon you are strong enough to stand the truth." Truth was what he gave her then, and she was strong enough anyway to go on sitting upright. She even let him take her hand—good Doctor Craddock, who in forty years, since he came to Cumberland, had never misled her. She knew he was right, of course, but knowing was not the same as believing.

Alison Sansing was not afraid of dying. Everybody had to do it. People went on and on about birth and what a miracle it was, but it wasn't any miracle; it happened every day, every hour; no living thing, not even the least, came into life without it. Death was the same. A little jolt and you woke again, like waking to life, and there were all the myriads who had gone before, waiting for you. *That wasn't so bad, was it?* they would say.

Father, brother—they would be there, loosed from the sorry, rain-filled grave where Cass Wakefield had laid them long ago. She would see them all again. Everything that had happened, all the years without them, would be forgotten, burned away like the fog on Leaf River winter mornings.

No, not forgotten, she told herself. The fog was made more beautiful by its passing, like flags in the spring; like the last drone of cicadas in a dying summer; like the brief yellow of hickories, the purple of sweetgums, in the fall. You loved most the things that passed away, that you couldn't hold to, no matter how much you loved them.

Not long after the war, some well-meaning soul had given her a popular book about the afterlife. In the book, all the dead were happy, the terror of life forgotten. They were gathered in a green, shaded garden scented of lilacs, drinking tea, and chatting, pausing now and then to welcome a new arrival likewise pink and new, carrying no baggage. She wondered how the author, never having been dead herself, could know these things. And what did the dead, without memory, have to talk about? In any event, she had read only a few pages, then thrown the book away. If heaven was nothing but tea parties, she would just as soon not go. And if the terror was forgot, so too must be the good, fine things that made living bearable, that made you want to stay.

Nothing, not even hell, could be worse than forgetting

what you loved. *Maybe that's what hell is,* she thought. *Where the soul is only itself, lost, and no marks to navigate by.*

She had tried long ago to imagine the violence that came down on Father and Perry, and she wondered if they remembered it and how it would seem to them. She had given up trying after a while, for nothing in her experience, nor even in the soldiers' telling, could frame it. Cass told her once, swore to her once, that they felt no hurt, that Death came quick among the smoke when the blood was up and all reason vanished. They felt no hurt, Cass said; flesh and blood gone to vapor, mind and heart to spirit, all whisked away before pain could reach them. Cass was sick that day he sat in her front room, his hat on his knee, and told her how they could not have suffered. His hands shook, his face was still pale and thin, and he could not keep still but sat and paced, sat and paced again, up and down the stifling room that smelled of ashes and dust. Father, brother— they had lived well and died with honor—Cass promised they had died with honor. He paced through a slant of August sunlight, while she sat with hands folded, listening to his sad voice. He said how, after the battle, he had seen them put in the ground side-by-each with only a board to mark their resting, in a muddy backyard near the place where they fell. *It was pretty bad,* he said. *I will not lie to you.* She believed what he said then, and believed it still.

She drew tighter into a ball under the featherbed, ran her hand up and down the shanks of her legs—still pretty, the hair and skin still soft, though she could feel the veins. She could smell the glycerin and rosewater on her hands. With her fingers, she traced the little swell of her breasts, probing for the knots. "How long till I believe *this?*" she asked aloud.

The lamp had long since guttered out; the jalousies were closed; the fire on the hearth was only a dull red blur. In the shadows of her room huddled the comforting shapes of wardrobe and dresser, chair and table and washstand. The world was in order, hushed and peaceful, with nothing to harm.

She knew she would believe when the pain started. Doctor Craddock had given her a bottle of Black Draught for when it did; she had put it deep in the cedar chest in the attic. He had given her some quinine, too, to thin her blood, because she demanded it.

Through the flannel nightgown she could feel the knots, felt soreness but no real pain. They were just clots, was all—nothing to be upset about. She had taken a big spoon of quinine before bed, and already the knots were smaller, she thought. The doctor had said, "Maybe in Memphis, maybe in New Orleans—"

"What?" she demanded. "What could they do?"

Culver Craddock wiped his brow, though it was cool in the cluttered room where they sat. "They have surgeons," he said. "They can . . . they could remove—"

"No," she said, disgusted by the notion. "No, I will not have that."

Now, in the quiet room, she began to cry again. She prayed to Saint Agatha. "Protect me," she said to the darkness, where a vision hovered: the martyr's severed breasts presented on a charger while a serving girl wept and caught the blood in a winding sheet.

"Then I don't know how long you will have," said the doctor, though she hadn't asked. She saw the pain in his eyes and hated him for it. "When it's time, you can come here," he said. "I will watch after you." As if she had no kin, no friends.

Well, she had no kin, that was true. Her mother and baby sister were buried in Alabama before the journey to the new country. She remembered dimly her mother's face, her voice a comfort in some forgotten darkness. The sister, stillborn, she never knew at all. The rest were far away in alien ground—she could not imagine *Tennessee*—hidden from the light, with nothing to mark them but a board torn from a paling fence.

Still, she had plenty of friends who would watch with her. The women, the ones who had been through the war, could bear it; otherwise, grief would have killed them long ago. Some had died of it—Perry's betrothed, poor child, had lasted a year—but the strong ones bore it, watched the seasons pass, the months and years spool away, until they learned that grief was too much of a coward ever to kill them. A coward, a thief, a murderer of children—but they had stood it.

Grief had done no noble thing by Alison. It had not strengthened her, as well-meaning people often predicted, nor did it bring her closer to God; that was for people who blamed Him for their troubles. She had always been close enough to God to satisfy them both, and anyway she had seen for herself that He was present in hell as much as in heaven—maybe more, for He always went where people needed Him the most.

But what if He asked for a tally? God had given her four-and-fifty years, a reasonable span. Yet, though she had done the best she could, she had little to show for it—an old maid living in her father's house. "I never wasted it!" she insisted to the dark. And if she had, it was not her fault, for grief had accomplished this much, at least: it barred the door to every possibility and closed her away in a room alone. Outside her window, beyond the tight-shut jalousies, lay a world she knew little

about, save that her people had gone there long ago and never
returned. She had lived with that fact, accepted it, since the
letter came from Franklin. Beyond that, she had done nothing.
Was that what she would tell the angel at the gate?

The pain was what she feared the most, more than death,
more than judgment. She told herself, *I will make it their pain—
Father's and Perry's. I will bear it so they didn't have to.* Still, the
thought of it, the cancer spreading like foul black water
through her veins, the smell that would drive people from the
room—she had seen it in others, had stood it herself when nobody else would. Sally Mae would stand it, and Morgan
Harper, but not the men. They couldn't stand anything. The
thought of it made her cry, not in fear, but in anger that they
had all cheated pain but her.

She pulled the cover from her face and wiped her tears. She
breathed the cold air. She touched her throat, felt the blood
pulsing there. Blood and breath were all she needed to prove
she was alive. No, not all, she thought, for even the blind worm
could claim those things. Some other proof was needed: an act
of will, of movement, to demonstrate that what she had lost
had not subdued her, that she was worthy of the life remaining.
She had thought about it a long time, had wanted it a long
time, but never dared to believe she could do it. It was the one
thing she had asked for herself but never given.

When the town cemetery was first laid out, her father
bought an ample section and ringed it with young cedars and a
fence twined with iron vines and berries brought all the way
from a foundry in Nashville. The cedars were tall now; they
threw too much shade, and the grass would hardly grow, and
the fence was rusted. For twenty years, whenever she walked

through the cemetery, she had lingered by the fence among the drowsing cedars and considered that plot of empty ground. The ones who should be there—father and brother—had never come home, and others who might have preceded her—husband, in-laws, a child perhaps—had never entered her life to leave it. When she stood at the fence, she had no one to grieve for but herself. She always thought she would tell the undertaker to plant her right in the middle and order a big pedestal with a weeping angel so she wouldn't be alone: a single, preposterous grave that people would show their visiting kin and say, "Now here is Alison Sansing, a lonely old woman, never wed, a tragic story . . ."

Yet, now and then, she had given herself to imagine something different. She had always said that people had more choices than they allowed themselves, and the gift of Possibility was greater than most people had courage to grasp. It was not always truth that set you free, for some truths were strong as prison walls and offered no chance for freedom. Rather, it was the power to imagine and the heart to make a truth of your own. Thus she would think, in the pale twilight by the iron fence, that maybe she did not have to be satisfied with truth. Father and Perry were dust—that was true—but even dust could be brought home, whatever remained of them that she could call her own, that could be laid to rest in the place where they belonged.

The courthouse bell rang the half hour, a single note drifting out over the town and dying away. She listened until it faded, and then she heard the clock on the mantel. The chime must have wound down, but not the mainspring. She listened, holding her breath, thinking it might stop at any moment, but it went on, ticking softly, and then the little *chunk* where the chime should have been. *Running slow,* she thought, and smiled at the ordinary thing.

She flung the featherbed aside, crossed the cold floor to the jalousies. She stood there, afraid and doubtful, with her hand on the latch. She had never told anyone of the thing she wanted. Instead, she had kept the possibility in her heart, and it had sustained her for a long time, even if she could never really believe in it. Well, now she had to believe. She would die—the day and the hour were practically laid before her—and compared to Death, every task that Life could offer seemed easy and small. *Why not, then?* she asked herself. The question hung in the cold air like the voice of the bells, and, after a while, like the bells, died away.

She opened the shutters. Her neighbor's house was dark, the town sleeping—all but an old hunting owl who queried from the oak tree by the road. Looking up, she saw the stars fading. She knew they were traveling toward morning, as she herself must be. She had tomorrow, then, and a few days after. That would have to be enough.

❖ 2 ❖

TWO BRICK CHIMNEYS FLANKED COLONEL SANSING'S old house, each lifting a narrow plume toward the gray underside of heaven, filling the air with the odor of burning coal. Nearly everyone had grates now, and Cass Wakefield usually paid the coal smoke no mind, but this afternoon, as he stood before the house, it made him think of St. Louis. He could not have said why, but the vision drifted back to him across the years: the sloping levee crowded with boats, ice on the river, the grimy red-brick faces of the buildings, and the smell of coal.

Cass Wakefield was a pilot of steamboats once, before the war when the river was booming. He was a soldier once, too,

and once a husband. He had done pretty well by them all—
save the last, he supposed. Since the war, twenty years almost,
he had traveled for the Colt's Patent Fire Arms Company of
Hartford, Connecticut—a handgun drummer, purveyor of
home protection and personal defense. He had done well
enough that he didn't have to travel much anymore, filling orders by telegraph and the new telephone for customers from
Vicksburg to St. Louis. A woman of his acquaintance once
asked how he could bear to look at guns, knowing as he did
their sole purpose. Cass agreed that it was contrary to good
sense and order, but the fact was, he liked guns. He liked to
shoot, too. He could punch out the ace of hearts at fifty feet
with any Colt revolver, a skill he hadn't known about when he
went to work for the company. He hadn't been much of a shot
during the war, but then, he hadn't used a pistol either.

Cass would be fifty-five in August, though he might have
passed for a younger man, so lean he was, and all his brown hair
still present for duty. He had all but four of his teeth, and his
hands were steady, his eyes still sharp except for close-up work
like playing dominoes, writing, filling out orders, perusing the
labels of patent medicines. Then he had to use reading glasses,
which he was always misplacing. He had to hunt for a pair so
he could read the note from Alison Sansing, the small, careful
hand on good paper delivered yesterday, which had brought
him to this corner in the January afternoon.

He had the feeling that time was gaining on him. In the
last year or so, his mustache had gone mouse-gray, and a
paunch was growing amidships where there had been none before. That was a mystery, since he rarely ate and took no pleasure in it when he did. Sometimes the sight of food, especially

in abundance, made him sick. Sometimes he was afraid to eat lest the hunger come again, which he knew to be illogical, but there it was. Yet the paunch grew, straining against his waistband. Well, let it strain, was his reaction. He was not about to have his breeches let out.

Lucian had the same problem with food, fried meat in particular. Worse, since just after the war, the boy was visited by headaches that blinded him but made him see visions. For these he took laudanum, sometimes paregoric, and sometimes smoked a plant the Negroes called Injun Weed, which was really cannabis.

Cass wore a bowler hat, a muffler, a suit of houndstooth wool, the pants correctly hung over white spats and shoes streaked with the mud of January. He carried a walking stick and, in a custom-made pocket of his coat, a blued .38 Colt Lightning (one of his best sellers at $19.95, including cleaning rod, brush, and oil can). In his waistcoat, at the end of a thick silver chain decorated with a Masonic fob, lay the big Howard watch his uncle Lewis had left him. The porcelain face was cracked and fretted now, but the delicate blue hands still measured precisely the innumerable hours. Cass was aware of its weight in his pocket, and he could hear it ticking in there, so he thought.

Colonel Sansing's house, where Alison had lived alone since the war, wanted paint, but so did all the houses in Cumberland, Mississippi. It needed new gutters, too, and someone to trim the hedges and scrape the grass from the brick walk and repair the rotten fence. In the yard were the composted leaves of twenty autumns, the latest drained of color now under the white oaks that shed them. A trifling wind stirred among them so that they moved like the ghosts of birds, though the clouds aloft were motionless. Cass felt the stillness around him, the emptiness of the winter afternoon when the streets off the square were vacant, the trees barren, the birds hushed, and the smoke seemed the only living thing. The cold reached deep inside him to the place where he used to fear it, where he feared it still in certain moments of awareness. He was safe from the cold now, of course; any time he wanted, he could cross the street to Alison's parlor where it was warm. Yet Cass did not move, as if to flee might taunt the cold, encourage it, spin him back to some place from which he could not escape so easily. Such a notion was silly, he knew, but his memory was like one of those moving picture machines in the city arcades. If he wasn't careful, somebody would drop a coin in the slot, and the cards would begin to flip, and figures jerk to life in a dim, flickering light. He frowned at the house where Alison Sansing was waiting to meet him. With her note, she had dropped in a whole handful of pennies. Cass might well have resented it, but he didn't. He would not do her that discourtesy, no matter how contentious she was.

She had not always been contentious. Cass had known her all his life, was close to courting her once, in fact. She was pretty of face, eyebrows arched over her brown eyes, a mouth quick to laugh. She could play the violin, after a fashion, and her father gave her real books to read: Emerson, Thoreau, Aquinas, Homer, Dickens. She was lively, a dancer with a happy spirit. Then Cass went out on the river, and in due season met Jane Spell in the old French Opera House, and married her, and brought her home. Then the war came and took from Alison Sansing not only her kin but all Possibility forever. Now

Janie was dead, and here was Alison, an old maid, and . . . well, who could blame her for being contrary? Not Cass Wakefield, surely, who was sufficiently contrary himself at times.

And who could blame her if she wished to raise the dead? Time, no doubt, was gaining on Alison as well. *You can help me,* she had written. In a little while, he intended to tell her in person that he could not.

He lifted his face into the breeze and found it laden with a dark perfume: cedars, perhaps the ones in the cemetery beyond the ridge. But no, it could only be his imagination. You couldn't smell cedar trees that far.

The street was empty, the houses mute. No curtains moved in the windows. To the west, a locomotive blew for the Oxford Road crossing; at the same moment, the courthouse bell began to toll. Three o'clock. He was late; he needed to go and put this foolishness to rest. He leaned against the fence—it creaked and nearly fell over—and fished in his greatcoat pocket, where he kept a silver flask shaped like a little canteen. It was inscribed, *To Cass from Lucian, Christmas, 1878.* Cass looked at the date. The summer of '78 was a yellow fever time, the worst ever. The men of Cumberland had taken turns guarding the depot to see that no one got off the trains from the south. The refugees got off up at Holly Springs instead, and before long, half that town was wiped out. That's how it was in those times. Cass took a long draft from his flask, then tucked it away and steadied himself. In a moment, he passed through the open gate.

⁜

Two hours later, he was walking back to town. A few lamps burned in the stores and houses, and sometimes Cass saw a fig-

ure move across a lighted window. A number of his old comrades would rise late in the night and walk the quiet streets for
hours, no matter how cold it was, but not Cass Wakefield. He
would roam the house perhaps, or pace the rooms of boarding-
houses and hotels, but he would not go abroad in the hours
when the lamps were dark.

Ordinarily it pleased him at this early hour to look in people's lighted windows, to see the life going on inside, to see
how they arranged their furniture and painted their rooms. Of
course, Cass had been inside every white person's house in
Cumberland at one time or another—and many of the
Negroes'—but the night made each dwelling different and
fresh, as if a secret were being revealed. Tonight, however, he
took no pleasure in the act. He felt as lonely as he had when he
stood night watches on the river; when, from the pilothouse,
he would see the wink of a cabin on the dark shore or pass a
town spread out on the bluffs. Then the lights would only
make him feel more lonesome, as though he had been born to a
vanished race.

By the time he reached the square, the warmth of Alison's
parlor had deserted him. It was only half past five but felt
much later. When the sun went down in the winter—or, like
today, when the gray merely faded from the sky—the hour
seemed already far advanced. Every small thing was asleep that
made the summer so busy. He heard no night birds, no voices
from the porches, no children in the yards. All the doors and
windows were shut tight, so he heard no pianos, no dishes rattling, no babies squalling. Even the hung-out wash was stiff
and motionless. What he *did* hear was dogs barking, horses
stamping in their stables, a steam engine popping off down by

the depot, his own footsteps on the plank walk. These seemed more melancholy than any silence, as if God had created them just to illustrate how lonely mortals were, and how helpless in the vast mystery of night.

Cass leaned against a lamppost and looked out at the square. Drops of rain hissed against the hot globe of the street lamp. A horseman went by, huddled against the damp and cold, his mount's hooves squelching in the mud. Cass took out his flask and drank.

Alison Sansing had a house maid, but when Cass had knocked on her door, it was opened by her minister, who was of the Presbyterian species. This gentleman, as chaperone, said nothing past a cool greeting; he thought little of Cass Wakefield anyway, who frequented taverns and was an Episcopalian and a Mason and therefore a freethinker and heretic, not to be trusted. The minister spent the whole time sitting by the window with his legs crossed, pondering, no doubt, the inscrutable Will of God, who, in the minister's view, had known about Cass Wakefield's appearance in this parlor since before Eden bloomed. So Cass thought anyhow, who had a low opinion of Calvinists in general and this one in particular.

Cass could ignore the clergyman, but he could not take his eyes from Alison Sansing. Cumberland was a small place, isolated from the wide world, and full of people who had been together too long. Somehow, though, Cass had missed Alison over the years. When Lucian was still a boy, she would sit with him night after night while his head pained him, reading to him when he could stand the light, listening to his visions when he lay in darkness. Then Lucian grew older, and Cass was busy traveling, and Alison Sansing fell away from them into that closed, lavender-scented world where old maids were thought to live—peering at the world through drawn jalousies, taking tea in the long, empty afternoons, clipping items from newspapers, and working on their genealogy. From this world she emerged only on Sundays for church, and sometimes Cass would meet her on the street and pass a little while with her, and meanwhile the clocks ticked on, the hands moved across the porcelain faces, marking the hours, weeks, years. Cass thought it might have been a year since he'd seen her at all, and he saw with startling clarity how time had gained upon her. Her face was still pretty but lean now, hollow of cheek, with arcs of shadows under her eyes. She had cut her black hair, shorn it like a boy's, and roughly, as if she'd hacked it off with pinking shears. He saw a frailty in her and, stranger still, a hint of mortality. Cass realized he had never thought of Alison Sansing as mortal.

There was nothing frail about her voice, however, or the way she paced before the mantel as she offered her plan in the same words she had used in the note, without enlargement. It was simple enough: she wanted him to go with her to Franklin and find her long-dead kinfolk and bring them home. She did not say why, after all this time, she had determined such a thing. Cass never asked, for he understood the quest as one of those that didn't need to make sense except to the one making it. Moreover, he agreed to go, all his arguments and misgivings dying away as he watched Alison's face.

He had plenty of time on his hands, and he knew where the men were buried, though he was not sure he could find the place again. It only made sense that she would ask him. The only thing left was to wish she had not asked at all. He stood a mo-

ment longer by the old square, then pulled up his collar and
started up the street toward home.

At the Wakefield house—a paintless single-story cottage
almost invisible behind a forest of untrimmed privet—he went
around back to get a fresh jug from the mildewed, spider-
haunted cellar. Then he went through the creaky back door and
into the tacked-on kitchen, greeted by the sound of mice high-
tailing it to safety. The kitchen had not been used in decades,
but the mice still preferred it, as if hope burned eternal in their
tiny breasts. Cass swore and fumbled for a lamp, then gave it
up and felt his way into the hall, where a pale glow defined the
sidelights and the milky glass panel of the front door. This
panel had been cracked by the discharge of an artillery piece in
the front yard during the fighting for Cumberland, and in the
wintertime, the crack admitted gusts of cold air.

Along the walls, barely visible, huddled shapes of furniture. Near the door stood a gaudy hall stand, resting place for a
quartet of rotting umbrellas that once belonged to Janie. Her
hats still hung on the hooks there. A low horsehair settee, piled
with old newspapers, lurked by the north wall; in the center, a
wing table with a lamp no one ever lit, flanked by a brace of
spindly chairs no one sat in anymore. On the table lay a loaded
28-gauge shotgun. By daylight, the walls themselves were yel-
lowed and grimed with the smoke of fireplaces, pipes, cigars,
French cigarettes, and Injun weed; the original white existed
only behind the pictures—oil portrait of Janie and her father,
the old fart, a charcoal of her sister, who died in New Orleans, a
chromo of Notre Dame de Paris—and behind the furniture, re-
gions only spiders and mice had visited in the last two decades.

Cass followed the smell of cannabis to the office and discovered Lucian sitting cross-legged on a cushion, drawing on one of the pipes of his hookah. He had a candle burning, which gave just enough light to see that his eyes were closed and a wet rag was tied around his head. Lying open beside him was a fat, threadbare dictionary, and on top of this slumbered a fat yellow tomcat.

"Well, Cass," said Lucian.

Cass set the jug between his legs. He did not care to take the Injun weed himself, for it made his throat sore. When he was settled, Cass told of his visit with Alison. Lucian was silent for a moment, drawing on the pipe. Finally, he shook his head. "You don't need to be going back up there. She should not have asked such a thing."

"Well, she feels strongly about it," said Cass. "Strongly. And she can't go by herself."

"She ought to leave those boys alone," said Lucian.

The two men were silent for a while, each remembering how it had been the morning after the Franklin battle. Cass, as usual, found that the memory had lost all its hard edges and returned as a sad dream. The few who remained of the regiment had been searching for their dead when they found Colonel Sansing and young Perry only a few yards apart in the ditch before the cotton gin. They wrapped the bodies in tent flys left behind by the enemy, and carried them in silent procession to the backyard of a house nearby, where other men had been buried that morning, and where now the Sansings were laid in a common grave. *Down, down, down.*

In the dream, the boys buried them together out of sentiment; in truth, they were too worn out to dig two holes, and the one they dug was not deep and filled quickly with water.

Chaplain Sam Hook said some words no one could remember, though Cass often wished he could. Sam Hook was chaplain for the whole brigade, but he stayed with his old regiment that day. Since first light, they had buried a dozen of their comrades and would bury that many more (each a little shallower than the one before), but Sam Hook always thought of something eloquent and particular to say about each one, for he had known them. That evening, they would kneel in the oak grove by McGavock's house, and Hook would remember every one they couldn't find. It was his last homily. The chaplain was lost at Nashville; no one knew where or how, but they all knew no one had spoken over him before the mud was shoveled in his face. Cass had always been sorry for that, and many times, as he waited for sleep, he imagined what he might have said if he had only been there.

In Cass's particular dream, the boys were neither tired nor hungry nor afraid, and no cold rain fell. There were no bright colors, but at least the oppressive gray was softened to a kind of twilight, and no wounded men cried out, and the terrible land-scape all around was shut away. There were only the boys, and a great silence, and the mounded grave with a fence pale driven at its head, lettered by Cass Wakefield himself in the white paint one of them had found in a shed:

SANSING
Col. & Adjutant
Father & Son
21st Miss.
Our Comrades

Cass knew that the scene he remembered in this moment was a lie, but no matter. Plenty of time left to remember it as it was.

"I reckon the marker is long gone," said Cass at last. He uncorked the jug and took a long swallow. "I will have a devil of a time finding the place."

Lucian leaned back and rubbed his eyes. "I don't even remember the house," he said. "When I see it, I'll know it, though."

"You won't see it," said Cass. "You ain't going."

"Oh, I forgot," said Lucian. "I'm not invited. But then—I wasn't the first time, either."

"That is not funny," said Cass. He tipped the jug, trying not to regret the promise he'd made. Well, no matter. In the morning, he would board a northbound passenger train with Alison Sansing, and sooner or later they would return. That was sufficient thought for the night to come.

❖ 3 ❖

IT WAS A WONDER TO LOOK OUT THE WINDOW AND WATCH the woods and fields roll past, even barren as they were. In all her life, Alison had never been out of Mississippi, and now, pretty soon, she would be.

She wondered if the wintertime was the same in other places as it was here. She wondered if Tennessee would be full of snow. She was tired of winter, and the worst of it, the dreary month of February, was yet to come. In March, the crocuses and daffodils would poke up their heads, though the daffodils were usually humbled by a late frost. They never seemed to learn but always pushed up and peered around hopefully. According to the Prayer Book, Easter would be early in April this year, and after that—

She pressed her gloved hand to her mouth to keep from crying out. Death was supposed to be a surprise, she thought bitterly. No one should have to live with the knowledge that next summer's birds would light on her grave. But of course she didn't really believe that yet. That was how you stood it, by not believing. Alison told herself she would have the summer, just one more, and the long, drowsy fall, and then the winter to die in. Having arranged that, she felt better.

She was not sure why she kept her secret. Pity, most likely. She could not bear pity. Besides, a revelation would only complicate matters. When she came back, she would tell her minister, and he would help her get ready. The rest could find out in their own time.

No doubt it was unfair to leave Cass Wakefield in the dark after he had done this thing for her. Cass had been friendly that morning at the depot, but he had spoken hardly a word since. She put this down to the fact that he didn't really want to go. She accepted that, just as she accepted the fact that she could never have gone alone. Yet chivalry, even in the best of men (and Cass, for all his singular ways, was among the best), couldn't always mask reluctance when the circumstance weighed heavy, and it would be just as hard for him to mask pity. She risked a quick glance at her companion. Cass was leaned back in the seat, his eyes closed, pondering God knows what. He was no longer young, but he was still a fair-looking man, if she cared to think about it. As she looked at him now, it was odd to think that once he journeyed a long way down a road she could not begin to imagine, and saw and did things no words could shape even while they were happening. Her father and brother had done the same and had not returned to even try to tell how it had been or how they had stood it.

Once she had hoped Cass Wakefield would court her, but he never had—perhaps because of her father, a formidable obstacle, though he didn't mean to be. In any event, Cass went off to the river and, in time, married another. When Cass came home to join the army in '61, he left his bride in Alison's charge. Alison and Jane and Sally Mae Burke passed the war together, staying in one another's houses, praying, waiting for the news, trembling when it came. They rolled bandages, collected lint, went cold and hungry. They watched the yankees come and go, watched the Negroes run off, watched the square razed. After Franklin, Jane and Sally Mae kept Alison among the living by refusing to let her die. During Gault's Rebellion, when the whole world seemed to have tilted beyond the last mad precipice, they convinced one another it hadn't, if only because they would not allow such a thing to happen.

Then the war ended, and Cass and Roger and Lucian came home on the Pontotoc Road. A boy had seen them out there, and told some men on the square, and one of the men fetched Alison. She went to meet them alone, walking far out the road, past the cemetery and into the hot, empty countryside. Finally she quit walking and stood in the middle of the road, the sun beating down and the grass in the ditches dry and buzzing with insects. She stood there in her black dress and bonnet like the Angel of Death, waiting, and at last they appeared over the ridge. She had expected two scarecrows, but instead there were three shuffling along, talking in that excited way people will when they are almost home after a journey. When they saw her, they stopped. Cass spoke her name, and Alison beckoned. Even from that distance, she could see in Cass Wakefield's eyes that he knew she was a messenger. They came slowly then, the strange boy walking behind Cass and holding on to the rag of his shirt.

"Well, Miss Alison," said Cass. She could smell the stink on them, but no matter. She put out her hands, but Cass stepped back. "Careful," he said, "you'll get greybacks all over you." He ran his hands through the tangle of his hair, then held them out to Alison. "See? We got them, Alison, and fleas, too." He stood there, swaying in the sunlight, the boy peeking around him.

Roger said, "Alison, where is—"

"No!" said Cass. He began to back up the road. "I don't want you to tell," he said. "You must go away and not tell."

"Listen to me," she said. "You must listen." Then she told how Janie was dead of the typhoid a month past, and Sally Mae gone half mad of it. When she finished, she was crying, surprised to find her heart still beating, the blood still coursing through her veins. She watched them kneel in the dust of the Pontotoc Road, Cass and Roger, while the boy looked past her toward the town.

That was the homecoming she gave them. She thought Cass Wakefield might hate her for a long time, but he never did. In a few days, he came to ask her help with the boy, who was sick, and to tell her how her people had died, and to assure her they had died with honor. That seemed to be important to him.

Now, in the railway coach, she said, "This is hard for you."

He opened his eyes, but he did not look at her. "I have

studied on it some," he said. "We'll find the place. That part is easy."

"What is the hard part?"

Cass studied his hands. "I helped to put them there," he said. "That was a long time ago. When we find the grave, I would not want you to look in it."

"I will not promise that," she said.

He nodded and closed his eyes again. "We'll see," he said.

✣

The country had changed a good deal, something Cass began to notice when their train crossed into Alabama. It was a bleak country of wide fields and dead cotton stalks, ponds whose still waters shone like polished coins. Here and there a barren wolf tree or a cedar rose in solitude, and now and then a chimney with no house. But there were intact houses, too, and more cabins than he remembered, and as darkness settled, the windows began to wink with lamps. Nowhere rose any landmark that Cass could recognize.

The train sped on through the darkening country. The porter had not yet lit the lamps in the coach, so Cass could make out the passing landscape—the broad, dark fields like the sea, the shapes of trees along the creek bottoms. He cursed the early dark and the clouds that hid the stars. The lamps in the houses seemed futile in all that blackness, offering no comfort to the traveler. Cass had looked out of countless train windows in his day, up and down the Mississippi valley, up to Missouri and down to Orleans, and he had always felt the same sense of loneliness and loss when other people's houses passed in the night. Still, it was better this time, for between him and the dark was the profile of Alison's face. There was her forehead, her eyes half closed, the curve of her nose, her lips parted—and beyond her the ghosts of the old army lying on the land, of Roger and Lucian, Ike and all the rest, and himself, too.

Then, at Decatur, Cass had a rude shock. As they came around the curve to the depot, he expected, even in the dark, to see the Federal works. They would be decayed perhaps, worn down by the rains, but he knew they would still be looming over the town like the cone of a sleeping volcano. Instead, they were vanished. Nothing remained to match the image Cass had long held in memory, and he stared dumbfounded. He simply could not accept that they were gone, nor that the universe could sustain such a vacancy. This time, he gave voice to his thoughts, and Alison put her hand on his arm. "Well," she said, "maybe they only looked big at the time."

"No, they were monumental," said Cass. "They were eternal, like the Pyramids. The armies of Charlemagne could not have prevailed against them."

"I should like to hear about it, then," she said, as the train crawled over the Tennessee River bridge. "And about how Lucian came to you. This was the place, wasn't it?"

"The very place," said Cass. Then he told how Lucian, conscripted from an orphanage, appeared in the backyard of a house in Decatur just before the battle. He told of the fight itself and how the rebels dashed themselves against the Federal works to no purpose, and how, when the battle was over, they came back to the house and burned it and left the owners homeless with winter coming down. When the story was done, he turned to Alison and found her eyes moving across his face.

"You burned a house?" she said. "An old woman's house?"

"Well, I take no pride in it," he said. "It was a rough time. We were . . . different then."

She shifted in the seat to face him, the window a dark square behind her, the night fleeing past. "Different," she said. "I do not think you were different. I do not think you are different now."

"I would not burn a person's house now," Cass said.

"Yes, you would," she said. "You certainly would."

"That is a hard judgment."

She shook her head, her eyes never leaving his face. "It is no judgment. It is merely a fact."

"Very well," said Cass, and left unmentioned his belief that sometimes fact and truth were not the same thing.

Cass and Alison's train left Decatur on time, and luckily so, for an hour later a freight engine derailed on the bridge approach, and a half dozen trains backed up behind it. One of these numbered Lucian Wakefield among its travelers.

Lucian stood beneath the passenger shed watching the rain and the deep-blue night. The depot was hot and swarming with passengers and squalling children, so Lucian preferred the cool air of the platform. He walked off to the south end, his hands shoved deep in his coat pockets, and looked off in the direction of town. He was already tired of the rain. He never took long to grow weary of it in winter, though he liked it in the summertime when it fell hard, silver and green, and afterward steamed from the backs of horses, steamed up from the railroad ties and lay in a mist along Town Creek. In summer, the birds sang after a rain, but no such music rose from the cold drizzle of the dead time. Only silence, and only the dark.

He was tired of the dark, too, and the dark was worst of all. In winter, the day was hardly begun before it was already getting ready for night. Sometimes, in winter, they had to burn the lamps in the back of Tom Jenkins's store all day, and even when the sunlight fell in a shallow slant through the front panes, it was pale and watery and reluctant. Never enough light anywhere—no lamp, no thousand lamps, could light the rooms through which they moved—fire to fire, lamp to lamp, in the dead time.

The winter nights were hard to walk through, though walk they did: Lucian Wakefield, Roger, Tom Jenkins, and others—Gawain Harper wandering home from the depot, Ike Gatlin hobbling on his ruined feet. ("It's the nerves," Ike would say sometimes, and tap his feet with his cane, punishing the nerves killed years before by the ice on the long retreat.) They met, these wanderers; they passed on in solitude or walked on together, always in silence but for Tom's constant tuneless whistling, while the tree limbs rattled above them, groaning and creaking with cold, and the fence palings gleamed with frost. In summer they might talk sometimes, and remember, laugh even—but the winter closed around them, struck them silent, and the sullen dawn came late and sent no heralds before it.

Rain and dark. Lucian was tired of them both, but he kept his sentiments well hidden, at the very edge of thought, lest Fate mistake him. This rain, this dark, whatever cold might come—these were nothing beside what the soldiers had known once, and now they lived with the fear that, if they pressed too hard, the terrors they remembered would come again. Thus Tom Jenkins whistled in the night, Steven Peck always drank his coffee from a tin cup, Bloodworth often went without a coat in the coldest weather, the Craddocks stayed every month of November in hunting camp, living in dog tents, and Carl Nobles kept a bull's-eye canteen wound around his saddle horn. They did these things not from joy or sentiment or habit, but because they knew something was watching, waiting to snatch them up again if they let themselves get too comfortable.

Lucian shivered. He stood just inside the overhang of the platform, behind a curtain of rain, and turned his mind to his present purpose. He did not question this journeying; probably none of the old boys would either. Roger Lewellyn had not questioned it when Lucian told him. Roger declared he would go himself, but Lucian wouldn't let him. Roger needed to stay with Sally Mae, who was suffering from the old fever in her brain.

Nevertheless, when the cars began to draw away from Cumberland, Lucian went out on the platform and thought about dropping off the train. He thought about forgetting the whole thing, walking back to the house on Algiers Street, where he could smoke a pipe of Injun weed and settle his mind. Cass had told him not to come. Cass didn't need anybody following along to complicate things. Yet here was Lucian, following anyhow. It was simple, really: follow Cass Wakefield up the old road, come what may, and never mind the reason. There did not even have to be a reason. The boy Lucifer had asked for nothing, and Cass Wakefield had given him everything. That was reason enough.

Lucian was tired, but he had no mind for sleeping. He

thought, *Here is Lucian Wakefield in Alabama in the year Eighteen-and-eighty-five.* It might as well be Omaha, for he recognized nothing among the ramshackle buildings of the railroad district. Still, it did no good to reason. Just over there, beyond the town buildings, the streetcars, the electric lights, beyond the arbitrary designation of the day—he had seen it on a Union Pacific calendar in the depot, and he had tapped the date with his finger—over there, in the mist of a winter's eve, it was still November of Eighteen-and-sixty-four. If he had time, and if it was day, he might go and find the yard where he first saw Cass Wakefield leaning against a board fence. Lucian remembered a woman from the house. She was gone gray and stooped with years of meanness. *You'uns goddamned rebels,* she had called them. Well, they had been rebels, sure enough—even the boy, though he hadn't known it yet. He hadn't thought himself much of anything then.

Rebels they were, soldiers of an imaginary country that even on that afternoon was moribund and populous with ghosts. Lucian remembered how the woman's husband had struck him, and he remembered running across the cotton field, hair sticky with blood, trying to catch Mister Cass. That was the moment he saw, for the first time, the torn red battle flags break out over the lines. It came to him then, though he didn't know how to think it yet, that here was a thing not long for the earth, but immortal still, so full of sorrow, so terrible and grand that it would never die so long as any of them lived.

Lucian came to love the flag, though he never saw it planted on any piece of ground they could call home. He loved it yet for what it meant to him: not a country, nor any cause, for these had ceased to mean much in the war's twilight—after the

Nickajack line, they painted no more names of battles across their flag, and after Franklin, it never flew over the regiment again. But Lucian loved and remembered the flag for those whose epitaph it was, those still quick and those gone down to dust, epitaph for them all who had traveled the old road and never returned, not even the living, who left so much of themselves in the smoke: "the boys," they styled themselves in their old, easy way. They had names—Bushrod Carter, Jack Bishop, Virgil C. Johnson and Julian Bomar, Gawain Harper, old Bill Williams, Eugene Pitcock, Nebo and the archbishop of Canterbury, Hook and Bloodworth, and Craddock and Lewellyn— kind, dangerous, homesick, frightened, and exhausted men among whom he had come without a proper name of his own. He had appeared in their midst by God's peculiar grace, a cipher with no kin or any tomorrow he could imagine, and the soldiers had taken him in. One of them had given his own name in trust, without question or regret, and taught him how he could be proud of it.

Lucian stuffed a clay pipe with Injun weed. He lit it off with a Lucifer match and drew deep of the harsh smoke. By the time his train got under way, he ought to be feeling better. He peered south toward the old Confederate lines. He decided that, even if he had time someday, he would never go down there. He preferred to go on despising the old couple, alive or not, and he liked to remember Cass Wakefield leaning against the fence, the first time he ever saw him. He would like to be rid of some things, but not that. He would keep that as it was, and if it meant keeping all the rest, too, then that was all right.

❖ 4 ❖

ASS WAKEFIELD PACED UP AND DOWN OUTSIDE THE depot at Spring Hill, Tennessee, remembering. A dreary light rain was leaking through the platform roof, hissing on the lanterns that burned here and there. The village was dark and forsaken at this hour, the buildings mere shapes in the gloom. Cass remembered hours marching and countermarching in the dark, but he hadn't known what happened until years later when he read about how a full corps of Federals had slipped blithely past them in the night, marched to Franklin, and spent all day digging breastworks while the rebels marched themselves to exhaustion in pursuit. That was how the fight came to be at Franklin, and how it was lost.

Looking out from the depot, Cass could not place where his regiment had been that night. He remembered bivouacking near a big house, and a citizen remarked that General Van Dorn had been shot there the year before. Some of the boys who had been with Van Dorn at Corinth went to take a look, but were chased away by sentries. He recalled that Ike Gatlin lost a clay pipe here—his favorite, and many were the colorful words he sent aloft on account of it—and no doubt it was still out there, along with buttons and ammunition, forks, spoons, frying pans, empty sardine cans from the lot they had bought in Florence. All that truck was lying in the dark, buried in leaves or turned under by the plow, scattered like the long-dead ashes of their fires. It had been there all these years, and behind it a long trail of similar relics to mark their passage across the land.

Their train had been at Spring Hill for almost an hour, while others came and went around it on the passing track. The conductor had alluded to some trouble with the locomotive, but he was guarded with his information, as if it were nobody's business why they were stalled out here in the middle of the night. In return, the passengers had grown surly. They defied his injunction not to leave the train and were now crowded in the depot. When Cass went by the foggy window, he saw Alison Sansing in a chair near the stove, reading a newspaper. It occurred to him how unusual it was to see a woman doing that. He wondered why that was so. A child slept on a bench facing the window, and beside him his mother knitted. People drowsed in impossible positions or read tattered weeklies; their faces, the dull yellow walls, the calendars, and the railway advertisements were muted in the glow of the lamps. The effect was like a painting, a nocturne, whereas Cass, standing outside, felt he was in one of those photographs from the war—all blacks and whites and grays, ill-defined edges, grainy, and a little out of focus. All the scene required was a few yankee officers standing around with their coats buttoned, leaning on their swords, and maybe a little contraband boy sitting on the bricks with his knees drawn up, wearing a forage cap too big for him. Cass was reminded of how much he hated images from the war—all those goddamned smug yankees lounging against walls and fences, the background full of overloaded wagons and fat horses. Apparently, no one had taken any pictures of rebels—live ones, anyway. There were plenty of dead ones, however. One time, in Chicago, Cass went alone to view the Gardner images from Sharpsburg. He made it through the Dunker Church series all right, but the group in the Sunken Lane was too much—men swollen, faces like grotesque balloons, humiliated beyond all measure. Why would anyone take a picture like that, and why would anyone go to see it?

Another thing that bothered Cass about war photographs was that even those taken in summer all seemed wintry to him. He was curious if the world had really looked like that back then: drained of color, everything bleak, barren, muddy, and raggedy assed, the land devoid of trees. He hadn't perceived it that way at the time. Strangely, the color was leaching out of his memory, too, though he knew there had been plenty of color. The blue coats of the Federals had looked black from a distance. Their pants were light blue; their clustered bayonets shone like new-minted lead; their tattered flags, national and regimental, were gay. Trees were golden in the springtime, and chickens, like the rebels themselves, were clothed in every hue. Mud was yellow or red or black, fires winked like stars among the dark, and the moon was pale. Death had its colors, too. Blood was bright red, brains a pinkish gray, tendons and bones gleaming white. A dead man's skin looked like candle wax sometimes, when the blood was driven out of it. Lately, in memory, all these colors were fading, and movement, too. Cass saw too many tableaux now, in grays and whites, as if his mind were arranging every moment in an album.

He paced some more. Presently, a flagman carrying a red lantern came skulking down the flank of the halted train. Cass said, "Beg pardon—" The man didn't stop or raise his eyes. "Broke a drive rod," he said, and walked off into the dark.

Cass thought it astonishing that such a thing could happen thirteen miles from their destination. They had walked it once, of course, all the boys, the miles-long patchwork column winding up the muddy roads. Before that, they had walked infinite leagues, and would walk a good many yet before enough dead men were counted. Lucian once speculated that among all those myriads, yankees and rebels both, you could not render enough fat to fry a pan of bacon, and indeed the soldiers were lean then. Their legs were thin and knotted with muscle, their feet—many of the rebels were barefoot, and some of the yankees—horny and thick with calluses, nails cracked and yellow, so that they could walk through briars if need be. Ice would cut them, though, and freeze them, as they found out on the retreat from Nashville. Cass thought of Ike Gatlin hobbling around the streets of Cumberland—it was not fair. Why hadn't they gotten him some shoes, away back yonder in Nashville? Cass thought about it and decided that the answer was plain, if unsatisfactory: there were no dead yankees in reach of the works, and therefore no shoes to be obtained.

A man's feet ruined for want of corpses. The logic was appalling, but there it was.

Cass rubbed the mysterious bulge of his stomach. No matter how little he ate, he remained too well fed. His rendered corpus could fry a brace of hams now, he supposed. He was annoyed by the rain, too—further proof that he was no longer fit for campaigning. Back then, rain made no difference at all. They had walked this very road northward in the rain, sometimes in snow and driving sleet, and laughed at all of it. That was how Cass remembered it anyhow. But they made few jokes after Franklin, and none at all on the southward trek from Nashville.

He went back to the window and looked in at Alison again. He was glad she was comfortable and warm, but part of him wished she would come out to seek him. Cass wanted to talk to her, tell her all that had happened, but no doubt she was tired of such telling—and who could blame her? Cass was tired of it himself, tired of thinking about it. He walked to the end of the platform again and listened. Somewhere in the dark, a horse was kicking against the wall of a barn. The rain had stopped, leaving a mist behind, and heavy dampness clung to everything. Wood smoke lay ghostly in the low places; it drifted from the depot stovepipe and from all the stovepipes of the coaches and from the locomotives. The sharp reek of the smoke, and the smell of his own damp wool coat, reminded Cass of the way the boys used to smell; years and years he had smelled them, and himself, and the air wanted only the stink of unwashed bodies and the sweet sulfur smell of powder to complete. Cass took off his bowler and drew his sleeve across the crown, and settled the hat on the back of his head. He was tired of black humors, tired of dropping coins in the moving picture machine, but he had no notion of how to quit. Moreover, he was tired of himself, of his own company. He wished Alison would come out.

He drew his handkerchief from his sleeve and wiped his face. Another train, northbound, had come into view and stopped just short of the flag. Its headlight illuminated the mist and gleamed on the wet flanks of a cut of empty boxcars. Their open doors were rectangles of deep night.

He should not have told Alison about burning the old people's house in Decatur. He should have left that out, he thought. Maybe she had some of her own stories she would like to tell, but he never gave her the chance. Who else would she have to tell them to? He should have paid more attention to her. He should have paid attention to the way things had changed, rather than to the way they hadn't. *Should have, should have.* Voices on the platform behind told him that others had come out for the air. Cass walked away from them, out into the yard.

⊹

In the depot, Alison was nodding by the hot stove when a conductor announced they would be boarding. Another train had arrived to take them on their way. The conductor did not beg their pardon for the inconvenience.

A bright flame danced in the stove's isinglass window, and Alison realized she was fairly burning up. She fanned herself with the Nashville paper she had found. Ordinarily, she didn't read newspapers—too much sorrow in too narrow a space—but she had read some of this one. Sure enough, it was full of trouble: robberies, shootings, houses burning down. A despairing person had thrown himself under a streetcar; a mean one had butchered a family; a cuckolded husband had stabbed his wife, then drunk a quart of lye.

She had read a whimsical name, and as she came awake, she tried to think of it. Then she remembered the name: March Hare. It belonged to a lynched Negro. A lawyer, the paladin of the night riders (the paper had not called him a night rider but did say he was a paladin), boasted to the paper, and to the world at large, that he had personally dispatched the whimsically named Negro. He kept coming back to the name, as if it were stuck in his head. Emptied his pistol into the man, he said. A beast, he said, and if he wasn't a murderer then, he would be sooner or later. The lawyer was a distinguished member of the community and a candidate for the legislature. He was eager to point out that he had served with valor in the Army of Tennessee and for years had been secretary of the United Confederate Veterans bivouac in the chief city of the state, and he felt it his duty . . . and the women of Nashville and the South deserved . . . and the Negroes had to learn . . . and so forth, the old rhetoric spooling predictably from the page.

After the war, Alison had been sympathetic to the night riders around Cumberland—not that fool King Solomon Gault, of course, but the ones who came later, who styled themselves the Cumberland Rangers. She had known most of them well, Cass Wakefield and Roger Lewellyn among them. They looked ridiculous in their masquerade costumes and engaged in all manner of high jinks—moaning and wailing, burning holes in their wives' sheets with torches, thundering up and down the roads at night with pumpkins under their arms, and other foolishness—but they never killed anybody until the very end. Two white men from Illinois were lounging on the square when a disguised man in a long duster and slouch hat and green sunglasses walked right up to them and shot them both and walked away. No woman of Cumberland, to Alison's knowledge, ever learned who did the shooting. The men knew, of course, but the secret stayed among them, and it would no doubt die with the last of them.

When the yankees finally got tired of reconstructing and went away, the Cumberland Rangers disbanded, and its members went back to being Freemasons and Knights of Honor and Knights of Pythias and so on. How they loved to band together: Lodges and Camps and Bivouacs, gangs and mobs and armies— always an army somewhere. She thought about that and decided that maybe war was the greatest Lodge Meeting of all. Death was the Grand Master, no women allowed, and the men, under their costumes and banners, were all the same, all playing at brotherhood, wallowing in tradition, ritual, pageantry, allegory . . . and secrets, she thought. Plenty of secrets.

She jammed the newspaper into the kindling box and stood up, a little shakily, and felt the tiredness deep inside her. She wore out quicker these days—Culver Craddock had warned that she would, and it made her madder than anything. Still, the journey had brought her closer to the place where her father and brother lay. What the grave held—bones, or dust, or perhaps no more than a dark stratum in the mud—did not matter. Bones or dust or mud, she would bring them home where they belonged.

Her intention was selfish, of course, and was causing Cass Wakefield no end of trouble, but she believed in it still. Cass would be all right—or at least no worse off than he was before—and her people would be home, and she would not be alone among the cedars.

She pulled up the hood of her cape and made her way across the waiting room and into the damp night. Cass was wandering out there somewhere, and she would find him whether he wanted to be found or not.

✠

Cass was watching a switch engine shunt the cars from their train onto another, and from that he surmised they would be leaving soon. The new train blocked the lamps from the depot, so he was standing in the dark when he heard footsteps in the cinders. He turned, and there was Alison, her face a pale oval under the hood of her cloak.

"I'm sorry," he said. "I didn't mean to wander off."

"It's no trouble," she said. "I just looked for the lonesomest spot I could find—and, sure enough, here you are." She drew her cloak tight around her and shivered. "What are you doing out here in the dark?"

"Nothin'," he said.

"No," she said, "you were out here thinking." She walked a little way and looked off into the dark. "I suppose you all came through here. Father was here, was he not? And Brother?"

"Oh, they were here," said Cass, "but I have no idea what they did. I hardly know what *I* did." He watched Alison peering into the dark as if she could see them out there: the bivouac fires and men moving across them, the pacing sentries, the sleeping guns parked hub-to-hub, her father standing with his hand on his sword hilt, and Perry breaking little sticks for the fire. Then Cass understood that she could see no such thing—the images were all his own. He said, "It was a grand confusion. We marched around in the woods, then we stopped, and wherever we stopped, we built fires and made coffee. Meanwhile the yankees marched right by us. I remember your daddy—"

He hushed then, embarrassed. He had not meant to speak at all.

She turned and came back to him and put her palm against the lapel of his coat. "Go on," she said. "What was Father doing?"

"He was standing there," said Cass, pointing as though he had found the spot in the darkness, "and the road was just over there, through the trees. He had his sword buckled on and his cap tilted down over his eyes, and he was watching the men passing on the road. We could all see them, but we didn't know and didn't much care who they were—but I think the colonel knew. He shook his head and turned away and walked past us where we were laying down. . . . He spoke to us, but I don't remember—"

He hushed again because he didn't know how to tell it: Colonel Sansing walking by them in the firelight, for a moment seeming taller than any man, and stronger than any of them, and his voice a comfort because he was the best of them all, and he was theirs. Then he vanished into the trees, leaving in his wake a cold place as if he were already gone forever. *I knew it then,* Cass thought, but he would not say it to the woman watching him in the drizzle of the train yard. "It is only an ordinary thing," he said. "A man standing by the fire, walking off into the woods . . ."

Alison's hand closed briefly on his lapel, then dropped away. "I will settle for ordinary," she said.

"Only he *wasn't*," said Cass. "He wasn't ordinary. He made . . . he made people want to follow him."

"You did follow him once," said Alison, "and now you have again." She took his arm and pulled him toward the train. As they walked, she said, "I do not flatter myself to think you came because I asked you, Cass Wakefield."

Cass did not reply, for it was only truth. He let himself be carried along. He wanted to tell Alison all that had happened, all the things he might have told Janie once. *Tomorrow,* he thought. *I will tell her tomorrow,* knowing all the while that it was too much ever to tell, no matter how long Tomorrow was.

Some of
the Boys

———⊷◈⊶———

❧ 5 ❧

THE REGIMENT TOILED IN COLUMN-OF-FOURS THROUGH the dust of its own passage, under a sky empty of cloud, over ground baked hard by the killing sun. The men moved through brittle grass and pans of curious flat cactus where fat grasshoppers leaped in their faces and clung to their jackets, or buzzed dryly away in the dust. Nothing stirred in the pines: no wind, no birds but the watchful crows. Overhead, a kettle of vultures circled patiently. No one spoke—talking was too great an effort to spend on the obvious or the trivial—but from the column rose a dull murmur of shuffling feet, a clank of tin cups and canteens, the creak of dry leather.

In the last company, the men struggled in a mysterious

void. They perceived the sun as a copper disk floating just beyond reach; the sky they could not see at all. In spite of the
heat, many had wrapped themselves in blankets or shelter
halves so that, in the cloud of bitter red dust, they seemed a
procession of terra-cotta monks. They hacked and coughed;
they spat; they stumbled up the road they could not see, following blindly the rumor of the men before them.

At the end of this unhappy company trudged an old man of
thirty-four, lean like a fence rail, of long brown hair and mustache and hawkish nose, his head full of bad thoughts and visions. Cass Wakefield had once been a pilot of steamboats. Now
he was a sergeant and file-closer in the Twenty-first Mississippi
Infantry of Adams's Brigade, Loring's Division, in the fabled,
though seldom victorious, Confederate Army of Tennessee. His
charge on this hot afternoon's stroll in Georgia was to watch for
stragglers, to encourage the weak and faint of heart, the exhausted and the lame, the sunstruck, the shirkers and con-
scripts, and the merely lazy who littered the column's wake,
who might otherwise be snatched away by the yankee cavalry
that had been harassing them for days: the despised, arrogant
horsemen of Illinois and Indiana and Ohio who appeared out of
nowhere, carbines snapping, sabers glinting, as if the vultures
themselves had suddenly descended and taken the shape of
armed and dangerous men. Cass hated all cavalry, even his own,
but right now he hated the stragglers more, and this for complex reasons. They were the cause of his discomfort; if conscious,
they groaned and complained; if swooned, they were pitiful and
beyond his help, though he had used nearly all the water in his
canteen to revive them. But most of all, he hated them because
they were himself, and if he could, he would join them.

What's keepin' you from it? The old question intruded on the moments of conscious thought that clotted from time to time in Cass's mind. *Honor,* he might have said in reply. *Duty.* But these words seemed to have dried up, withered like squashed frogs in the terrible sunlight. *Pity* might have answered in the early hours of the march. Then Cass had done the best he could, prodding, kicking, cajoling; doling out scorn and shame where they served; fatherly concern, even compassion, when they were called for. He bathed the faces of unconscious men from whom the sun had drawn all strength and will. One of these, a lad of perhaps sixteen, had cried out, *Cass, oh, Cass— Jesus, I ain't been baptized!* Cass said, *You're all right. Just take some of this good water,* but the boy shook his head. *No, I can't see anything. Cass, I am goin' to hell, and it is black as night.* Cass took the boy's face in his hands and whispered hoarsely in his ear, *Do you repent you of your sins, known and unknown?* The young soldier choked, gasped, his face all blistered and red. At last he nodded frantically, forcing the words: *I do, I do! I am so sorry. I ain't always been good. I ain't*—Cass patted the flushed cheek. *Hush,* he said. He tilted his canteen and poured the last of the rust-red water over the boy's head. *I baptize you in the name of the Father, the Son, and the Holy Ghost.* Then he took the boy's hand. *Go in peace—your sins are forgiven you.* The other tried to speak again, but a convulsion took him, and he crossed over quick as a bird. Cass folded the lad's hands on his breast, then rose and staggered on after the column, knowing the buzzards would come pretty soon.

Another man, a veteran of many campaigns, had leaped from the earth with sudden energy, squalled, *Pap, you tech me agin, I'll bash yore goddamn head in,* then ran off howling through the pines and scrub oaks. No doubt someone would find his bones out there, years hence.

As the day wore on, Cass Wakefield gave up trying. He'd passed several unfortunates and malingerers in the last few miles without taking any notice. Indeed, Cass seemed unable to take notice of anything. He had pulled his blanket so close around his head that he could hardly breathe. The sweat ran in muddy rivulets down his face. His mouth was full of grit, his head ached, the blood drummed in his temples. All he could see of the world was a twilit circle where moved the vague outline of the man to his front, who might have been Bushrod Carter—he had a broad blue patch sewed over the seat of his breeches—though Cass couldn't tell for sure. He had no sense of anything beyond the moment through which he passed, though strange, disconnected images crept through his mind: a girl with a flute, white geese on a pond, a window sheeted with ice, roaches scurrying over the deck of a wharf boat in the rain. These did not seem to have anything to do with his own history, nor even with any world that he knew of.

Beside Cass Wakefield stumbled his comrade Roger Lewellyn, who had not spoken for hours, except to himself. Roger was betrothed to Cass's cousin, Sally Mae Burke. Cass had been looking after Roger for three years now, and the man was forever a trial and a penance to him. Cass could hear the pattern of Roger's voice rise and fall as if in conversation; he seemed to be bringing up a lot of questions, though on what subject Cass did not know or care. He was not interested in speculation any more than he was in stragglers. He hadn't the energy. It was all he could do to accommodate the phantoms that wandered uninvited through his own head—the pelican, for example. He hadn't seen a pelican in years, yet here was one flapping along above a placid sea, folding its wings now and then to dive, rising again in a spray of water, a fish flapping like a silver ribbon in its beak.

Then, around two o'clock by the coppery sun—Cass couldn't get to his watch, and the hour was of no importance anyhow—the woman came. She appeared so suddenly, and seemed so real, that Cass could not be sure if she was inside his head, or if he were really seeing her through the opening in the blanket. *Cassius Wakefield,* she said. She stood hipshot, one hand on a gallery post. She was thin and pale, her graying hair pulled back. Her sunken cheeks were a faint rose color like in a tinted daguerreotype, though no picture of her existed anywhere but in Cass's memory, a facility that never seemed to rest and that now erected around his mother a gallery with rocking chairs and barrels and a set of deer antlers over the door: Frye's Tavern, away back home. A breeze stirred in the woman's apron and moved leaf shadows across her face. *Cassius,* she said, *what you mean, wearin' that blanket in the heat of the day?*

Ma? said Cass.

Her face softened, and she smiled. *You want some water?*

Cass shut his eyes tight, but the woman was still there, only now it was not his mother but his young wife, Janie, moving lightly down the steps of Sally Mae Burke's house. She carried a clay jug in her hand and wore a loose summer dress of palest green. By the way it moved, by the way it clung to her, Cass knew there was no corset, no stays, under there, only the flesh damp and warm. Her brown hair was pulled up off her neck in the heat, though wisps of it were fallen loose and moved in the breeze.

Janie, he said, *you ought not to be here.* He put out his hand, wanting badly to touch her. His heart was beating fast, he grew dizzy, and the girl was of a sudden diffused in a red light. The pain settled on his breast like an anvil. *You ought not to be in this place,* he said.

But the girl did not seem to hear his voice. She looked about her, then tilted the jug and began to pour water on the nodding caladiums by the porch.

"Don't do that!" cried Cass aloud. "You ought not to be here a-tall!"

Roger Lewellyn jumped as if slapped. "What? What did you say?"

"Go on *away* from here," said Cass, but he needn't have, for his wife was already gone.

"Well, that's rich," Roger said. "Where am I supposed to go?" He was shrouded in a quilt Sally Mae had sent him long ago. It was greasy now, and the colors all faded. Roger flung the quilt back over his shoulders and glared at his companion through the settling dust. "Well?" demanded Roger.

"I was not talkin' to you," said Cass. "I thought I saw—"

"Fine!" shouted Roger. He stopped, turned in a circle until he was facing rearward. "I shall go over there," he said, pointing to the tree line. "That's Leaf River, right there!" He struggled wildly against the quilt as if it were a living thing, and finally flung it away. He unslung his rifle and threw it clattering to the hard ground, followed by his hat, then all his accoutrements. He stood swaying in the road, babbling about Leaf River, which, like Frye's Tavern, was hundreds of miles away in Cumberland, Mississippi.

Cass traveled a little way on momentum, then he, too, stopped in the road and watched for a moment as the column moved on. When he looked back, Roger was sitting in the road, rocking back and forth, moving his mouth without sound. Cass turned back then, gathered up rifle and hat and quilt and accoutrements, and pitched them off the track under a stunted blackjack oak that gave of a little shade. Then he seized Roger by the collar and pulled him to his feet. "Come along, pard," said Cass.

He led Roger to the oak and stripped his jacket off, then shed his own jacket and cartridge box, belt, and haversack. He spread his blanket under the tree, and the two of them sat down. A big copperhead snake slid away in grudging accommodation.

"That's a deadly serpent, Cass," warned Roger. "You will find them in these river bottoms."

"Never mind him," said Cass. "And this is not a river bottom."

"His mate is around here somewhere," said the other, peering about.

"Shut up," said Cass.

His canteen was empty, used up on the dying lad who lay back down the road where the vultures, no doubt, were already busy at him. Cass could imagine them huddling around, squawking, jostling one another, their black clothes whisking and rustling. He shook the thought away. Roger had a cupful of water remaining in his own canteen; it was hot, and it stank of the green pond from which he'd drawn it, but Cass put it to Roger's mouth and wet his lips, then dampened a handkerchief and wiped the boy's face. He took a drink himself, then poured the rest over Roger Lewellyn's head. In a moment, they were both breathing again, the flush diminished in their faces.

Roger said, "I wish we'd of got married before we left."

"I can't marry you, Roger," said Cass. "People would talk."

"I was not speaking of you and me," explained Roger patiently. "I meant Sally *Mae* and me."

Cass did not need to be told how Sally Mae and her Own True Love had put off their marriage until the war's end, which they all believed would be by *summer's* end. That was another summer, a long time ago. Discussing the postponement was like watching a sad play over and over again: you kept hoping the end would change, but it never did. Cass said, "You did the right thing. Just think how nice it'll be when—"

Roger said, "How long is it?"

Cass did not want the boy to think about it. He did not want to think about it himself. "A long time," he said. "Now, shut up. Think about somethin' else."

"Two years and a quarter, since after Shiloh Church," said Roger, holding up two fingers. "That is a long time not to see her face." He dragged his haversack over on his lap and stared at the buckle. Cass knew he wanted to get out his tintype of Sally Mae, which the sunlight (Cass had warned him time and again, but Roger never listened) had faded until little more than a ghost of the image remained: a beautiful girl ghost in a patterned dress, dark of hair, with olive skin like a Spaniard, and hands prettily shaped. Cass had no tintype of Janie. He had not seen her either in two and a quarter years, and the mail was unreliable, so that Janie lay on the other side of long silences. Lately these facts had been worrying at him. Anything could happen in all that time. Too much could happen. They had not been together long when he left, and she might have forgotten him. Sometimes he could not see her face clearly. Now that Roger had brought it up, Cass wished more than ever that he hadn't. A little moth of panic fluttered in his heart.

"Redbirds mate for life," said Roger, his fingers puzzling at the buckle. "I think rabbits as well, and badgers."

"What the hell you know about badgers?" said Cass, anxious to change the subject. "God damn the animal kingdom and their habits! Now, listen to me: this is not a good topic for conversation. We must rest, then catch up with the boys, lest we get snatched by the cavalry." He peered around at the thought, half expecting to see armed troopers encircling them.

Roger said, "Snakes, I do not think, do, though they stick together when they are. Still, nature is rife with examples." He gave up trying to open his haversack. He put it aside and drew his bayonet and began to thrust it into the orange clay, *chuff-chuff-chuff.*

Cass lowered his voice to a whisper, though no one was around to hear. "Roger, sometimes I think I am goin' to desert. What do you think of that?"

"You can't," said Roger. He picked at the flakes of skin on his sunburned face.

"Why not? Others have."

"You promised Sally Mae you would look out for me until we returned. We have not returned yet. Anyway, what would you do?"

"I want to go back to the river," said Cass. "I can pilot on the gunboats. You can go with me, and I'll show you—"

Roger waved his hand. "Bosh," he said. "I am not doing any such thing, and you would never make it to the river through all these yankees. Besides, don't change the subject. I know what you promised Sally Mae." He turned now and pointed the bayonet at Cass. "You promised her you'd watch out for me. I *know* you did."

"Now, listen to me," Cass said. "I am beginnin' to have visions. I am not well and cannot stand the strain. I could of swore I saw my mother just now, and her dead these many years. I also saw—"

"Sometimes I wonder if those people ever were at all." Roger sighed. "Still, you see them, the ones that are gone, I mean—when you get too close, like we are now. There is only a little way between us and them—you ever think about that? I see them, oh, all the time—" He nodded off, then caught himself. "What was I saying?"

"Forget it," said Cass. "Take your rest."

"Who was that you saw?" asked Roger. He yawned, and Cass yawned in sympathy. They sat with their long, aching legs outstretched. If they stayed here too long, Cass knew, their muscles would cramp, but he didn't much care right now. A fence lizard came, gaped at them, then scurried away. After a moment, Roger spoke again, his voice drowsy and slurred. "Your mother, yes," he said. "I never knew her." He yawned again. "More and more, I have trouble remembering things. Seems like now I can't much remember any way but this. Can you?"

Cass's problem was just the opposite: he couldn't quit remembering. He leaned back against the galled, knobby trunk of the oak. He imagined the gallery of Frye's Tavern again, the moon vine, the woman who had been his mother for ten years of his life. He wondered if she had really looked that way. He thought of Janie, of her hair and eyes, her talking, her boyish, miniature body that he might never know again. He shut his eyes and tried to call them back, but they wouldn't come. Just as well. Maybe Roger was right; maybe they had never been at all.

"Go to sleep awhile," said Roger. "You will feel better if you do."

"Might," said Cass. He thought about telling Roger to keep watch, and almost did, but the words drifted away from him like leaves on the water.

The first time Cass saw Roger Lewellyn, the boy was practicing for a recital, playing Mozart to the empty seats of the Cumberland Opera House. His long hair fell over the collar of his frock coat. His thin face, painted by a single gaslight, was smiling: not with pride, for he was unaware that anyone was listening, but with wonder at the music rising on the air, the beautiful dalliance of which he, like the piano itself, was only the instrument. Cass stood with his cousin Sally Mae in the shadows of the hall and listened, Sally Mae practically swooning on his arm. Cass had already decided to hate the boy, the more so because he had promised to look out for him in the adventures to come. *What does she see in this waif?* he asked himself. This creature of light and water, devoted to beauty, ephemeral as an elf? And this boy was going to the army?

Then a year passed, another April came, and Cass found himself wandering in the shredded, tangled woods beyond the sunken road at Shiloh. Cass and Roger had been together most of the day but were finally separated in the blind chaos of the fight. Cass was frantic that Roger was dead. How would he stand it, hating the boy as he did? Worse, how would he explain it to Sally Mae? He struggled through the vines and creepers, through briars, smoke, the confusion of intermingled divisions and brigades—soldiers everywhere, some of them belonging to the enemy, all bewildered as children lost—wounded men reaching out, flames crackling in the underbrush, riderless horses galloping by all flecked with foam, blood on the new leaves, a man without a jaw, a man carrying his own arm, another with his ribs showing white—this was what they had made, all them who had fought that day. Surely it could not be real, Cass thought—surely not this ruin, this shambles, this Valley of Death (nobody ever said it better than that, Cass thought). But Janie was real, and Sally Mae Burke was real, and Cass had failed them. Whatever terrible dream this was, he had failed them in it, and now they would have no more of him forever.

The field was enormous, there was no end to it, but still he searched. Cass was done fighting. He had failed, no question; he was humiliated, ashamed, a shambling figure stuffed with straw, but he would search if it took a lifetime. He would be an old man, gaunt, wild of hair and eyes, dressed in rags, frightening picnickers in the wood: *Have you seen him? A boy with long hair? Frail? He played the piano!*

He found Roger in a smoky glade, came upon him all at once and unexpected as one might a unicorn, and with the same sense of unbelief. The boy stood to his shanks in dead men, these already swollen and anonymous, of weight and mass but without substance, their faces blurred no matter how close you looked at them. Insects swirled around them. The white blossoms of some flowering tree drifted in the air.

The high green boughs bent their heads; the sky promised rain before night, and the night was fast approaching for them all. Roger, his cap gone, was drenched in blood; his hair was greasy with it, his jacket stained dark with it, his hands slick with it so that his musket kept sliding as he brought it up and down, up and down, jamming the butt again and again into the face of a man who lay at his feet. The face was broken now, all the bones yielded, and made a wet, sucking sound when the steel buttplate struck. Meanwhile, Cass watched, helpless and immobile, as Roger struck until he could strike no more. He rested a moment, panting, muttering to himself, shaking his finger at the man at his feet. At last he turned his musket and drove the bayonet deep into the center of the man's chest. Then he backed away, leaving the musket quivering upright. He looked at his hands, then brushed frantically at his jacket as if something were crawling there.

"Roger!" said Cass, his voice a hollow squawk like a raven's: not his own voice but one he had found along the way. He approached, his hand out, but stopped when the boy waved him off.

"Keep away!" said Roger. "Don't you touch me!"

"Are you hurt?" Cass whispered.

The other's breath was coming in long, ragged heaves now, his thin chest rising and falling against his cartridge-box strap. His eyes were red; his teeth were clenched, white and rimmed with powder, his lips blackened and burned with it. "I swear to God, don't touch me," said Roger. "I must kill them all!"

Cass moved closer. "They are dead already," he said. "All these men are long dead, Roger. Come, let us go now."

Roger looked up at the sky, at the leaves beginning to turn in the wind. When he looked at Cass again, his eyes were empty. "Leave me alone," he said.

For the first time, then, Cass understood their fate. They might live or die or be broken according to the chance that befell them, but alive or dead or broken, the one thing they would all be was mad. It could not be otherwise now. Here, in this awful glade, these men must be killed again and again— and who was to say there was no sense in it? That it made sense to Cass Wakefield frightened him more than anything he had seen down his long passage from the first pink blush of dawn. And Cass understood this, too: that in all that terrible wood, nothing was more dangerous than the boy, the piano teacher, Roger Lewellyn.

"All right," Cass said. "All right, pard. We will see to it."

"Will you help me?" asked Roger.

That night the rain came in torrents; the trees thrashed overhead; the ground ran with bloody water. Shells from the yankee gunboats on the river burst in filthy yellow blossoms in the woods. All night, lanterns moved like wills-o'-the-wisp through the trees, and men called to one another, searching. Sometimes they would move through the glade and raise their lanterns over the dead men's faces. By midnight, all the dead men had been turned over, and their faces were like putty in the lantern light. Sometimes the searchers noticed the two living ones sitting together under a big oak tree, huddled under gum blankets taken from the dead. "Have you seen . . . ?" they would ask, and speak the name of a lost comrade. But the living ones would only shake their heads, and the searchers moved on.

A dark hour came when the earth held its breath for morning. The rain, gentling now, pattered in the fallen leaves, the fallen blossoms, the sodden clothes of the dead men. The rain fell on their faces, washing away the blood. In this dark hour, when the searchers had long since returned to their regiments, Roger said, "Cass, you really ought to try and sleep." His voice was annoyingly calm; he spoke as if they had just returned from a late night at the theater.

"I may never sleep again," said Cass.

"Well, you'd feel better if you did."

"Might," said Cass, but Roger Lewellyn was already asleep himself, trembling with dreams.

✛

That was two and a quarter years past, and now it was high summertime in Georgia. Cass and Roger were both asleep, hats over their faces, when the horseman came. Cass heard the hooves scuffing on the road, sat up, opened his eyes, blinked in the sunlight. The horseman towered over them, leaning on his pommel.

"Great God!" said Cass, rubbing the sweat out of his eyes. "It is the Angel of Death!"

It was not the Angel of Death, but Lieutenant Perry Sansing, the regimental adjutant, come to close up the column. He said, "Gentlemen, what are you doing?"

"God damn, it's a popinjay, then," said Cass. "Wake up, Roger, and see. Do popinjays mate for life?"

The other did not move. "I do not think they mate at all," he said from beneath his hat.

"How come there's so many of 'em, then?" said Cass. He shielded his eyes and looked up at the horseman. "Mister Sansing, how do you do, sir?"

"I am well, sir," said the adjutant, and shifted the cud of tobacco in his jaw. Perry was from a distinguished line, a handsome boy in a butternut frock coat whose breeding showed in
his face. He had enlisted as a private, though his father was colonel of the regiment, and advanced through the ranks by pluck
and enterprise. When he was made adjutant, young Perry was
presented his father's Mexican War saber and great howitzer of
a Dragoon Colt, which Perry carried in a holster on his civilian
saddle. His mount was a sleek, nervous racer known through-
out Loring's Division for her speed and endurance. Cass had
won a good deal of money on the little mare, and besides, he
was fond of young Perry himself and actually glad to see him.

"I am glad to hear you are well," said Cass. "Why don't you
light awhile and join us?"

The boy shook his head. "No, I can't," he said, "though I
should like to. Now, Cass, you boys mustn't be lying around
like this. It is indecorous. It looks bad. You are cluttering up
the countryside. And besides, we are likely to be engaged
soon."

Cass shifted uncomfortably. "Perry, say it ain't so."

"It is so," said the lieutenant. "Furthermore, we are dangling out here like a ram's balls, and if we don't hook up pretty
soon—"

"I am engaged already!" said Roger suddenly, and laughed
in a strange, girlish way that shuddered the nerves. The others
did not laugh. Young Perry was betrothed himself, to a sweet
child so sprightly and gay that Cass had expected to hear music
every time he saw her. She was Perry's great weakness, and
sometimes Cass was afraid the boy's yearning would kill him.

"Shut up, Roger," said Cass. "Don't be talking about that."

He rose stiffly to his knees and looked at the adjutant. "Roger is a little pixilated," he said. "The heat has infected his brains."

"I understand," said the lieutenant. "My fleas are all dead of the sunstroke." He unwound the strap of a wooden canteen from the brass horn of his saddle. "Here's some good spring water," he said.

Cass uncorked the canteen, and the smell of whiskey coiled out like a jinni. He took a sip, then nudged his companion. Roger sat up, his hat sliding away. "What?" he said, blinking.

"Take a little," said the adjutant. "It will quicken the blood."

Roger sipped at the canteen. "Cass says he is goin' to desert," he said.

"Hah," snorted the lieutenant, and spat. He had only lately taken up chewing, and was not accurate.

"Damn you, Roger," began Cass, "I only mentioned—"

A distant splatter of gunfire broke across the quiet afternoon: the skirmishers had found somebody. Perry's horse sidestepped nervously, her ears pricked toward the sound. "Damn!" said the adjutant, tightening the reins.

"Hi-ho!" said Roger merrily. "This is no time to swap knives!"

Lieutenant Sansing looked at Cass. "You want to light out, now's the time."

"God dammit," said Cass, "I don't *want* to light out—I only mentioned—"

"All right," said the adjutant. The little horse was backing now, and suddenly Perry was talking in the peculiar strained way that officers had when events were closing down around them. "Join your company, then," he said. "Be quick."

Cass handed up the canteen. "I never meant I would run away," he said.

"I know," said the adjutant, and smiled, and for an instant was the boy again. "Hell, Cass," he said, "my daddy whipped the Mexicans twice. These yankees are nothin' but a Sunday stroll." Then he clamped his heels down, and the mare scratched in the clay and gravel until she found her footing and was gone, just like that, her tail streaming out behind her.

"We may rue this day," said Roger, watching the adjutant ride away. His face screwed up into a mask of worry. "I forgot it was Sunday. I wish those fellows would leave us alone."

"Well, so do I," said Cass, rising stiffly to his feet, his muscles cramped just as he had known they would be. "Now get up. Get your traps on."

Roger got to his hands and knees. "Where are my things?" he said. "I must roll up my quilt." Up ahead, the firing swelled to a steady roar, then in the midst of it the sudden thump of artillery—one report, then another, then another, a battery firing by gun, the concussion jarring the air.

Cass fumbled at the buttons of his jacket, his hands shaking. He was not ready for this.

Roger was rolling his quilt, slowly and deliberately, muttering to himself. Cass reached for his accoutrements, picked up his cartridge box; the strap was tangled in his belt and haversack, and everything came up in a wad, as it always did, no matter how carefully he laid it out. Cass was having trouble breathing again. Up ahead, the guns fired by section, and he flinched, feeling the sound, the terrible detonation like a blow to the chest.

Roger was up now, puzzling out his own tangle of equipment. Cass slung his cartridge box, then strapped on the belt with its dangling bayonet and cap box, and the bayonet was twisted, of course, and he had to straighten it and pull the cap box around front, holding both ends of the belt together, then fasten the oval buckle with the star for Mississippi, far away as any star that burned. Then the haversack and canteen—forget the blanket, he would have to get another one somewhere; it was too hot for blankets anyhow, just as his mother had said—then his hat, then his musket. He picked up the Enfield by the barrel and dropped it straightway; the piece had been lying in the sun and was blistering hot. Cass sucked his fingers and thought, *How will I ever get a charge in that?* and time ticked away.

Roger, fully accoutred now, was brushing the dust from his sleeve. "Come along, Cass," he said. "Don't dawdle, and a big fight just up the road."

"What makes you so goddamned eager all of a sudden?" said Cass. He thought, *This is not real; somebody is dreaming it. Sally Mae is real. Janie is real.*

A throaty cheer rose above the firing: the yankees applauding themselves. Cass looked at his musket, reached for his canteen, remembered it was dry as a cob. What, then? Only this remained, one more humiliation: he unbuttoned his fly, summoned his will, thinking *Please, please,* and sure enough he felt the pressure, and in a moment he was thinking, *Well, I am pissing on my rifle,* while Roger shook his head in disapproval and the steam rose from the hot barrel.

"Was that *really* necessary?" asked Roger, but Cass ignored him. He unbuckled his haversack, dropping the tin cup and frying pan that dangled from the strap, and fumbled inside until he found his rosary. Father Denby Garrison had given one to all the Episcopal men before they left Cumberland, at great expense to himself, since they had to be brought out of Cincinnati, no easy trick even in the early days of the war. A good many were already underground, twined in the hands of the dead. In any event, it was Father Garrison's rosary that Cass carried now. He pressed the crucifix to his lips, looked for an instant into the face of the suffering Christ, then took off his hat and slipped the beads around his neck, which was his custom in a fight. He replaced his hat, picked up the cup and frying pan, buckled his haversack, bent to retrieve his rifle. When he straightened, he was as much an instrument of war as he would ever be.

In a moment, they were shambling after the regiment, Cass holding his musket upside down by the small of the stock, smelling the reek of it. Cass thought of all the foul things he'd smelled in the war: the leavings of men, the unwashed living and the swelling dead, burning houses, the stench of powder and of fear. He cursed the sense of smell from which there was no escape. His feet pounded on the hard clay; he stumbled once, skinned his knee, was up again and following Roger Lewellyn toward the battle that loomed before them in a cloud of white smoke and flashes and yelling. And then they were in it.

The regiment, about to make contact with the right flank of the division, had been ambushed. A full brigade of ragged yankees had risen from the fields to meet them, had overrun the skirmishers and struck the column head-on. As the regiment maneuvered into line, it was caught in enfilade by a battery masked in a pine grove and supported by infantry.

It was a tight place. Once upon a time, a regiment of the Army of Tennessee would have stood in line of battle, taking the hot canister, slugging it out with the lads across the way. But those days were gone, and now the regiment was going to ground. The boys dug frantically with bayonets and tin plates and frying pans and with unsoldered canteen halves kept just for that purpose, while the enemy's twelve-pounders showered them with chunks of red clay and iron fragments, and the foul smoke rolled over them, and the officers snarled and bellowed like demons, and the regiment's drums beat to no purpose. In the midst of these things, Cass and Roger arrived on the field.

They struck the line midway where the color company lay, where the ragged banner of the regiment was shaken loose and waving in the smoke. Men were kneeling or lying on their backs to load, the rattle of their ramrods unaccountably loud amid the firing. The air was quivering with detonation, holding the sound and pressure as if it had jelled, so that to move through the sound was like moving in deep water. The air, too, was alive with the hum of fat minié balls passing, each one searching with malice for a living heart.

Officers prowled upright behind the line, their swords drawn, pausing now and then to fire their pistols into the smoke. One of them spied Cass and Roger. "Look here!" he cried. "Get in the line!"

"Captain Sullivan's company!" shouted Cass.

The officer grew apoplectic. He was so crowded with opinion that he could not speak, could only move his mouth and gasp for air. He raised his sword, but a ball came and struck the base of the blade—it made a distinct sound in all that uproar, like a stone striking a tin roof—and the officer howled and dropped the weapon and thrust his fingers in his mouth like a child, and Cass and Roger fled toward the right of the line.

Meanwhile, the battle grew on itself, consumed itself in the fury whirling at its center. The regiment, too, would have been consumed—nothing left but surrender or death—had not the balance of Adams's Brigade, in contact at last, come loping to the rescue across the broad savanna. Quick the scarecrow rebel infantry came, running in the killing heat with muskets at the shoulder, eager to possess this land between the ridges— every grain of sand, every gully, every wind-shook pine and rag of struggling grass—as if no other land in all the earth could be worth their dying. They lifted their voices, so that over the guns rose a quavering eerie cry like harpies descending, which drowned the manly hurrahs of the yankees and shivered the soul of every man. The smoke was riven with stabs of fire, here with a glimpse of tattered colors, there a man caught for an instant with arms outflung. The smoke rolled toward heaven, toward the gates of night, and under it no man could see its ending.

Cass and Roger ran bent nearly double but moving fast, carrying their long rifles horizontal to the ground, every step jolting through the thin soles of their shoes. Cass was trembling, his heart seemed about to explode like a dropped melon; he saw through a red haze swimming with planets; he could hardly breathe. All the broad earth, all of life, and all of past and promise had narrowed to the moment where he still lived—one moment, then the next, then the next. He ran. To his left, the line: rifles and ramrods moving like levers in a complex machine, driven by the pawls, the pistons of men. The line seemed poised on the rim of a volcano—nothing visible but smoke and eruption, streaks of flame, beyond the clattering, beyond the frantic churning of the machine. To his right, the mad wilderness of the rear: province of file closers, the crawling wounded, the limping and staggering, now and then a man running who could bear no more. Held horses pulled at their bridles, musicians huddled, all in a roil of dust and smoke, while a kneeling surgeon presided calmly, remotely, over a boy he could not save. Cass ran, himself a part of the vast engine now, though some agency of his soul detached itself, kept watch still, gathered and sorted and stored all he would remember in distant, uncreated hours if he lived. He could no longer feel the ground under his feet.

He collided with a man shot in the face, who reached blindly, clawed at Cass's jacket, then spun away. Voices, some at his ear, clamored in strange tongues, chattered like wheeling flocks of birds. They passed Perry Sansing's fleet mare; she lay on her side, flanks heaving, her legs moving as though she might still outrun the thing that was closing on her. But her bowels spilled from a gaping slice in her belly, and her heart was gone, and Cass saw a deep sorrow in her eyes. The adjutant himself was nowhere to be seen, but he wasn't dead, Cass knew. He was somewhere in the smoke.

"There!" shouted Roger, and pointed with his musket.

Captain Byron Sullivan had bent the company back at a right angle to refuse the flank; they were dueling with the infantry supporting the guns, and trying to kill the gunners and their horses. The artillerymen had to stand the fire; Cass saw one of them struck in the breast just as he pulled the lanyard, the final gesture of a life begun far away but ended here. The gun bellowed and leaped backward and caught the man's body under its wheels.

Lieutenant Tom Jenkins strode behind the line in his shirt-sleeves. A pistol was thrust in his waistband; on his shoulder rested a short Enfield. When he saw Cass and Roger, he grinned. "Now come on, boys," he said, and pointed with his free hand toward the men huddled on the line.

Some pines stood here, but canister from the guns had hewed them down to splintered stumps and chewed up the ground, and Cass wondered how Jenkins could live standing erect. Cass squeezed prone into the line, the men on either side making room. He scrabbled in his box, found a cartridge, tore it with his teeth; he bit too deep, of course, and filled his mouth with powder. His hands were shaking, but no matter, they always did, and still he got most of the powder down the barrel that was still too hot; the powder flashed while Cass's hand was still over the muzzle. Cass cried out, looked at his hand. It was speckled with powder grains deep in the flesh, fingers glazed white and already blistering, that quick. *The blood poison,* he thought.

The guns fired by battery, a devastation, rocking the earth and showering the riflemen with cascades of dirt and pine boughs. A man, thrown up in the air, landed with a thump across Cass's legs. He sat up, looked at Cass, waggled his beard. "It ain't hurt me any," he said, and grinned, his yellow teeth outlined in red. Almost at once, the guns fired again—these were veteran gunners, good at their trade—and Cass curled himself into a ball, hugging his rifle while the shower of dirt poured down and the iron hummed in the air, searching. He looked at his hand again, moved the fingers. *Not so bad,* he told himself, though the hand was already swelling. It burned, too, but not so bad. He felt better then, knowing it would fix itself. Lying on his back, Cass loaded his musket, no flash this time, and capped it, and was about to take a shot when Roger passed him, bent low, his teeth showing white in his face. "Come on, Cass," said Roger.

They were extending the line, thinning it out in an attempt to lap around the guns. Once more Cass was running, breathing hard, the blood throbbing in his hand. A man stood up to fire. The crown of his head vanished, and he dropped his musket; he stood a moment longer, arms outstretched, fingers drooping. He tilted his chin, like a man trying to read through a pince-nez, turned then and took a step toward Cass and folded to his knees, where he remained. Cass ran.

"Here!" shouted Roger, pointing. Cass flung himself to the earth, drew his bayonet, and began to dig. "Fix bayonets!" Captain Sullivan cried, but Cass dug. He dug with frantic joy, as if some great treasure lay just below. The ground was soft here, yielding, happy to embrace him. *Thank you thank you thank you,* Cass murmured in his mind.

Tom Jenkins came along the line, bent low now. "Get ready, boys!" he shouted. "Get ready!" But still Cass dug, using his good hand now, scooping the dirt and flinging it behind. He knew that in a minute he would be up and running, following the company into the pines where the tormenting guns lay, but he was determined to finish this hole. Just another minute and he would be done; then he could go. He plunged his hand into a sudden cavity in the loose earth, drew it out—

And stopped, blinking, trying to understand what he was seeing. He seemed to be holding a glove in his hand: a pale, translucent, oily glove that had come from no place he could imagine. He stared at the thing, trying to make sense of it, until all at once everything came into focus: a spray of white grubs squirming blindly in the sunlight, an eruption of ants and beetles, the blue sleeve, the delicate bones of the hand he had grasped and stripped—a man buried here after the fighting a week ago, who had lain all this time cooking in the hot earth. And now the man himself burst from the grave, not in body but as an exhalation of gas, violated, crying outrage and humiliation against the still-living man who had shamed him. The smell hit Cass Wakefield full in the face. He screamed, flung the skin away, scrambled to his feet in horror, and so was standing upright when the guns fired for the last time, and a round burst just in front of the line. The iron whirred and hummed around Cass's head, missing him, but a chunk of rock-hard clay the size of a fist struck him in the temple. He staggered, trying to flee, but there was no use in it.

✛

Roger Lewellyn was played out. He sat cross-legged in the rear of the line, retching a thin gruel, while the company rose from the earth with a shout, charged madly into the pines, and overran the battery. But these things seemed infinitely remote to Roger, like a tale of some epic clash that had happened long ago, and to other brave lads than these.

In a little while he stirred, lifted his head, and saw Cass Wakefield lying in the sunlight. Slowly he rose, swayed for a moment, then stumbled to the place where his comrade lay. The smell from the shallow grave struck him, and he bent over, hands on his knees, and retched again. He pressed a handkerchief to his mouth, knelt, and examined his friend. Cass was lying on his back, hands over his face. "Cass," Roger said, "what's the matter? Are you killed?"

"Lemme 'lone," said Cass.

"Well, fine," said Roger. He rose, took hold of Cass's jacket collar, and dragged him to a stand of pines where some cavalry men had left their horses tied. The effort took all his strength, and for a moment he sat among the horses, who seemed to take comfort from him, whickering and nodding their heads in a gentle way. He spoke to them and waved at the swarming flies. He rose again, found a canteen tied to a saddle and drank greedily from it, then returned to his comrade. He wetted the handkerchief and swabbed Cass's face, careful of the bloody knot rising on his temple. At last he sat down with the canteen between them and listened to the diminishing noise of the fight. The boys were cheering among the captured guns, and he could hear the wounded crying. For himself, he seemed to have lived, and Cass had lived, though many had not. Once he would have thought it God's will, but he understood better now.

He took another drink and afterward felt much improved. He looked at Cass and noted that he had curled on his side like a sleeper. That was fine; he would feel better if he slept awhile. Roger fumbled in his haversack and found the tintype of Sally Mae, which he placed on the ground beside him. Then he took out a pencil and a sheet of brown paper. He looked at the girl smiling up at him—the image was faded, and he could not see her clearly anymore—then spread the paper on his knee and began to compose a letter. He began: *Dearest Sally Mae, I hope this finds you well as it leaves me.* He paused, looked up through the pines at the indifferent sky, then turned once more to his letter. *Today I had a glimpse of the ending of the world.*

Meanwhile, Cass Wakefield, curled as one sleeping, dreamed of white egrets, and of willows like green smoke along the river.

✛

For several days after he was knocked in the head, Cass Wakefield was more addled in his mind than usual. He could neither eat nor sleep, though these things were no particular inconvenience since there was little to eat and no time for sleeping anyway. He could compose a sentence in his head, but when it came out, it was often gibberish. Worse, he could not seem to walk in a straight line. He would start out all right, then go wandering off in the fields until Roger came and got him. His vision was blurred, and his head buzzed with annoying galvanic shocks. Worst of all, his right hand had swollen like a melon and was useless.

The regimental surgeon took a scholarly interest in Cass's afflictions. He questioned Cass about the "electrical episodes," as he called them, and measured Cass's head and made notations in a memorandum book. He poked and prodded at the hand and speculated about the chemical composition of gunpowder—did the niter, in fact, retard corruption? Probably not, but what if it did? That corruption had not spread already was a medical curiosity, the surgeon proclaimed, and he might get a monograph out of it for the professional papers. He told this with more relish than Cass thought appropriate. Finally, the surgeon insisted that the hand come off. Cass refused, maintaining he would just as soon die with it as without it. The surgeon took offense at the implication, and on the third night some of the boys held Cass down while the surgeon pried out most of the powder grains with a pen knife and drained the pus. Then he damned Cass to hell and left him alone.

The next day, Cass was unable to walk at all, so he rode from daylight to dark on a litter strapped to the sticky floor of an ambulance. The back door was open, a square of violent sunlight, and the interior full of flies. Roger had found Cass a full canteen of water. Cass bathed his face and soaked his handkerchief and lay it across his eyes. He was as comfortable as he had been in years, it seemed. He was the only passenger, and the comparative solitude was a luxury. He had ridden in an ambulance only once before, after the battle now called Shiloh Church, or Pittsburgh Landing by those on the other side. That had been a bad time. Now, Cass felt as if he were being borne along in a sedan chair.

As the little wagon jolted and heaved over the road, Cass Wakefield's mind drifted into other lives—stories he had heard; confidences he had received; incidents of lives now finished, of lads who once were quick and now lay along the road behind. But not forgotten. Never the least nor the sorriest of them forgotten, these sparrows, nor even the ones across the way forgotten, some of them. Once, among various plunder, Cass took a letter from the still-warm body of a man he had killed—the letter of a father who never dreamed his words would fall to a stranger who had loosed his boy's soul with a single lucky thrust of a bayonet. Cass made himself read the letter:

Son, the Ice is thick on the River & on the Pond
we dug, you remember how hot it was that summer.
Now you should see Marly & your Mama skate
out upon it & how they twirl so graceful cutting
Figures & I laugh to see it. No fresh snow for a
week but the sky is lowering out the window & I
expect some Falling Weather ere morning. Had a
calf born, nearly lost it. All are well.

He swore for days he would write some answer, that the father might know the truth. But simple shame kept him from
it, and at last he threw the letter away.

All these lives commingled in the foul, sun-cooked box of
the ambulance, together with the sounds of the march: the
groaning of wheels, mules braying, men talking, the urgent
passage of couriers, and the endless dry shuffling of feet as the
army fell back toward Atlanta. Meanwhile Cass lay dozing on
the mildewed canvas litter that smelled of death, among whispers and phantoms. It was as though his own life were not sufficient company, but he must draw into himself the days and
years of others who clamored to be heard.

So it was in a world where the quick and dead no longer
had any clear distinction between them. Around Cass's neck
were the cool obsidian beads of his rosary, token of a faith he
had come to shyly, but with gratitude. He knew the black scattering of night without faith, and from this he fled as one pur-
sued by crows. Cass believed in the soul, and, believing, he
treasured every one and would hold every one cupped in his
hand if he could.

But souls could not be held—not by him, anyway, nor by

any mortal man. They had to fly, and light and air were their province. He was not surprised, then, by the brush of others' lives through his unsettled mind, nor by the unfamiliar voices he heard, nor by a glimpse of places he had never been: a kitchen in firelight; a bed still warm and damp, the counterpane tossed to the floor; a schoolroom, a broom-swept yard, a handkerchief lying in the blue shadows of a fence corner. These were the remnants of other lives now ended. They had been real once, and now, set free from time and earth, they needed a place to rest awhile. He did not mind they chose him as the vessel, and though they crowded him sometimes, he took comfort in knowing that he, Cass Wakefield, by the same measure would not be forgotten.

The ambulance halted momentarily, and when it jerked into movement again, Cass was shaken from his drowsing. He drew the handkerchief from his eyes and found that another passenger had joined him. In his current state of mind, he was neither surprised nor afraid to discover Rufus Pepper, who had been dead for more than two years, hunkered in the dried blood on the ambulance floor. Rufus was gangling, thin as a lath, and whiskery. An old converted flintlock lay across his knees. He wore a gray forage cap tilted back on his head, and Cass thought how odd it looked, for the boys had not sported those in a long time.

Well, Cass, you look like a warm turd, said Rufus by way of greeting.

"Thank you, Rufus," said Cass. The thought struck him that he didn't know *what* he looked like. He hadn't seen a mirror in months. "You lookin' mighty fresh yourself," he said.

I reckon them Romish beads ain't hepped you any.

"They are not a charm," said Cass. "They are a guide and a reminder."

Hmmm, said Rufus, who was a hard-nosed Presbyterian from the country. The ambulance took a hard jolt to starboard, and he steadied himself. *What's the matter with you, anyhow?* he asked. *What you doing in this amba-lance?*

"Well, Rufus," said Cass, "I have had my brains shook loose by a bomb shell. And look here at my hand." He held up his swollen hand, which burned hot as a lighter knot.

Well, that looks bad, I guess, said Rufus. *Likely it will kill you directly, if a tree don't fall on you first.* Rufus grinned, and Cass remembered how they were driving the yankees from a sunken road in the great Shiloh Church battle, and an aerial bomb shell had snapped off a big hickory limb, and the limb came crashing down and flattened poor Rufus like a hoe cake.

"I am grievous sorry we never buried you," said Cass. "I know some of the boys looked that night but never could find you, though they did find others."

Oh, never mind about that, said Rufus, waving his hand. *I have no hard feelings in the matter.*

Cass understood that Rufus Pepper was only an illusion coiling out of his own head; nevertheless, he seemed as real as anything else at the moment. Cass raised to one elbow, slow and careful, trying not to stir up the electricity. The rotten fabric of his shirt was stuck to the stretcher, and some of it tore away. "Well, Rufus," said Cass, "do you have some message to deliver, or are you just haunting around generally?"

Rufus rubbed his chin. He looked away, then back again. *I have gone down home,* he said.

"You have been home?" said Cass. He knew the lost ones

stayed with the regiment, but somehow he had never considered them going home. The notion disturbed him somehow. "Can they see you?" he asked.

The gaunt man shifted uncomfortably. *Yes, they can, sometimes,* he said. *They see something, anyhow. They will shiver of a sudden or glance at the place where you are. My old woman saw me, I know. She spoke to me, sat right up in the bed, and said, "Rufus, what happened? I got to know!" I tried to tell her, but I couldn't.* His voice seemed to fail him then, and he moved his hands over the stock of his rifle. *Durn it, you can't talk to 'em,* he said at last.

"But you are talking to me," protested Cass. "How come you can't talk to them?"

Hit's different, said Rufus. He waved his hand in a futile gesture. *I don't know how to tell it. They are in a different place, somehow.*

"But we are not?"

You all are closer than them, said Rufus. *Some of the boys is closer'n ere others.*

"Can you tell which ones?"

No, no, said Rufus, scratching his whiskers.

"Well, that is no encouragement," said Cass. He lay back and pressed his good hand to his eyes, and tried to imagine Rufus's wife alone in the cold cabin, rising in her bed to meet such an apparition. "Damnation, Rufus, you must have scared your old woman half to death."

Outside, the crows were cawing and talking in the pines. They always followed the ambulance train, drawn by the sweet smell of blood. Cass said, "Rufus, can you do me a favor if you go home again?"

I will, said the other.

"You go through Cumberland next time," said Cass, "you

find Sally Mae Burke's house—you know it, a fine place back in some oak trees. Look and see—"

Oh, I been there already, said Rufus.

"You *been* there?"

Where your Janie lives still? Surely I been there. I been to all them kind of places touching our comrades.

Cass felt a tightening in his heart. "What did you see there, Rufus? What did you come to tell?"

Miss Sally Mae was in the front room making a letter. I found your Janie sleeping in a hammick by the heat of the day. She was in a dress of green, and her hair all a-loose. She was so pretty, I made to touch her, but she got a chill and waken up. Said, "Cass?" and looked right at me.

"She spoke my name? What else? Is she going to be all right?"

Rufus grew uncomfortable again. He fidgeted with the stacking swivel of his musket. He took off his cap and wiped his brow on his sleeve. Finally, he said, *Cass, I'm sorry. It don't work that way.*

"What way, Rufus?"

Now, Cass, I can't tell you what you ain't supposed to know yet. That would put things out of order, don't you see?

"Oh, that's a fine thing," said Cass. "A fellow has to be dead to get all the news."

Rufus was growing dimmer. His voice seemed to come from far away. He said, *Janie's all right now. I can tell you she ain't forgotten. That's what you're worried about, ain't it? Why you want to run away?*

"I got to get home, Rufus!" said Cass. "I got no choice!"

Only the voice remained now. *Aw, you always got choices, pard.*

"You—" Cass began, but a spark of electricity arced and capered through his head, and he shot upright, reaching blindly. "You don't know anything about all that!" he cried.

But he was alone. His visitor was gone, and where he had been was only a little dot of sunlight shining down through a hole in the ambulance roof.

6

Cass Wakefield deserted the Army of Tennessee while they were fighting in front of Atlanta on the Nickajack line. He said nothing to Roger; he simply put down his musket and accoutrements and walked off from the company without a word. His head was still foggy, but he could walk in a straight line now, and his hand had ceased burning, though it was stiff and still leaked pus into the rag he'd wrapped it in. Cass walked toward the rear; nobody paid him any mind, and everything was so easy that he wondered why he hadn't done it long ago. He made three miles, in fact, before he was snatched up by the cavalry and bound hand and foot with a picket rope.

At the company bivouac, Cass was delivered to First Sergeant William ap William Williams, an old Regular Army man who ordered the old Regular Army punishment known as the "buck and gag": a bayonet was jammed lengthwise in Cass's mouth, his hands tied behind, and the picket rope wound around the bayonet and around his drawn knees and tied around his feet. This was supposed to last for an afternoon; within five minutes, Cass was in such pain that his spirit forsook him and perched in the branches of a pine tree overhead, and from there he watched the approach of Roger Lewellyn.

Roger looked down at Cass where he was trussed up. "What is this?" he demanded of the guard.

"It is a God damned abomination," said the man, "but you must leave him alone. He deserted and was caught. Go on now, Roger, and mind your business."

Roger said, "Cass Wakefield deserted? Nonsense. He would not do that without telling me." He knelt and put his hand on Cass's shoulder. "What is all this, Cass?" he asked.

Cass tried to answer from the pine tree, but he could make no sound.

Roger departed, only to return a few minutes later with an open clasp knife. He knelt and cut the rope, unwound it, and took the bayonet from Cass's mouth. At once, Cass's spirit returned, and he looked up at Roger through a haze of scarlet.

The guard hissed, "Damn you, Roger, now you've done it. I must call for the corporal of the guard."

"Well, call for him, then," said Roger.

The guard called the corporal, and the corporal called the first sergeant. "Here! What are you about, then, Lewellyn, you snipe?" said the first sergeant when he arrived.

"Well, I am cutting him loose, as you can see," said Roger.

"God damn you, then," said the first sergeant. "You will join him in the traces, by God."

"No," said Roger. By this time, a crowd of soldiers had gathered. Roger faced the first sergeant, the knife in his hand. "Bill," he said, "you shan't do it to me, and if you truss Cass Wakefield up again, I will kill you."

Here, all at once, was a novel situation to interrupt the afternoon. The men spread unconsciously into a circle, with Roger, Cass, and the first sergeant at the center. They were silent, with none of the jeers that accompanied fights of lesser import. Their silence was their testimony: here was a solemn trial, no longer of authority but of the principals themselves. No one understood this better than the first sergeant, who had been soldiering all his life.

"Is it so, then?" the first sergeant said mildly. He lay down his rifle and began to remove his accoutrements. He was a big man, a Welshman, with muttonchop whiskers and a lean face and eyes that always squinted. He had fought Indians on the plains of the mysterious West. No one knew why he had cast his fortune with the state of Mississippi, but here he was.

By comparison, Roger looked small and lost. The long campaigns had not altered his appearance. He had been gaunted at the start and could not be gaunted further. The sun would not brown but only burned him. His fingers were slender and delicate, like a girl's, and he guarded them above all his person. You would not find Roger Lewellyn clumsily ramming a charge, or reaching in the fire for an ear of corn. In fact, the thing that surprised the boys most was that Roger was using a clasp knife, which might close on his fingers in a fight.

He was soaked with sweat, his hair plastered with it, his thin, filthy shirt transparent down to his bony chest. He was gone pale under the sunburned flakes; his voice had risen a full octave, but the hand with the knife was steady.

Williams stood before him, now divested of coat and equipment, the symbols of his rank. He, too, was soaked in sweat, but his body was hard and knotted of muscle. He gave no glance at the circle of men around him. He said, "Lewellyn, I have sworn to gag you and Wakefield both for your treason. It cannot be unsaid, though I take no pleasure in it. You have stated that if I do, you will kill me. How, then, are we to resolve this?"

"I . . . I mean what I say," said Roger. "This is no fit punishment for a gentleman."

Williams nodded. "I see. A gentleman. Does a gentleman desert his comrades?"

The words stung Cass like a hornet. "Roger," he croaked.

"Be quiet, Wakefield," said Williams. He looked at Roger. "You must answer me, lad."

Roger shook the hair from his eyes. He was trembling, all but his hand, as if it were bent by a will of its own. "You don't"—he hiccupped—"you don't know the circumstance!" he said.

Williams spread his palms. "All right, then," he said. "Have at it, as you will."

The sun beat down hot upon them, and there was no breeze. Somewhere, crows were cawing in the pines, the only sound. It was so quiet that when Cass moved, he heard the grating of his elbows in the red dirt, the groaning in his joints as he pushed himself erect. "Roger, for God's sake," he said.

Roger turned to him then, his face white and stricken, not with fear but with pain. "I don't know what to do, Cass," he said. "I won't allow—"

"Remember Sally Mae Burke," said Cass. "She is all you must think on."

Roger drew in his breath, let it out in a sob. "I am," he said. "I *am,* don't you see? She would want—"

"I know," said Cass. "Honor. She would ask no less of you than that. But you cannot fight the first sergeant." He took the knife from Roger's hand, closed it, tucked it in his breeches pocket. He turned to Williams then. "Bill, I am your man," he said, "but I won't be trussed again."

The first sergeant stood with his hands on his hips. He shook his head. "Well, fuck me all around," he said. He seemed to notice for the first time the men gathered about. "I am be-fucked," he said to them. "This is honor, then? Would you care to take a vote, lads? Draw up a referendum? Shall we schedule a debate? What say you, then?"

The men looked at one another. They shuffled their feet and studied the sky. "Well, it *is* a mean thing to bind a man so," said one.

"I never said 'twasn't," replied the first sergeant.

"Um . . . you could have him dig a trench," said another.

"A trench?" said the first sergeant, his whiskers quivering.

"A large trench," the man said, spreading his arms to demonstrate.

"Yes, and fill it up with rocks," said a third man.

"There ain't any rocks around here, fool," said a fourth.

"Well, goddamn, fill it with frogs then—and don't be callin' me a fool."

"Or bullshit," said a bearded man. "He could fill it up with bullshit. They's aplenty of that around here."

"Nobody asked you, Joe Clem," said the third man. More words were exchanged, a shoving match broke out, and the crowd shifted its circle in accommodation. Soon, the four men were trading blows and curses, and the soldiers were jeering and laughing. Bets passed between them, and more hard words, and old insults were recalled. Cass, Roger, and the first sergeant, outside the circle now, watched as the scuffle turned into a general melee, raising a great cloud of dust, lasting a good five minutes until some officers arrived and broke it up. Finally, the men wandered away, all of them in good spirits, relieved, satisfied that honor had somehow been preserved.

First Sergeant William ap William Williams took up his jacket from the ground, shook out the dust, and drew it on. He buttoned it up to the neck and flexed his shoulders. "Lewellyn," he said, and pointed.

Roger picked up the worn accoutrements and girded and belted the first sergeant, adjusting cap box and bayonet. He handed the first sergeant his hat, then his rifle.

"Very well, then," said Williams. He looked at Roger, then at Cass. "You understand," he said, "how all this might have turned out different."

Roger made to speak, but Cass hushed him. "Yes, First Sergeant," said Cass.

"This is not a play," said Williams. "You should know that by now. The ending is not always the same."

"Yes, First Sergeant."

"Therefore," said Williams, "you must not press me again. Not ever. Do you understand?"

"Yes, First Sergeant," said Cass and Roger together.

"And Mister Wakefield," said the first sergeant, "you will take your place in the line henceforth. We do not need file closers who run away."

Williams turned then and walked away. He limped, where a Comanche arrow had taken him in the thigh years ago. When he was gone, Cass sat down in the dirt and rubbed his jaws. "Goddamn, Roger," he said.

"You're welcome," said Roger, and sat down himself. He looked at his hands. "How come you wanted to run away, Cass? You are no more worn out than anybody else."

Cass could say nothing to that. They were all walking shadows now, these lads, and only the strongest remained. Some invisible wire held them in place or pulled them here and there, but bound them together nevertheless, even Cass Wakefield. He remembered what it was like, only a little while before, to divest himself of it, uncoil the wire from his heart and lay it aside. For the first hour, a great weight seemed lifted from him; after that, only something lost.

Roger had found a stick and was poking at the dirt with it. After a moment, he threw the stick away and looked at Cass. "Old Bill was nearly right," he said. "When he told how this isn't a play, I mean. But not entirely right."

"Roger—"

"It *is* a play, after a fashion," said the other. A horned, pincered beetle, glistening black, crawled between them, scuttling along like a model for some great siege engine. Roger watched it pass, then looked at Cass again. "You wear the worn-out mask," he said.

"Ah," said Cass. "And which one do you wear?"

Roger laughed. "You should know. I took it off a minute ago, and you saw what was under it. I was scared pretty nigh to death."

"There is no man here," said Cass, "if you took off his mask, wouldn't show that. You did damn well, for a piano player."

"You were going home to Janie," Roger said. "I don't know why you don't just tell the truth. How long since you heard from her?"

Cass tried to remember. The days, weeks, months had a way of running together, and only places had any meaning. "I'm sure it was at Ringgold," he said. "The letter was written in March."

Roger counted on his fingers. "That's a long stretch," he said. "Truth is, you are afraid she has forgotten. That is your circumstance; there is no shame in it, and if you are bent on running away, I wish you success, as long as you tell the truth. I will tell the boys you acted with honor. They will know it anyway. They know you are not a coward."

"I am obliged," said Cass. He felt as if he were filled with straw. He could almost see it leaking out his pants cuffs, his sleeves, the collar of his shirt. He unwound the filthy rag from his hand and dropped it in the dirt. The pus had drawn some maggots, which he flicked away like grains of rice, as if it were a thing every man did in the course of the day. You shaved, oiled your hair, chose a shirt and cravat, brushed the maggots away. Then you put on your mask, so that when you ran away, the boys would say you were brave.

Roger had brightened some, drawn up his knees and

linked his arms around them. He turned his face toward the sky. "I acted with honor," he said, and nodded once. "I can tell Sally Mae someday."

"Yes, you can," said Cass. He put his arm around the boy's thin, sweaty shoulders. "You surely can. Remind me at the wedding, and I will tell her myself."

⚜

In the world the soldiers inhabited, a man could be dead any number of ways: by gun, bayonet, knife, saber, canister, by all the chance of battle, but not by battle only. They died by tree limb or sun or the slow freezing of the blood; of dysentery, measles, fever, the bloody flux; by standing too close behind a horse or coming unexpected on a picket line in the dark. Cass watched a man die from the prick of a thorn, another from drinking cold buttermilk. Once the company, flung out in skirmish line, was crossing an abandoned farmstead when one of their number vanished like a wraith before their eyes. They found him at the bottom of a well, his neck broken. One day, a boy, cleaning his revolver, let the piece discharge. He apologized to everyone, then, a half hour later, went to waken his father, asleep against a rail fence with his hat over his eyes. The boy called out his father's name, then lifted the hat. The pistol ball had struck the old man at the bridge of his nose. The boy cried all day, and that night hanged himself in a barn. Sometimes men died for no apparent reason: they simply quit; they sat down, arranged themselves, and ceased to be. The Death Angel was everywhere waiting, counting them over and over, eager to subtract. He marched beside them in the ranks; he moved among them when they slept, peering into their faces.

He was eager for the little slip, the moment of weakness or for-getfulness. He courted them all.

They grieved. True, after so long a time among the slaugh-ter and waste, they no longer seemed capable of sorrow. Cass remembered crossing an old battlefield sown with dead; from a shallow grave reached a hand, all bone and leathery skin, a tin cup's handle hooked in its fingers. But the cup was not joke enough. Into it, the passing troops had thrown pennies, but-tons, IOUs, even a wedding ring. They laughed going by. They said, *Look! See the poor soldier begging for back pay*. They said, *Look! It's somebody's darling*. But secretly they grieved for the unknown lad whose hand, strangely graceful still, beckoned to them. They would not admit it, not even to themselves, but they sorrowed. And behind them, on the long road they had come, followed the faces, the voices, of those they could never forget. The sorrow grew in them, though no one from the old, the other world, could have told it. Grief crowded the secret rooms of their hearts. Now and then, it passed a shadow over their own faces, trembled in their own voices. Now and then, a man, sitting by a fire perhaps, or strolling through the camp, would suddenly begin to cry. He would weep without shame until he was done, while the boys looked away and were silent. No one ever laughed or ever brought it back again in jest.

So they grieved, and more: they were harried by guilt. That, too, was the work of the Death Angel, who chose one and let another live, who dropped this one by the roadside while his comrade walked on. The soldiers traveled always in the company of those who were gone, who were transformed by memory into better men—gentler, funnier, braver men—than they might have been in life. The Death Angel reminded the living always of how much promise was lost, and how, beside it, their own possibilities shrank to no consequence. He whispered how they could never do enough, be enough now to be worthy of the gift of life. *And yet, are you not relieved?* he would whisper. *Tell yourself truly—are you not glad it was him and not you?* The soldiers might speak of tomorrow, of what good deeds they would do, of redemption or love or promise or hope, but deep in their hearts, they knew it to be a lie, a tale they told themselves to beguile their shame.

Consider a line of battle advancing under the red, tattered, star-crossed flags. The line wavers; it is hewn by musketry, shredded by canister, consumed in the bitter smoke. A man makes this terrible passage, and when it is done, he wakes from the dream that has possessed him and looks about in wonder. He is alive. For a moment, the world is Eden born anew for him, and life so precious it cannot be comprehended. For that moment, his very flesh seems pink and warm, just fashioned from the clay. Then he looks again, more closely. In the regiment's wake lay the ones subtracted—some trembling, others crawling, most quiet as stones. All at once, the illusion of life gives way to its hardest truth, and the living man chills his heart, or so he believes. It is easy now, he thinks, after so long and so many lost. Yet, in the company of the living, he is drawn back over the field of the dead, ignoring the shouts of officers to rally, to pursue. All that is over now, and new business must be attended to. A tally must be made, seeds gathered for future dreams. The living must see for themselves, this last time, who will follow them on the road.

Here lies a man who found beauty in all things; in birds, in the uncurling of a fern, in the shadows made by candlelight on a tent wall, and he would say to them, *Is that not beautiful?* trying to teach them how to see. They had learned from him, and because of him the world would never seem without grace in the smallest things. Now he has no eyes at all.

Here a man is crawling, intent on some destination only he could name, if he would. But there is no name for it he could give them that they would understand. He pulls himself along by handfuls of broom sage, unmindful of the coils of his innards and the coppery, dust-covered bag of his liver dragging behind. A while ago, he was a cheat at cards, a thief who bragged of Negro girls he had taken in the corncrib at home. Now he whimpers and crawls like an infant, and at last is still. The soldiers cover him with a blanket, and one of them remarks that here is ol' J. D. Cunningham, who had never run from a fight until now, and they laugh. But they remember one cold midnight when he walked into a burning house to find if any could be saved. That is what they will tell, as long as any remain to tell it.

In a bombshell crater lies a man who fell in love with another's sister. He saw her in a tintype dropped from a letter: a plain girl in white, hands folded, sitting in a chair. He was smitten and begged permission to write, and the brother had a little fun with him, then gave him the picture for his own. *Jes' so long as the chaps don't look like you,* said the brother, though later he told them all in secret, *Here is a good man for young Polly; let's see what comes of it.* What came of it was this: a half-dozen letters interchanged, a promise made and accepted, and now the brother's body in fragments at the smoking bottom of the hole, and intermingled the lover's broken limbs, his face buried in the mud, while Polly, somewhere, snaps peas in a bucket, unaware for a little while of what she has lost.

Now here is a boy with both his legs splintered at the knee, the white, shattered bones gleaming wetly. Beside him lies his severed hand. The living man kneels, ponders the hand turned upward, the curled fingers, the grooves in the palm black with dirt. A month ago, when Roger Lewellyn was weak with fever, this hand had made a letter for him in fine cursive script: *Dear Sally Mae, I am feeling poorly so have asked Charlie Ables to write a few lines in response to your thrice welcome letter received in May. I hope this finds you well, as it leaves me.* Now the hand lies mute and helpless, and young Charlie Ables lifts his head from the bloody grass. "Cass, is it bad?" he says.

"Oh, no, Charlie," says the living man. "It is nothing." There is one hand left, and he takes it. The hand fastens on his own, so tight there is no pulling away. The living man sits a long time, unwilling to loose the fingers, while all around men's voices call to one another, and a burst of firing erupts on the flank, and the hot sun travels overhead as if nothing at all had happened. The regiment is in line again, and the old flag broken out and whisking its tattered fringes in the breeze. On the cotton bunting they have painted, one by one, the names of their battles. These are barely readable now, but no matter; they are sufficiently graved in memory. An officer passes, touches Cass's shoulder.

"Come along," he says gently. "We must leave them now."

"All right, Perry," Cass says, though he knows there is no leaving. Still, it is what they say. He pries the fingers free and closes the dead man's eyes. He touches the rosary about his neck, a reflex like the jerk of a cooling muscle. He picks up his musket and takes his place. Behind him, the drums begin. The officers shout. The regiment moves forward.

✤

So they grieved and were ashamed, though only in the secret provinces of their hearts. To the citizens lining the fences, leaning from the windows of houses, or peering from their shops, the men appeared reckless and defiant in their long ragged columns. They seemed dangerous under their banners and the gleam of their bayonets, in the cadence of their drums, among the prancing of the officers' horses. And so they were dangerous, though not by any implements of war. They were all more or less insane now—the mild ones, the dull-witted ones, even those who believed and accepted that God's inscrutable Will was being done. This, above all, made them dangerous. The citizens would not comprehend, but the soldiers understood it in one another, and none of them had been surprised when Roger Lewellyn, mildest of boys, offered to kill the first sergeant on the road to Atlanta. Certainly Cass Wakefield, who knew him best, was not surprised.

They fell back on Atlanta in the summer of '64, and in that time Cass discovered he wished Roger Lewellyn dead. He would be wandering among the dark trees of his dream, and the thought would come suddenly from the air, darting, buzzing like a foul horsefly: *If he were dead . . .* Then the Death Angel would stroll by, lean into Cass's ear, whisper, *Did you hear that? Wouldn't everything be simpler then?* Cass knew it would. He could run away then, and Janie would not forget him, and Sally Mae would forgive in time. And Roger would forgive him surely, looking down from the stars. Then, with daylight and waking, Cass was horrified and ashamed at what he had made in his dream. He clung to Roger Lewellyn like a tick and prayed for forgiveness. He watched for Death, to interpose himself if he could—a vanity that always made the Death Angel smile.

Once, in the works before Atlanta, when Cass was in the dark place, the shade of Rufus Pepper came again. This time, Rufus was not soldiering but wandering through his days before the war. He was dressed in linsey-woolsey trousers held up by a single gallus, a faded gingham shirt, and a straw hat wide as an umbrella. He was barefoot. His long, mud-crusted, calloused feet with their horny nails were appalling to Cass, who was revolted by the sight of any male feet but his own.

Hidy, said Rufus.

"Damnation!" said Cass. "See here—what you haunting me for anyhow?"

Rufus was hurt. *Well, you was my pard,* he said.

"Yes," said Cass, "but sometimes you scare the dog shit out of me, dropping by like this."

Well, I'll jes' go on, then, said the man, and began to dissolve.

"Now, hold on," said Cass. "I don't mean to offend. Don't go away. I am glad for your company—honest Injun I am. You just take some getting used to, is all."

Rufus was satisfied and made himself solid again. He squatted on his heels, his toes splayed in the mud, and looked about. *This is bad ground,* he said. *You ought not to come here.*

"It is not a place I come to by choice," said Cass. "You ought to know about that."

I do know, said Rufus. From his pocket, he extracted a

peeled willow twig and began to work it among his yellow teeth.

"Well, I suppose you have come to tell me about Janie again," said Cass after a moment. His visitor shook his head and was silent. "Then I expect you want to see what moves in the stream there," said Cass. "Perhaps that will interest you."

Rufus chewed on his twig. The mysterious light of that place shadowed the planes of the man's cheekbones, the sunken hollows of his jaws, the stubble on his chin. Rufus picked up a black gob of mud and let it slip through his fingers; left behind in his palm was a wriggling mass of worms. Rufus flung them in the water. *There ain't nothing real here, Cass,* he said.

The tree limbs rattled as if in protest. An indistinct shape slid from the bank and swirled the scum among the reeds.

"Those worms were real," said Cass. "The mud, the trees, that water there, the things that swim in it—they are real as anything."

No, said Rufus, *you make it all up.*

"Don't be saying that," said Cass. "I do not choose—"

Look yonder, said Rufus, and lifted his hand.

Cass followed the pointing finger. The trees had parted, leaning inward toward a channel of dark water where a black steamboat, gleaming all of polished ebony, was nosing down the stream. Its wheels churned the water without sound; its chimneys brushed the gray curtains of moss, but no smoke rose from them, nor any steam from the pipes. All the railings were hung with crepe, the windows shuttered. The pilothouse was dark, though something moved there, Cass thought. He knew the movement: the pilot crossing from the wheel to the window and back again.

"What does it mean?" said Cass, his voice hushed.

What you will, said Rufus.

Now the boat grew closer, and Cass discerned on its bow a catafalque adorned with dark angels, and beside it the Death Angel, smiling, wings folded like a black frock coat.

What you will, said Rufus again.

On the catafalque lay a patent iron coffin with an oval glass, a window on the dead, and toward this the Angel moved his hand. Cass felt himself rise up among the moss. He smelled the boat's cold chimneys and its rotting wood, felt the chill breath of water dripping from its wheels. He looked down on the coffin, and in the glass saw a thin pale face watching back, the lips open in a smile, forgiving—

"I don't mean that!" cried Cass Wakefield, and sat upright, the blanket flung away.

A sentry stopped, looked once in his direction, then moved on. It was nothing; men were always crying out in the night. The moon was late, rising full, and the earth was crossed by the shadows of stacked arms, the rags of tents; of battery horses and the wheels of guns parked nearby; of restless men who moved among the pine grove. Beyond, encircling for miles, shrouded in wood smoke and the smell of frying fatback, lay the Army of Tennessee like a vast encampment of gypsies. Roger Lewellyn sat hunched by the dying fire, feeding it with scraps of bark. He turned; a brand flared up and lit his face. His long hair was pulled back in a queue, and his cheeks glistened with sweat.

"What is it, pard?" said Roger. "Were you dreaming?"

"Yes," said Cass.

"Well, don't tell it before you eat," said Roger, "else it will come true."

Cass propped himself on one elbow. His hand burned, and his skin felt as if it had been rubbed with bacon grease. A mosquito whined in his ear, and he swatted at it. After a moment, he said, "Roger?"

"Right here." The boy was turned from him now, a dark shape against the fire.

"Roger, I will not run away again," Cass said.

"That's good, Cass," said the boy. "Now, why don't you try to sleep? You'll feel better if you do."

Cass nodded and lay back again, settled his head against the sweaty leather of his cartridge box. He looked up through the pines at the glittering spray of stars, and he thought, for an instant, that a dark, familiar shape moved across them. Then he slept, traveling toward morning in the careful hands of God.

✧ 7 ✧

ONE MILD INDIAN-SUMMER AFTERNOON, THE ARMY of Tennessee was sprawled out all over the city of Decatur, Alabama. Their commander, General John Bell Hood, had given up Atlanta and been rewarded for his loss with an ambitious new campaign. Hood, the cavalier, planned to rescue the ladies of Nashville from the yankees and drive on up into Ohio. First, however, he had to cross the Tennessee River, and to that end, a sporadic, futile fight had been going on since daylight around the formidable yankee works, behind which a handy pontoon bridge lay beckoning. Adams's Brigade, including the Twenty-first Mississippi, was in reserve and had not been engaged, so, after the custom of all soldiers, they improved the time by building big fires and making coffee. Some of them went chicken hunting. Hood was a great fighter but not a great provider.

A little after one o'clock, a boy appeared suddenly, unaccountably, in the regimental midst. No one had seen him approach. "I am lookin' for the Twenty-first Mississippi," he announced to a group of men playing marbles on a gum blanket. The game was not going well, for the mud made a various landscape under the blanket. The soldiers looked up at the boy in wonder. "For what?" said a thin man in spectacles.

The boy turned his head and spat. "If I was you and was goin' to play marbles," he said, "I'd get a table outen that house yonder."

"You would, would you?" said the thin soldier.

"Yep," said the boy. "I'd take the legs off and set it in the mud. Then you could play."

"How come you never thought of that, Jack?" said another man. He looked at the boy. "This is the Twenty-first," he said, "but we are fresh out of sugar tits."

"Huh," said the boy, and spat again. "I 'spect you are."

The man started to rise, but the thin soldier waved him down. "Look here," said the thin soldier, and pointed toward the next house. "You go see General Wakefield over there. That's his headquarters. He'll fix you up."

The boy looked in that direction. "What'll he be playin'? Dolls?"

"You'll have to find out for yourself," the thin soldier said. "Now go away."

The boy made to spit again but didn't. The soldiers watched as he turned without a word and moved away.

Cass Wakefield, Roger Lewellyn, and Ike Gatlin had built a fire out of some boards from a house, a handsome dwelling far enough from the enemy's works that it hadn't been razed for their field of fire. The occupants had objected to the rebels dismantling their weatherboards, but Cass reminded them how lucky they were to have a house at all, and a few boards less wouldn't matter, and if they didn't go inside and be quiet, his boys would tear the whole *God*-damned house down around their ears and burn it all. After that, they had no more trouble; in fact, the scrawny old wife had slung them a mess of fall turnip greens and a pitcher of water.

Now Cass was sitting on his gum blanket against a paling fence, smoking. He was a sergeant again, elevated by simple subtraction in the battles around Atlanta. He could hear the rattle of musketry, the shouts of men, but it wasn't his fight yet, so he pushed these portents to the back of his mind. What rankled him at the moment was the ungrateful conduct of the citizens, whose interests, theoretically, the army was here to accommodate. True, the old wife had brought them some greens, but she'd been grudging about it. Probably they were full of boiled worms or spiders. Well, Cass thought, if the boys stayed long enough, they would burn the fence, too, except the part he was leaning on. He could smell the greens cooking and wished they didn't cause him to bloat up so. He might eat some anyhow, he thought. He was debating the issue when a shadow fell across his legs.

In the pale afternoon sunlight, Cass saw a boy of perhaps sixteen, slender of frame, with blond curly hair and a face that was not handsome but beautiful. He wore linsey-woolsey breeches too short for him, and a stained gingham shirt, and carried a carpetbag, which he put down at his feet. "You General Wakefield?" he said.

"Beg pardon?" said Cass.

The boy produced a paper and handed it down to Cass. It was a note from the provost marshal, a single line:

Sullivan: Here is a boy. Good luck.

Cross

Cass pulled himself reluctantly to his feet and knocked his clay pipe against the fence. "This ain't for me," he said. "It's for Captain Byron Sullivan."

"Huh," said the boy. He shrugged and thrust his hands in his pockets. He had round brown eyes with long lashes, and a spray of briar scratches across his nose. "You all got anything to eat?"

Ike and Roger came up. "This a fresh fish?" said Ike.

"Just hatched," said Cass.

Roger had a little corked bottle of salt in his hand. He examined the boy. "He doesn't look like much," he said.

"You don't look like much yourself," said the boy.

They all laughed at that. Cass gave the note back to the boy and said, "Well, you'll have to see the captain, then the colonel, then the general, but they are all busy today. Come back tomorrow."

"Oh, let's keep him, Cass," said Ike Gatlin.

"I ain't goin' no fu'ther," said the boy, and sat down on Cass's gum blanket.

Roger said, "Come along, Ike. We should leave Cass and his orphan to get acquainted."

"Wait a minute," said Cass as they strolled away. "He ain't any of mine."

In a moment, Ike and Roger were hunkered by the fire, watching some boys haul a table out of the empty house next door. "He ain't *my* orphan," shouted Cass, but the men around the fire grinned and ignored him.

A swell of musketry broke out upriver, accompanied by the mad cheering of the yankees. *We will never take this place,* thought Cass. *It is all a waste of time.* He looked at the boy. The sound of the fight did not seem to move him; in fact, he appeared to be asleep, leaned against the fence, his arms crossed tightly over his chest.

"Now, see here," said Cass, "you have got my place."

The boy opened his eyes. "I never seen your name on it."

"Well, you are a smart-ass anyway," said Cass. "You'll fit right in. Where'd they find you?"

"Aberdeen, Mississippi."

"What's your name?"

"Lucifer," said the boy.

"The hell you say!"

The boy shrugged. "It's the name they give me down at the orphantage. They said it means 'light.'"

"Well, that's one thing it means," said Cass, "but probably that's not why they gave it to you. I guess you really *are* an orphan."

"Born and bred," said the boy.

"What's your other name?"

"They never give me ere other. I reckon they thought the one was enough."

Cass wanted to question the lad further, but all at once the drums of the regiment began the unwelcome summons of the long roll. Cass groaned, and a slender knot of fear tightened around his heart. He did not want to go anywhere. He wanted to stay in this backyard and camp out and wash his shirt, sleep awhile, smoke, drink coffee, and talk to the boys. Nevertheless, he started for the color line, buttoning his jacket. He was almost there when he stopped, walked back to the fence, and kicked the boy's foot. "You, Lucifer," he said.

"What?" said the boy, cocking one eye open.

"You hear those drums?" said Cass. "That is the call to arms. It means we are goin' into this broke-dick fight."

"I won't wait up," said the boy, and closed his eye again.

"By God," said Cass. He knelt and pried the boy's eye open with a thumb. "Listen here, spawn," he said. "You keep watch over that fire yonder till we get back. Don't let anybody steal those greens. Understand?"

The boy brushed Cass's hand away. "Do I get some if I do?"

"You may," said Cass. "I may also kick your ass if you don't. Do I make myself clear?"

"Clear as horse piss, squire," said the boy.

Cass started for the color line again, and along the way met First Sergeant William ap William Williams.

"Here, Wakefield, damn you!" said the first sergeant, and pointed at the sleeping boy. "What is that, pray?"

"Oh, that's my substitute," said Cass. "Can I go home now?"

"Could I be shut of you so easy," said Williams, "I would pay the man myself. Now, that yonder is but a whelp. Where did it come from?"

"Well, damned if I know, Bill," said Cass. "It just showed up."

"All right, all right," said the first sergeant, and gave Cass a shove. "Go on, now. See to your lads."

The company was already in line, the stacks of muskets disassembled. Roger handed Cass his musket and accoutrements—a trifle smirkish, thought Cass, as he took his place behind the line.

Captain Sullivan strode out in front. "Load and come to shoulder arms," he said.

The men went through the drill, complaining. They had grown lazy over the space of the day, content to let their comrades in other brigades knock their heads against the yankees. Now Adams's Brigade was forming up at last, scattered across backyards and streets and alleys. The customary rumors made their rounds: they were going to attack the works, they were going for the pontoon bridge, an Angel of the Lord had appeared on high, and so on. Even the men who spread the rumors did not believe them. No one was taking this fight seriously.

Cass refused to believe they were really going into battle. He declined to consider an attack on the Federal fortress. General Hood, in the last few weeks, had made it clear that, in his view, attacking entrenched positions was the only true test of a soldier, but here was an array of works even the cavalier must find daunting. Cass had read newspaper accounts of fortresses that "frowned," and he had always thought the phrase an exaggeration, but this one frowned. It glowered at them like a living thing. It was dark and muddy and sinister, bristling with armed men, and there was no end to it. You could see it down every street. From the ramparts, a big National flag waved defiantly, as if posing for a correspondent or a sketch artist. Somewhere behind the works, a Federal band was playing, and the Adams's Brigade band began to play in reply.

The brigade moved out in columns of regiments, crowding into the narrow street. Citizens watched from the windows of their houses or from the porches. They did not cheer or offer encouragement; they did not wave any contraband Confederate flags or sing "Dixie"; no old codgers emerged with flintlock or pike to join the fray. The citizens merely watched, benumbed and resentful.

The soldiers paid them no mind, for the citizens were irrelevant now, inhabiting a world removed across an unbridgeable chasm. All the homely elements of that world—the houses, the furniture inside, quilts, buckets, fences, a child's wooden toy left in a yard—were known to the soldiers once, but now they seemed to lose all dimension, like a photographer's painted backdrop. The men quit their talk and laughter. The mud pulled them down at once, so that their passage became a slow struggling. Drummers gave up trying to beat a cadence. Companies got mixed up with other companies; the press of bodies lifted some men off their feet, pushed others into fences and ditches. Men who did not swear by custom swore now. Some fell and had to be helped from the mire, and valuable shoes were sucked away and lost.

Still Cass did not believe. He gritted his teeth and pushed and shoved his men forward. Like the rest, he was only dimly aware of the scene through which they passed, but it nagged him nevertheless. Here in the street was chaos, a mad current running down to death, bearing the men along—and just over there curtains fluttered, a pitcher sat in a windowsill, sheets lay over a line to dry. Both sides of the chasm could not be real, he thought. They could not possibly exist at the same time. No, the one over there had to be real. That's where Janie was, he thought: safe among the quiet streets. *Keep her safe,* he prayed silently. *Let the angels watch.*

The street ended abruptly, and the brigade emerged into a vast, brick-colored field. Great clouds of blackbirds rose from the earth and swirled into the sky, chattering and complaining. The field was already churned to morass, but the soldiers were driven into it anyhow, their shouldered rifles wobbling every which way. Cass dragged himself along. Surely they would be called back any minute; surely they would not be sent against that loom of earth.

Now the colors were uncased, opening out in the breeze, and the brigade went into line of battle facing the river. Cass could glimpse the pale shine of the stream, but it worked in him no yearning for rivers. He was beginning to believe what was happening, and he was already detaching the part of him that would participate from the part which would remember. Between the brigade and the river was a railroad fill, and on this slight elevation, insolent Federal officers peered at them with spyglasses. Presently, the space behind the railroad became crowded with shining bayonets and the dark masses of the enemy. It was a sortie in force; the yankees were coming out to meet them.

Another fact became immediately apparent when a gun fired from the ramparts. The brigade was exposed, spread out in the field like geese. Here, at last, was a thing to be taken seriously. They heard the report, saw the white smoke snatched away on the breeze, heard the whistling of the shell. The round splatted in the ground to their front, exploded, showered them with gobbets of mud. Soon other guns were firing, and in a moment men were tossed into the air, legs flailing, rifles spinning away.

Colonel Sansing rode along the front of the line on his big gray charger, one of the few times Cass had seen him mounted in a fight. The colonel waved his hat, his white hair streaming. "Get ready, boys!" he shouted. "Remember ol' Mississippi!"

"Ol' Mississippi!" the men shouted in return.

"Close it up, now, boys," said the officers. "Make ready."

They fixed bayonets. They were going to stand and volley, like in the old days. General Hood would not have them dig, not for the world. Across the railroad, they could see the enemy lowering for a volley. They could see the rifles come down, and every man ached to run, but the wire coiled around them and held them fast. "Stand by, lads," said the officers. "Steady, now." Meanwhile, the Death Angel rubbed his hands. The volley came, a rolling boil of white smoke lit by flashes, then the *fizz* and *hum* of fat minié balls, and men were tossed backward, or spun about, or dropped in place like stovepipes kicked over. Now, time to return fire. The orders were given: Fire by volley! Ready! Aim! Behind the line, Cass watched the rifle muzzles lower. Fire! The regiment let go in a single crash—Cleburne's old boys took pride in their volleys—and the white smoke

whipped back over them, obscuring the field. Load! The ramrods were hardly out when the countermand was given: Cease
loading! Charge bayonets! Forward at the common time. . . .

Another volley boiled out from the railroad. Colonel Sansing's horse went down, all legs and flapping stirrups. The colonel rose, mud-covered; he cursed and stomped forward with his
sword out. They pushed ahead through the mud, into the
white veil that hung before them like a cloud. They always argued the point afterward: was it better if you *could* see, or better if you *couldn't*? In any event, they were all believers now,
and the rage was leaking from them like steam. Cass kept his
rifle at the shoulder, pushing the men with his free hand
against their backs, pulling them up from the mud when they
stumbled, dragging them from the line when they fell. "Close
up. Close up," he said, over and over, thinking, *It's all right.
This is not real. It's not real. Janie is real.* He was intent on his
work, fixing his mind on the instant he was walking in, so he
did not notice at first the pulling at his jacket skirt or the voice
behind him.

"Hey. Hey, mister!"

Reluctantly, angrily, Cass was jerked back into the stream
of time. It was the boy Lucifer. Cass looked at him in astonishment. "What! What are you *doing* here!"

The line was moving. A man broke ranks to run away, and
Cass pushed him back with his rifle. "What!" he said to the
boy. "What, what, *what*!"

"I come to tell you—" the boy began, but his voice was
swallowed in the *bam-bam* of an exploding shell, this one to the
rear of the line, so close it knocked Cass and the boy off their
feet. Cass scrambled up, hauled the boy erect by the coat collar,

and shook him. "What!" he cried. Blood was trickling from his ears and from the boy's nose.

"That ole woman!" shouted the boy, wiping at his nose. "You all wasn't gone five minutes, she come out and—"

Another shell exploded, and they were showered with mud and old cotton stalks. Cass pulled the boy along, trying to keep up with the line. They were running now, closing in, the terrible cry rising from their throats.

"She come and took all them greens, pot and all!" shouted the boy, running beside Cass. "The man hit me with a ax handle!"

They stumbled over a deep furrow. Cass stopped, shoved the boy down, and knelt beside him. "I don't care about that!" he shouted in the boy's ear. "Don't tell me that! You stay right here, you understand *me*!"

But it was too late. The yankees swarmed over the railroad bed, the two lines clashed, and in an instant Cass and the boy were in the midst of a wild melee of shouting, cursing men, of officers firing their pistols and the *clack-clack* of bayonets, all swirling in the smoke. Cass did not even have time to be afraid. He straddled the boy and set his feet, and here they came. Cass parried a man's blow, struck him in the jaw with the butt of his rifle. Another man thrust and missed, stumbled off balance; Lucifer grabbed his leg, and he went down in a clatter of accoutrements, and Cass drove his bayonet in where the straps crossed on his back. The boy pushed the dead man off, pointed, shouted. Cass turned in time to fire his musket into a little man with hairy knuckles. Now Cass was in a rage, his blood hot and poisoned. It always happened: one minute he was begging in his mind for it to stop; in the next, he wanted it to last forever, wanted them to keep on coming so he could kill them. He parried and thrust, nearly blind with the smoke. He was only dimly aware of the men around him yet fully aware of himself. He could feel his clothes move across his skin, feel his shoes slipping in the red mud, hear his own breath rasping. Someone let off a rifle next to his ear, and powder grains burned his cheek. His hands were so slippery now that he could hardly hold his rifle; his mouth was full of grit, eyes stinging with sweat, nerves quivering. *Keep on. Keep on.* You couldn't quit. You had to believe you could beat them, no matter how big, no matter how fiercely they yelled. You had to believe that.

Then, all at once, the fight was over. The Federal drums were beating retreat from the works, their soldiers scrambling back over the railroad fill. The boys made to pursue but were held in check by the officers, which only made the soldiers madder. They were hot for blood now—anybody's, no matter.

The men howled and complained; the officers cursed. Lanky Paul Caudell threw his rifle in the mud and stomped on it. "*Every* God damned time!" he cried. He looked at Cass. "Every time they run, we quit! *Quit!*"

In a moment, the brigade was passing in column over its dead, hurrying back to town. Cass pulled the boy out of the mud and got him to moving. He tried not to look at the dead men as he passed—men lying singly or locked or piled together, friend and enemy all the same now, dead. His nerves still jumped and fluttered, and he looked on the rooftops of the town with disgust. He wanted to be clawing at the works, driving the sons of bitches into the river. He was invincible, immortal, an Angel of Death.

"Man, oh, man!" said the boy. He was digging in his nose with a bloody finger. "Lord God Almighty!"

Cass pulled the boy's hand away. "Don't be doing that," he said.

"Lord, *that* was a circus!" said Lucifer.

The boy's hair was wet with blood, and the sight of it made Cass's anger swell renewed and vigorous. "You say that fellow hit you?" he asked.

The boy rubbed his scalp. "Feel of my head. They's a knot right there where he laid into me, the son bitch."

"Don't be cussin'," said Cass. He touched the boy's head, felt the knot. "He hit you with a *ax* handle?"

"Well, it might have been a hoe," said the boy.

"Goddammit," said Cass. He set out at a trot up the flank of the regiment, the boy running beside. When he passed Roger and Ike Gatlin, he pulled them out of line. "Come on," he said, and the two followed without question.

"Where the nation *you* goin'?" demanded Captain Sullivan as they passed, but Cass trotted on without answer. In a moment, Roger said, "Where *are* we going, anyhow?" Cass outlined the circumstance.

"Good," said Roger. His face was speckled with blood. "Good. Let's go."

"Good," said Ike.

It was as if they had not stopped from the moment they set their feet against the charging enemy. They went into the streets, scattering citizens before them, their bayoneted rifles at port arms. They entered the yard, passed the dying cookfire, and came around the front of the house. Cass clattered up the steps, across the porch, and drove his rifle butt into the door, splintering the latch. The door swung open a little; Cass kicked it so that it slammed hard inward, the sound echoing through the house. Cass and Roger and Ike Gatlin and the boy Lucifer burst all together into the front hall. It was empty of furniture, but firewood was stacked by the stairs. Halfway up the staircase stood the man and woman, the man in front with a single-barrel bird gun in his hands.

The woman screeched, "You'uns goddamn rebels get outen my house!"

Cass never stopped; he was on the stairs in an instant. The man was about to speak, was raising the shotgun when Cass grabbed the muzzle and pulled hard and sent the man tumbling past him. The woman screeched like a hawk, was on Cass in a moment. He retreated, the woman clawing at him, shrilling, until Ike Gatlin grabbed her from behind.

"Hold her, Ike," said Cass. "Get her outside!"

"Goddamn these yellerhammers!" said Ike. "They are full of meanness!" He dragged the woman out the door with her kicking all the while at his shins, and biting, and flailing with her fists.

The man was pulling himself off the floor. He was fifty, maybe, but stout, with big hands and purple veins in his face. He was fumbling for the shotgun when Cass pulled him up by his hair and slapped him hard across the face, and again, and again, driving the man back across the stack of wood. "Strike a boy, would you?" snarled Cass.

"Hit him again!" cried Lucifer.

The man made to rise again, but Cass swung and laid him

out. He kicked the shotgun away. "Roger," he said, "there a fire on the hearth?"

"A good big one in the parlor," said Roger. He was already gathering up chunks of firewood, piling them in the crook of his arm.

"Stoke her up," said Cass. "Throw in some furniture!"

In a moment, the fire was blazing, bulging from the hearth, spitting fat coals over the puncheon floor. Lucifer found some chairs and threw them in. He tried a horsehair couch, but it was too big, so he broke up a spindly table. The dry wood caught up like tinder.

When they came out the door, Cass was dragging the man by his coat collar, and smoke was already boiling out the downstairs windows. Cass bumped the man down the front steps and let him drop. The woman was silent now; Ike had her backed up against an oak tree in the yard.

Soldiers were running past in the street. "It's a big skedaddle!" one shouted. "We leavin' town!" said another. Some stopped to look at the house. "Say, that house is afire," one pointed out.

"Too late, can't save it now!" said Cass. "All we could do to get these folks out!"

Roger shook his finger at the woman. "Ought not to leave lighter wood so close to the hearth," he said.

The soldiers went on, satisfied. It wasn't their house. Cass knelt by the woman. "Anybody else in there? You better tell me now."

The woman gritted her teeth. "Did you kill Homer?" she snarled.

"No," said Cass. "Now, is anybody still—"

The woman spat in his face.

"I already ast her that," said Ike. His cheek was bloodied where she'd scratched him. "I reckon if she had chillun, they wouldn't burn anyhow."

All over town, drums were beating assembly. Companies, regiments, brigades were forming up in the crowded streets again. Horsemen spattered past. The house was spouting flame now, popping and crackling, the smoke rising in a dirty gray column. They could feel the heat of it.

They stood a moment longer and contemplated what they had done. The woman pulled herself erect and leaned against the trunk of the oak. In the twilight, the flames were harsh on her face. "I lived in that house all my life," she said.

"Well, you sold it cheap," said Cass. "A mess of god-damned turnips." He shook his head. "Come on, boys," he said. They gathered up their traps, and in a moment they were in the road, running to find the regiment.

❖ 8 ❖

THE DAY AFTER THE FUTILE BATTLE OF DECATUR, THE army was near Muscle Shoals, halted for a while. Cass and the boy were walking through the camp. Cass said, "Lucifer, how did you come to be here, anyhow? Why ain't you off rolling hoops somewhere, or turning over privies like a natural boy?"

"Well," replied Lucifer, "one day some officers come to the orphanage and culled out thirteen of us boys, said we was able-bodied and must go to the army. I was glad of it at the time."

"I expect you were," said Cass. "How do you feel about it now?"

"Well, I have been in a battle, and got hit with a ax handle, and burnt down a house, and walked two hundred mile, seems like—I am having a bully time so far."

"Hmmm," said Cass. "Well, let's go see the ole Massa."

Colonel David Sansing's headquarters were under a precarious woodshed that was nailed to a big gum tree. Cass and Lucifer found the colonel in residence, together with Adjutant Perry Sansing and the regimental clerk, a man named Moses Teasdale who was famous for a book he penned before the war, *Is Freemasonry a Threat? or, The Libertines of the Lodge.* The work sold widely, but since then Teasdale had suspended his prejudices, or at least their utterance, against the brothers, of whom many were in the regiment. He was said to be at work on a book damning the Catholics, of whom, in the regiment, there were none at all. In any event, Teasdale was now bent over a rickety folding desk with the regimental muster roll spread out before him.

"Now, then," said Colonel Sansing when Cass presented his charge. "What is your name, my lad?"

"Lucifer," said the boy.

Teasdale looked up in astonishment, and Perry laughed. Colonel Sansing glared at Cass. "Is this a joke, sir?"

"No, Colonel. It is the name they gave him at the orphanage."

"Why, God damn," said the colonel. "He can't have a name like that around here! The boys would light up the woods with him!"

"Why not call him Lucian?" said Perry. "That's a good name."

"First-rate suggestion," said the colonel. "Write 'Lucian'

down there, Mose." The clerk scratched with his pen, and the colonel looked at the boy. "What's your other name, if I dare to ask?"

"I don't have one," said the boy.

"Don't have one?" said the colonel. "Mighty irregular."

"It's Wakefield," said Cass. The boy looked up at him in surprise.

"Hmm," said the colonel, regarding Cass with suspicion. "Kin of yours?"

The boy scowled at Cass. He said, "I ain't kin to nobody."

"Well, nevertheless, Wakefield it is," said the colonel. "Put it down that way, Mose." The clerk nodded and scratched with his pen.

"Now then," said the colonel, "how old are you, about?"

"Eighteen year," said the boy.

Cass thought, *Ah, you lying little shit.*

Colonel Sansing stepped out from behind his clerk and gathered the boy's shirtfront in his hands. He knelt among the soggy wood chips and dragged the boy down with him. "Now, look here," he said. "First off, you call me 'sir.' Second off, you lie to me again about how old you are, I will slice you open and count the rings. You understand *me?*"

"Well, you said *about,*" muttered the boy. "I'm six . . . I mean, *four*teen. Goin' *on* fourteen. Sir. Colonel."

"Great God," said the officer, and released the boy, and rose to his feet, joints creaking. "Well, there's younger'n you out here, I expect. In any event, you'll have to do." He looked at Cass. "Take him back to the trains, see if the quartermaster is sober enough to find him a rifle and a blanket."

"Yes, Colonel," said Cass, and saluted, which drew a snort from the adjutant. They had gone a little way from the wood-shed when the colonel called Cass back. "A word with you," he said.

The four soldiers stood under the lean-to a moment and watched the boy throw sweetgum balls at a cat.

"That whelp is no Christian," said Teasdale. "He may be a papist. Have to be watched ever minute, or—"

"Shut up, Mose," said the colonel. He put a fatherly hand on Cass's shoulder. "Now, Cass, I am depending on you to watch after this infant. He—"

"Aw, Colonel," said Cass, "I already got Roger. Can't you—"

"Roger is pretty well brung up. You can wean this one now and keep him out of hot places. I am counting on you."

"Yes, sir," said Cass.

The officer rubbed his nose. "One more thing, by the way," he said. "There was a woman waylaid me back on the road a while ago. Cass, did you and those other boys burn down a house in Decatur?"

Cass pursed his lips. "Well, it was an accident," he said.

"She was not of that opinion, sir," said the colonel.

"Well, she must of been hysterical," said Cass.

"Goddammit, sir," said the colonel, "I will hear of no more hysterical accidents, you understand *me?*"

"Yes, Colonel," said Cass, and saluted again, and stole away.

As they made their way back to the trains, the boy said, "How come you did that?"

"Did what?"

"Give me your name."

"Well, I wasn't using it at the moment," said Cass.

"Well, all right," said the boy. "But, say, how come they didn't like 'Lucifer'? It *does* mean 'light,' don't it? Joanna told me it did."

"Who's that?"

The boy reddened. "Was a teacher down there."

"Ah," said Cass. As they walked along, he explained about Lucifer being a fallen angel. "The story goes, it was a big battle up in heaven. It was Satan and Lucifer on one side, the Lord God and Jesus on t'other. They had armies of angels, *hosts* of 'em, and lightning bolts for artillery. Guess who beat?"

"I haven't any idy," said the boy.

"Well, who's in charge now?"

Lucian thought a moment. "God?" he said at last.

"There you have it," said Cass.

"Huh," said the boy. "What become of Lucifer and them?"

"Well, they were cast into perdition—that's hell, of course—and there they remain, stirring up trouble for everbody."

"Well, if God's in charge, how come He don't just put 'em out of business? Then there wouldn't be no more trouble."

"It is only a story," said Cass. "It is"—Cass searched for the word—"it is . . . an *allegory*! We must make of it what we will." The fact was, Cass didn't know what to make of it himself.

"Well, I am not surprised," said Lucian. "What I know about God, He spends all His time hatin' niggers and yankees and infidels, and casting people into hell left and right."

Cass was shocked. "Where you hear such a thing?"

"Reverend Pelt, the old chaplain down yonder," said the boy, stopping to scratch his ankle. "That's all he studied. Come to think of it, maybe that's why God keeps Lucifer and them around. Way old Pelt went on, I bet they's a thousand people in hell by now. Somebody's got to look after 'em."

"You may be right," Cass said.

The boy said, "Did Lucifer cause this mess we're in?"

"No," said Cass, "that was Abe Lincoln."

"Hah!" said the boy. "I am not surprised. Reverend Pelt always said old Abe—"

"God damn your Reverend Pelt to hell," said Cass. "I don't see *him* out here anywhere!"

"You won't, neither," said the boy, and laughed.

They walked on, down a lane bordered by fences and trees. After a while, they arrived at a scattering of broken-down spring wagons, mules, patched harness, and bewhiskered teamsters, white and black, most of them drunk. This was the brigade trains. The quartermaster—a pale, slender man who, in another life, might have been a woman, and probably ought to be a woman in this one—took Cass's order for a musket. He disappeared into the maw of a wagon, under a mildewed canvas top with *U.S.* stenciled on it. There came a great deal of banging and tumbling around, and presently articles of astonishing variety began to fly out the back of the wagon: a coffeepot, a cane-bottom chair, a dictionary, some ice tongs, a plaster parrot, a pair of long drawers, a lap desk, several blood-stiffened blankets. Finally, the man himself emerged with a rifle. "It's a Springfield," he said. "It'll take the five-seven-seven ball, though it might wobble a little on the outbound trip."

"Ain't you got any old two-banded guns laying around?" said Cass. "This one is taller than he is."

"Well, sir," said the officer, "this is *not* the Crystal Palace."

The remark made no sense to Cass, but the quartermaster thought it hilarious. He only quit laughing when Cass snatched the musket from his hand.

Cass picked up the cleanest of the blankets and the dictionary. Lucian wanted the parrot, but Cass reminded him that they were on the march. "The quartermaster will keep it for you," he said. They collected some caps and ammunition, which the boy stuffed in his pockets, then ambled down to a creek that wound its way among sycamores and oaks. Cass showed the boy how to load and prime, then let him shoot a round at the creek bank. The boy could hardly lift the musket, and the recoil knocked him flat.

"You got to tuck it into your shoulder and lean against it," said Cass, careful not to laugh at the boy spraddled in the mud of the creek bank. "And open your eyes, for God's sake. You can't hit what you can't see. Now, that rock yonder—that's your mark."

A big heron sailed over them and lit on a mud bar a little way distant. The bird lifted one foot and glared at the water.

"How about I shoot *him*?" said the boy.

"Why, no," said Cass. "Just shoot at that rock."

When the boy shot, the heron flew away squawking. The boy shot three more times and was fairly true to the mark. His next round sent the rock spinning into the air. The boy grinned and rubbed his shoulder. It was the first time Cass had seen him smile since they burned the house down. The boy said, "Now, that's somethin' *like*!"

"Well, we'll see how you like it after you've carried it a few years," said Cass. "Anyhow, we better quit using up the government's powder and ball."

"What else can you show me?" asked the boy.

"Well," said Cass, "there's the School of the Soldier—but never mind all that. You just watch what the other fellows do, and you'll—what's the matter?"

The boy's face was turned away, the smile gone. His hands were jammed in his breeches pockets. "You ain't goin' to show me that?" he said.

So Cass went through the manual of arms, and the Load-in-Nine-Times, and the facing movements. They spent half an hour on it while the sun fell behind the trees and the air grew cool. When the time was over, the boy could do the drill as well as any in the ranks, and better than some.

"Well, you are a quick study," said Cass finally. "Let's go to camp, see what there is to eat."

"Can I carry the gun?"

"It's yours forever," said Cass.

After they had gone a little way, the boy asked, "You reckon we'll leave in the mornin'?"

"We always leave in the mornin'," said Cass. "If not by dead of night."

"Huh," said the boy. "Say, can I get a jacket like you got?"

"We'll get you one," said Cass.

They walked back through the chill early twilight, Cass with the dictionary under his arm, Lucian carrying his rifle and the blanket Cass had showed him how to roll. Cass had told him, "Get shut of that citizen's carpetbag. You don't want any-body to mistake you for a congressman."

That night, the boy bedded down between Cass and Roger under a white oak tree. There was no moon, and the camp was dark when the fires burned down. Now and then, a picket let loose at something. Cass was almost asleep when Lucian poked him. "Say, did you know a possum's got two peckers?"

"I did not know that," said Cass.

After a moment, the boy said, "Say, are you married?"

"Yeah. You?"

"Naw," snorted the boy. After a moment, he said, "I bet you got folks, too."

"Some," said Cass. "Most of 'em's in the ground, but some are still quick."

"Is your wife comely?" asked the boy.

"Oh, yes, indeed," said Cass. "She is an ornament."

The boy was quiet for a moment. He said, "I bet these fellows won't like me."

Cass raised on one elbow and peered into the dark. "That's up to you," he said.

The boy shifted in his blanket. Cass could see the pale oval of his face. "I bet I get kilt right off," said the boy.

"Now, that's four subjects," said Cass. "Pick one and stay with it, or go to sleep."

"I reckon I'll go to sleep," said the boy. "I always feel better afterward."

Great God, thought Cass.

After a moment, the boy poked Cass again. He said, "Say, what is a allergory, anyhow?"

Roger grunted. "That makes five," he said.

⁜

The next day, Cass took Lucian foraging. Along the way, they practiced marching and doing the manual of arms at the common step, and the Frenchy bayonet drill, which Cass had always enjoyed. They traveled north of the army, toward the river where houses might be. They were gone two hours, had collected nothing but a brace of rabbits, when they happened on a farmstead where recent violence had been done. Buzzards and crows flapped away at their approach, settling in the trees nearby, and a bony cur slunk away through the broomsage. The farmhouse and outbuildings were still smoldering, the grass all burned. A dead hog lay in the cinders, skin black and blistered. Cass read the signs easily enough. "A cavalry fight," he said. "This mornin', I guess."

"Well, how can you tell it was cav'ry?" asked Lucian, his voice gone quiet.

"Well, lad," said Cass patiently, "I see the prints of shod horses, I observe a great scattering of horse shit, I see a dead horse there, and one over there—and that pitiful thing yonder is a dead yankee cavalryman, the like of which you will not see many, believe me. Taken all together, these things point to an engagement of our mounted brethren-in-arms."

The boy looked at the dead man, a blue, swollen shape barely visible in the broomsage. "Can you tell who beat?" he whispered.

Cass found himself whispering too. "I would say our side, since the others left their dead behind. Thing is, the cavaliers are only interested in fighting. Win or lose, it don't matter much to them; whatever they gain, they don't get to keep it long."

In truth, Cass didn't want to talk about it. He was bothered by the scene, which actually suggested a serious combat— house and buildings all burned, and more dead than the horsemen usually suffered in their brief clashes. There were plenty of boot and shoe tracks, too, so they must have fought dismounted. They had got in one another's faces, these bold cavaliers. Cass did not feel it necessary to point out the other corpses he saw. There were too many to bury, and the birds, already restless in the trees, would pick at them. The dog would get his share and the bugs the rest.

Cass said to the boy, "Go look behind the barn. See is there anything we can use."

Lucian was still looking at the dead man. "Oh," he said. He turned his face to Cass, and there was a shadow in it. Cass knew the look well. The boy said, "I'd just as soon stay with you."

Cass put his hand on the boy's head. "You have come out soldiering," he said, "and you must act like a soldier. These fellows won't hurt you. They are past hurting anybody."

Lucian thought a moment. "This is worse than being in the fight t'other day," he said. "It is way too quiet."

"I know," said Cass, "but you must get used to it. Now, go on, do like I said."

Lucian nodded, then turned and went off around the smoldering skeleton of the barn. Cass watched him trudge away, the musket tilted over his thin shoulder. "Lucian?" he said, but the boy didn't hear. Cass almost called him back but didn't. There was no really no reason to send the lad on such a scout, but the practice wouldn't hurt him, Cass supposed.

He knelt and examined the hog carcass. It was too far gone and blown with flies to scavenge. "A waste for everybody," he said aloud. He thought how the boys would have shouted Glory if he and Lucian had come into camp leading such a prize on the hoof. "God damn the cavalier sons of bitches for killing this hog," Cass said.

Kneeling, his musket across his thighs, Cass pushed his hat back and looked around him. Somebody lived here once, milked a cow, fed this hog, planted cotton. Frolicked, maybe, and fished in the river. Now they were gone, and only God knew where. These yankees, around their breakfast fire that morning, had dawdled and joked and complained, proud to be soldiers, though they would never admit it to one another. Now they were humiliated and dead, removed from the earth in the space of a morning's ride. No room in the chronicle for such a little fight; only a mention in dispatches, a brief nota-tion in some junior officer's hand. The officer would remember them when he wrote the names, Cass thought, but beyond that, beyond the closed circle of the company, the regiment, the families who would not know for a while yet—beyond that, history would not mark these boys. Cass took no joy in the knowledge that they were enemies; it was a waste, and all for nothing.

Over all hung the peculiar silence of a recently abandoned field. The restive squabbling of the birds, the wind, the sudden leap of a flame, the creak of a limb—these things had no voice in the quiet. It was a vacuum all to itself where time had no mean-ing, where men were made to whisper and walk soft lest they waken something they did not want to imagine. Too much was done in such a place, and it didn't pass easily. He had told Lucian he must get used to it, but that was only something a man said. The lad would have to learn for himself that he never would.

A light touch on his shoulder. "Jesus!" Cass cried, and leaped to his feet. It was Lucian. "*Dammit,* boy," said Cass sharply. "Don't *ever*—"

Then he stopped. The boy held his musket by the barrel,

and behind him was a long furrow in the mud where he had dragged it. He looked at Cass and made to speak, but no sound came. In his face was more than shadow now, more than fear, more even than knowledge. Cass knew that look, too.

"What is it, lad?" he said, whispering again. "What did you see?"

The boy opened his mouth and a sound came, but only a sound, like a mouse in the cellar.

Cass said, "You must show me."

The boy shook his head. "Lucian," said Cass, but the boy shook his head again. He began to cry, fighting it, trying to be a soldier, managing only to be a boy.

Cass said, "There's a good lad. Never mind. We can go on back; we got two rabbits—"

"Uh-uh," said Lucian. He dropped his musket and wiped his shirtsleeve across his eyes. He pointed toward the barn.

Well, shit, thought Cass. "All right, then," he said. "You stay right here and guard this hog."

Cass did not want to go behind the barn. There could be nothing back there he hadn't seen on other fields, but he had never been far from his comrades then. Cass had always declined to explore alone the horrors left after a fight, yet that was what he had required of Lucian, and now he must do it himself. He must stand to it, if only to prove to the boy that dead men didn't bother—until later, of course.

He cradled his musket and walked through the scorched grass, smelling the burned wood and the faint whiff of decay that pretty soon would cover the homestead like a filthy blanket. He paused at the corner of the barn, listening, then stepped around.

He saw the horse first—a chestnut, blazed white, lying against the fence in a corner of the lot. All the dead horses were different colors; the regiment must have just had a remount from gathered stock. This one lay on his belly, legs curled under him, his muzzle pressed to the earth. His eyes were open, and Cass half expected him to rise, but he was dead like the others. Did he say ha-ha amid the trumpets, once? The saddle was a rampart of bedroll, saddlebags, overcoat, saber, picket pins, all the junk the yankee horsemen toted. Then Cass saw the rider.

"Aw, mankind," whispered Cass.

The rider had met a fate different than his mount, and unluckier. He had been thrown clear of the horse or perhaps dragged himself away, driven by some impulse to flee. He had found a rotten stump, and there he was leaned against it, his booted legs stretched out before him. He had done it all by feel, Cass supposed, for his face was a shapeless thing, like cherry cobbler spilled from the bowl. Around the mass, the man's hair, soaked in blood, glistened darkly. Only one eye remained, white and glutinous and blind; the teeth, without lips to define them, were fixed in a grin. Where the nose had been, a little red bubble grew and popped, grew and popped.

Cass felt as though he had discovered the bottom of time. He had been wrong after all, for in years of soldiering, he had never come upon a live thing like this. Now he was alone with it, the silence closing down. A rumble of gas came from the belly of the dead horse. Cass whispered, "Do you know I am here?" and the man lifted his hand. The solitary eye swiveled like a lizard's. The teeth parted, the opening webbed with blood, and a sound came, urgent and pleading.

"I know, sir," Cass told the man. "I know."

Then the boy was there. He came quietly, without his musket. He wrapped his hand in the skirt of Cass's jacket and pressed close. "What made it like that?" whispered Lucian.

"A shotgun, I expect," said Cass. "Don't say 'it.' He's a man still."

"Why would they leave him? Why won't they take him to the doctor?"

"They would have. I guess everybody thought he was dead."

"Oh, Lord," said the boy. "We got to do something!"

"Well, we are," said Cass. "You are going to go back and guard that hog like I told you."

The boy pressed closer. "I don't want to—"

Cass took the boy by the arm, bent, and spoke into his face. "*Listen* to me. This is a thing you don't talk about. You just *do* it!"

The man let out a sudden squawk, and Lucian jumped and covered his ears. "But what *are* we going to do!" he cried. "Are we going to take him to the doctor?"

Cass closed his eyes and steadied himself. He cursed the enrollers who gathered children, and those who allowed it. "No," he said at last. "I am going to shoot him, Lucian. That's what he wants."

"How do you *know* that?" sobbed the boy.

"Because that's what I would want," said Cass. He turned the boy back toward the house and gave him a shove. "Now, go on. Be quick. This man is in hell every minute, and us fooling around." Cass watched the boy until he was out of sight around the barn.

The birds had settled on the hog again but flapped away when Lucian came. He stood in the scorched grass, watching some ants rebuilding their nest where a horse had stepped on it. He tried some cuss words aloud, but they did little good. He tried thinking: *Lucian Wakefield. Lucian Wakefield.* He did not tell Mister Cass, but he knew the chaplain had named him Lucifer because he was bad, and he must be bad still. The reverend said, *Lucifer, you was born in hell, going to end up there again.* The boy never understood that till Mister Cass explained it. Maybe old Pelt was right, and here he was. But he was called Lucian now. That thing back yonder had tried to speak to him, and he couldn't understand. The eye had rolled at him, looked at him, and he ran away. How could it be alive? "I wish I hadn't gone!" he said aloud, but took it back right away. Mister Cass had watched over him in a terrible battle and given him his own name without even being asked—and now Mister Cass was back there with that—going to shoot it—what did that mean? The thing had scared him so bad, coming on it all at once, and all at once like falling down in a deep well, and how could he and it be in the same place? Cass said the thing was in hell, so maybe he was, too. But Cass said it was a man. He said—

Lucian jumped again when the shot came. It echoed in the trees down by the broad river. He was crying now, no longer ashamed of it, knowing he couldn't stop.

Lucian Wakefield. Lucian Wakefield. Way up in north Alabama in the year Eighteen-and-sixty-four. Them ants don't care about anything, they just go right on. I am growed now, I have been soldiering, my name is Lucian Wakefield now.

Cass came around the barn carrying his musket in the

crook of his arm, like a bird hunter returning, and a white scarf in his hand. "Lucian," he said.

The boy wiped at his eyes. Cass knelt before him and held up the scarf. "I got this out of his bags—you take it. You'll need it when the weather turns."

"But I don't want it!" said the boy, backing away. "I want a jacket like *you* got."

"We'll get you one, but this'll be good with a jacket."

"I don't want it!" said the boy. "What if he comes hunting it back!"

"He won't do that," said Cass. "All that's done with now. Kneel down here." Lucian came and knelt. They were facing each other, and Cass hung the scarf around his neck. "He don't need it. He might want you to have it. In fact, he told me to get it for you." It wasn't much of a lie; the man might have told him that, if he could have.

The boy made no reply. He could smell horse sweat on the scarf and thought about where it was last night, and just a little while ago.

"We all do it," said Cass. "It's all right. Not a single one ever came back looking for his goods."

"You promise?" asked Lucian. "He said that to you?"

"Honor bright," said Cass.

The boy nodded and seemed mollified. He touched the ends of the scarf. "Huh," he said. His face was a mess of dirt and tears, and Cass could see the sun's light paling on it. He could see blue shadows in the fence corners, and black shadows creeping along the ground where there had been none before. The day was falling quickly.

"I'd want to go back home," said the boy, "if I had one."

"Me, too," said Cass.

The boy twisted the scarf in his fingers. He looked at Cass. "Maybe you'll take me where you live, if I am good."

"Well, I . . . well, I never thought of that."

"How long before we can go there?" asked the boy.

"We have to whip the yankees first," said Cass.

Now Lucian started to cry again. He was worn out with crying, but there didn't seem to be an end to it. "I don't know," he said. "Don't know if I can stand it much."

"Well, I thought you were having a bully time," said Cass.

"I was," said the boy. "Goddamn, I can't quit this bawling! What a baby!" He struck at himself with his fist until Cass grabbed it.

"Here, don't be doing that," said Cass. He unlimbered his canteen and gave it to the boy. "Drink a little. Wipe your face. Here's my handkerchief. You are a regular Miss Nancy, all right."

The boy scowled but took the filthy rag and wet it and wiped his face. He held the canteen in his hands and stared at it. He said, "When you done for those fellows the other day, it never bothered me too much, and at the house them people were mean and I never minded, but now—Lord, that poor man back yonder, I come on him all at once, I never knew such a thing could happen to anybody—"

Then the boy's chest began to heave. He dropped the canteen and crawled a little way before he threw up, sobbing and hitting his fist against the ground.

Cass knew he had to decide then. The winter day was short, near twilight now, but all the days of man were short, and too much depended on what you did when you came to a crossing.

You couldn't stand there long, you had to decide, and whatsoever ye shall bind on earth shall be bound in heaven. *Janie, I wish you were here,* thought Cass. But Janie was far away, and the night was coming.

Well, fuck it, thought Cass. *This time next month, we'll all be dead anyhow.* He rose and waited until the boy was done heaving. When he pulled him up, the boy was limp, trying to catch his breath. Cass turned him, took the rag, and wiped his mouth. Then he stroked the boy's greasy hair, calming him, calming himself. "We'll go home one day," he said. "You and me and Roger, and whatever boys are left. You don't have to worry about being good."

"I guess that *was* too many," said Lucian, sniffling. "I'll tell you one damn thing, though."

"Quit your cussing," said Cass. "Tell me what?"

Lucian looked back toward the barn. "I won't never hurt anything again," he said. "You can tell 'em that, all them gilded sons of bitches."

It was full dark when Cass flopped the two dead rabbits down by Captain Byron Sullivan's fire, where the company stew was in progress. Into this stew went everything the boys could gather at foraging, so it was various of content and odor. "That all you got?" asked the officer.

"We left the pies and sweetmeats down in camp," said Cass.

First Sergeant Williams began to clean a rabbit. "How're you and that infant making out?" he asked.

"His name is Lucian," said Cass, then told about the incident at the farmstead. The captain leaned back on his heels and sighed. "Well, that was a hard lesson for a boy," he said.

"You know any easy ones?" said Cass.

"I still hope to discover one," said the captain.

Cass took a deep breath. "Well, I'll just tell you now and get it done," he said. "I am sending the rifle they give him back to the quartermaster. I won't have the lad bearing arms."

Williams looked up from his skinning. "*You* won't—well, goddamn—"

"Now, don't fuck with me, Bill," said Cass. He turned to the captain. "Colonel Sansing give him to me to raise, and I mean to do it as I see fit. I—he is—goddammit, Cap'n."

The captain held up his hands. "All right. We'll put him to cooking, bearing litters, and the like. Will that satisfy you?"

"Yes," said Cass. "Yes, sir."

The first sergeant put his rabbit down and regarded Cass for a moment. He said, "You put me in mind of a fellow I knew in Texas, used to hunt rattlesnakes for sport."

"Yeah?" said Cass. "What happened to him? He get bit?"

"No," said Williams, "he just got to looking like he'd seen too many of 'em."

✛

Roger said, "What have you been doing with that boy Lucifer? He is slinking around like a stray cat."

"He is called Lucian now," said Cass, and told the story again.

"Oh, my," said Roger. "No wonder he is in a dark study."

"Where is he now?" said Cass. Roger pointed to a stand of sycamores at the edge of a slough. Cass said, "Let's go see."

The boy was sitting among the roots of a big sycamore. Cass and Roger sat cross-legged before him, took out their pipes, went through the ritual of filling and lighting up. They were running short on matches, and the tobacco was dry as dust. Cass would wait to tell Roger about the good tobacco he had taken from the cavalryman's saddlebag. He said, "Lucian, do you smoke? Lord knows you spit enough."

"No," said the boy, "but I been meaning to take it up."

"It is a noble habit," said Roger. "Superior to chewing."

"Good for the humors, too," said Cass. "Lucian, tell Roger who taught you about the Lord."

"Well, old Pelt, the chaplain at the orphantage," said the boy.

"Orphan-*age,* dammit," said Cass. "Would this Pelt ever read the Bible to you?"

"Oh, yes. He would line out a passage, then tell us what it meant. He said we were to believe it, every word, else we would go to hell. Way he talked about it, I didn't much want to go there."

"No, me neither," said Cass. "Did you ever read any of it for yourself?"

The boy took up a stick, began to break it in pieces and throw them into the dark water of the slough. Cass thought about what Janie said of the Bible once: *Lord knows, I can't get much out of that dreary old thing.*

After a moment, the boy shook his head. "Naw, I never read it, though I did look at the pictures. Fact is, I can't read much a-tall. I never took to it somehow."

"Well, well," said Roger. He unlimbered himself from the ground and went away.

"Where's *he* a-goin'?" asked the boy.

"You never can tell," said Cass.

In a moment, Roger returned with the dictionary. He lay it in the boy's lap. "You study this," he said. "We'll do five words a day, if we can."

"What if I won't?" said Lucian.

"Be quiet," said Cass. "Now, you study those words like Roger says. What about prayin'? Did they teach you to pray?"

"Oh, we prayed *all* the goddamned time."

Cass sighed. "Well, what did they tell you about it?"

"You-all are making my head hurt," said Lucian.

"Nevertheless," said Cass.

The boy got another stick and broke it, *snap-snap-snap*. He rolled his eyes. "They *said* we was to offer praise, then thanks, then blessings for others, then ask for whatever *we* needed that was wholesome."

"Well, that's all right," said Cass. "What's so hard about that?"

The boy snorted and threw the sticks in the water. He put his grimy hands together and looked at the sky. "Thank you, Lord, for making me an orphan, and for sending me to the war where I'll get kilt, and for being hungry and cold, and for see-ing that poor man today, and please bless these holy men what keep badgering me about praying and reading and not cussing and all manner of torment."

"Well, hell," said Cass. "That was a mess. Plus, you left out the praise."

"Huh," said Lucian. "If God is so big, He don't need *my* praise—be like me swelling up ever time a cricket chirped at me."

They were quiet then, for a time. Now and then, a big sycamore leaf, finally letting go, rattled down through the branches. The slough was still and silent; it gave of no voices, and no movement save where Lucian dropped his sticks in the water. The twilight was coming, and cold shadows followed. It was the dying time: of the day, of the year, of men, perhaps of the army itself. Cass shivered and drew his gray jacket close about him. He would have to get one for the boy pretty soon. Tomorrow, come what may. A jacket was not too much to ask for.

Suddenly there came a stirring, almost imperceptible, in the fields and woods around. It resolved itself into the sound of men's voices rising, the stamping of horses, the snapping of blankets shook out, the scattering of fires, preliminary taps on the regimental drums. Cass and Roger knew what it meant, and the boy, too, perhaps, for he looked up questioning.

"Yes," said Cass, rising to his feet. "Time to get under way."

His judgment was confirmed by the appearance of First Sergeant Williams, fully accoutred, who said, "Here! What you peckerheads up to now?"

"Why, we are keeping school, First Sergeant," said Cass.

"Yes," said Roger, "and holding seminary."

"Well, it is no surprise to me," said the first sergeant. "But you must adjourn now and fall in, for we are about to travel."

"Yes, First Sergeant," said Cass and Roger together.

"What is that book the boy has?" asked Williams.

Roger said, "Well, Bill, it is a dictionary."

The first sergeant shook his head. "Jesus, such an army this is," he said, and limped away as the drums began to sound Assembly.

⊹

They marched through the night, through the growing cold, under a sky that little by little grew empty of stars. They could sense it coming: the cold that would eat down into their bones, that would shiver them, and kill some of them. The long columns marched in silence but for the clinking and creaking of their burdens. They marched with the long, swinging step that was their pride and trademark, up nameless roads, past dark cabins and houses where the occupants huddled, listening, sometimes peeking out to see the phantom shapes hurrying past.

Whence they were hurrying, and why, the soldiers knew only through rumor, reinforced now by a sure instinct developed over many such journeys in the dark. They were going to cross the river. They were going to outrun some yankees coming up from the south: cut them off before they could reach the works at Nashville. There would be fighting before Nashville, then. Cass knew the Death Angel was with the column now, already making his choices. He kept Lucian close by, dragging him along by the collar when he fell behind, lest the Angel come peering into the boy's face. Beside them, Roger marched in silence, keeping his own counsel.

They stopped just short of the river to wait for the pontoons. The cold had them now, and a drift of snow was falling. The men wrapped themselves in their blankets—no fires allowed—and sat or lay wherever the command to halt had found them. Cass could smell the river, the Tennessee. He knew it to be a clear, rock-bottomed stream that ran like a sluice between bluffs and rocky banks. Cass wondered about such a well-mannered river. He asked Eugene Pitcock, who had piloted on her.

"Not so mannerly," said Eugene. "There's some bad falls, and the shoals above Florence cuts the river in half."

"Can't you spar across 'em?" asked Cass.

"It's all rock and fast water," said the other man.

"Well," said Cass. The idea of rocky shoals made him glad he was a Mississippi man. Was once anyhow. Perhaps again.

Now he was leaning against a muddy bank where the road cut through, shrouded in his good Federal blanket, while the snow whispered down around him. Janie came to him, passing by out yonder in the swirl. She stood out well, for she was wearing a mourning dress and a black lace scarf over her head. Cass realized he was seeing her the way she looked on Canal Street once, when they paced behind the white hearse that bore her sister Madeline. The girl was twelve, and would be forever; she had a little boil cut off her neck on Thursday, and they were burying her on Sunday. Now, in Alabama, out in the snow, Janie raised her face to look at him. *I can't much stand this, Cass,* she said. He remembered how she said those same words over and over that day, but now he didn't know if she was speaking out of that time or this. *I can't much either,* he said, *but don't worry. It won't be always,* words as stupid and empty now as they were then.

Pretty soon, Janie went away, and it was only a soldier trudging along where she had been, his blanket over his head. The man's footsteps squeaked in the snow, and he was talking to himself. Cass was used to these apparitions, but he hurt in his heart anyhow. He counted the months back to August, the time when he had finally got another letter from Janie, dated in

June. The army was still in Georgia then. It was said that a good deal of their mail was burned when the Atlanta depot went up, and they had been on the move since. All that time, and so much could happen. People went so quickly. She could be long asleep under the cold ground. . . .

"No, she isn't," said Cass aloud. He prayed. "Keep her safe; let the angels watch."

Roger was sleeping, wrapped up in Sally Mae Burke's quilt. Between them, Lucian shivered in his crusty blanket. Cass thought he was sleeping, too, but in a little while the boy said, "Who you talking to, Mister Cass?"

"Nobody," said Cass. "Go to sleep."

The boy rubbed his eyes and looked about. "This is the first snow I ever seen," he said. "I feel like I ought to be looking at it."

"Well, it can be pretty in some circumstances," said Cass.

"Mister Cass, I been thinking," said the boy. He blew his nose on his blanket. "We cross that river, they's going to be a battle, ain't they?"

"I expect so," said Cass.

"Will it be like the one in Decatur?"

Cass thought a moment. "I will tell you what I know about that," he said. "The worse part of a battle is waiting for it. Then, when it commences, it's no matter how big it is. What matters is what's happening right where you are, and maybe you have an easy time, and maybe you don't. There's not any good ones. Some fellows like it, and I suppose it is well they do."

"Do you ever like it, Mister Cass?"

"Sometimes, when I am in it, but not before or after."

"Well, are you scared much?"

"Always at first," Cass said. "Everbody is pretty much afraid when he starts out, and some can't overcome it and run away. I have done that myself, and if a man tells you he has not, he is a liar. Mostly, in the thick of it, you let go of being scared; I don't know if anybody could do it otherwise. Some of this you'll have to find out for yourself. There ain't a way to tell it."

"Hah!" said Roger suddenly. He was wakened by their talk or by some dream that roused him, and he pushed closer to the boy for warmth. He spoke in a voice harsh with sleep. "If we live a thousand years, won't ever find a way to tell it." He coughed, and turned his head to spit. "In a battle, everything is wrong, nothing you ever learned is true anymore. And when you come out—if you do—you can't remember. You have to put it back together by the rules you know, and you end up with a lie. That's the best you can do, and when you tell it, it'll still be a lie."

Cass said to the boy, "You were in that fight the other day—what do you remember of it?"

Lucian thought a moment. "Legs, mostly," he said. "Smoke, fire, noise. Sometimes I think like it lasted twenty seconds, other times a month or so. All I *really* remember is you dragging me acrost that cotton field. I don't even know who beat."

"That's good," said Cass. "Put that in your memoirs, and you will be telling the truth."

"Who'd want to read that?" asked the boy.

Roger laughed. "Nobody. That's why, when Mister Wake-field writes *his* memoirs, he will come out a major general. It's what all the first-chair memoirists do."

Cass said, "How do you know about memoirs if nobody's written any yet? Anyway, I will leave your sorry ass out of 'em."

"No, you won't," said Roger.

"Well, now listen, you-all," said the boy. "If you are scared, do you . . . do you pray before?"

"I don't believe God takes any part to speak of," Cass said. "Not in these fights of ours, anyway."

"Well, why not?" asked Lucian. "He's in charge, ain't He—you said He was. Don't He pick a favorite?"

"It would not be fair if He did," said Cass. "Anyhow, I guess we're all His favorites. I mean, more or less. Some more than others. Me, for instance—I'm a great favorite. Now, Roger here—"

"Well, fine," said the boy, and pulled the blanket over his head. Cass poked him, and he put his head out again. "Never mind," the boy said. "I ain't likely to be a favorite anyhow."

"Well," said Cass, "you might be if you quit cussing so damn much."

"Huh," said the boy.

Roger threw off his quilt and sat up, fully awake now. He pointed at Cass. "You quit ragging this boy about his language," he said. "It is his way of being genteel. Besides, he has a natural talent for it."

"Roger," said Cass, "you do not know a goddamned thing about cussing. I have never heard you utter so much as a syllable that couldn't be trot out at solemn high mass."

Roger ignored his comrade. "Listen here, Lucian," he said.

"As a philosopher, your uncle Cass is only an amateur, and you have thrown him off by asking questions he is not equipped to answer."

"Now, see here—" began Cass.

"Never mind," said Roger. "The boy asked about praying, and all you can do is rag him." He poked the boy's legs. "Here—sit up, you."

Lucian obeyed, rubbing his eyes again, and gapping. "Lord, don't you-all ever sleep?" he said.

Roger passed him a canteen. Ice clinked inside it. "There's plenty of time for sleeping tomorrow, or the next day, when you're dead and your uncle Cass throws dirt in your face."

"Roger!" said Cass.

"You be quiet!" said Roger. "Or, better yet, deny it if you can!"

"Nobody's throwing dirt in this boy's face," said Cass. "He is going home with us."

Roger laughed. He looked at the boy and said, "What Mister Wakefield means, in his crude and belligerent way, is that he has faith. Tomorrow, or the next day, there'll be a fight, and it won't be such a little thing as Decatur was. Mister Wakefield believes that God takes no sides but hopes for the best for everyone. I happen to believe the same. In a fight, lad, it is not so much us and the yankees. The Angel of Death wants us all—that's where the real battle is, and why it's all so insane."

"Well, could you pray to *him,* then?" asked the boy. "The Angel of Death?"

"You could," said Roger, "but he wouldn't listen. Only God does, and He can't help you right then."

"Well," said Lucian, "there's no sense in praying a-tall, if you ask me."

Roger laughed again and slapped the boy's leg. "There you have it," he said. "No sense in it a-tall. To ask for protection is pure lunacy, lad, especially when the other side is doing the same, and to the same address. That's exactly why everybody prays, you see; it's all we have to offer commensurate with the madness."

"But if God—"

"Hush," said Roger. "Be still and listen. You must have your faith, and it will be sore tested when you see what's left after a fight, what's hanging in the trees and spread over the ground—that place you saw back at Muscle Shoals was a garden by comparison. You look around, and you might be tempted to ask where God was when all this happened."

"Well, where was He?" asked Lucian.

"He was there," said Roger. "He was there all along, watching and grieving. If we live, I will take you over the next field myself, and maybe you will learn what you can only learn the hard way: that God is there with you, and whatever sorrow you are feeling—well, how infinite must the sorrow be in *His* heart? It is the only way. Once a man decides God planned all this, once he points to God as responsible, then his faith is gone. No mortal can bear that, no matter what he says. We have lost pretty much everything, but faith we must not lose. That is why we pray, and fervently—but *not* for preservation, mind. That article is left to you and your pards, not to God. To ask Him for it, and be spared when so many are not, will only doom your faith."

"What *do* you ask for, then?" said the boy.

Roger pulled the quilt around his shoulders. "To be forgiven," he said.

They were quiet then. The snow swirled around them, borne on a cutting wind, and through it ghostly shapes began to pass, bending, searching, speaking softly. Little stars of candlelight pricked out in the whiteness as men gathered their belongings. A murmur rose from the camps; the army was stirring, its vast and myriad soul already in motion toward the mystery that waited beyond the river.

Cass and Roger stood and stretched and groaned. Muscles cramped in the cold, and the blood slowed. Lucian sat a moment longer, watching them. "Mister Roger," he said at last, "if I pray to be forgive, you reckon it will take?"

Roger knelt, took up Lucian's hat—Cass had lifted one from a gatepost along the march—brushed the snow from it, and set it on the boy's head. "You can ask the dead ones," he said. "They know better than us."

Lucian came slowly to his feet. He was shivering, and Cass took up the blanket and spread it over the boy's shoulders. He said, "Dern it, we got to get you a coat. We'll find one today."

The boy looked up. In the pale, ambient light of the snow, his face held no measure of understanding, but a great deal of wonder, a little less of fear. Together, fear and wonder made understanding of a kind, enough for a boy, and as much as any of them could hope for. "Can *you* see 'em, Cass?" he said. "The dead ones? No fooling, now."

"Sometimes, yes," said Cass. He looked at the ground. "They are close tonight, but they mean no harm. They are just lonesome, I guess."

"I will see them, too," said the boy, and turned his eyes toward the river.

"It will take, lad," said Cass. "When you pray, and do it rightly, it always takes just fine. They would tell you that, I think, should you ask them."

Lucian nodded, his eyes still fixed on the barren trees where the river flowed silent and dark. "It ain't much time," he said. "I reckon you better teach me how."

They crossed the river to Florence next day and set out northward. It rained and snowed and sleeted by turns until the weather broke, and Indian summer lay upon the land. At Spring Hill, Tennessee, the Gods of War looked down on the army and offered a splendid chance for victory, but orders were ignored or misunderstood, the darkness confused everybody, and next morning they woke to discover the great opportunity lost forever.

So they went on to Franklin, where, it was said, the yankees had halted with their backs to the Harpeth River. The rebels hurrying north tried not to think of what that meant. They swung along, talking at first, or complaining, or speculating, only to fall silent as the sun grew higher and the miles began to tell. Then it was only the sound of their feet on the road, the clank of their accoutrements, their coughing, and the voices of their officers: Come on, boys. . . . Close it up now, boys. . . . Keep it moving there, lads.

Still they knew—these boys from Tennessee and Mississippi and Alabama, from far-off Texas and Missouri and South Carolina—what lay before them. Somewhere up ahead, by a town most of them had never heard of, the enemy was strengthening his works and setting his guns in place, waiting for the moment when the colors of the Army of Tennessee would break out upon the plain. The soldiers knew that the fields they would have to cross were still marked with the furrows of last year's planting. No smoke hung in the woods, and the Harpeth had never run with blood, and the houses and churches and woodsheds were innocent, for a little while yet, of the cries of wounded men and the rasp of bone saws and the stink of chloroform and gangrene. They knew also that the Death Angel had made his choices, and, for some, the cold ground was waiting. For the rest, they were marching into a darkness like nothing they had ever seen, into a shadow that would fall across all their days remaining. They understood that no prayer or promise could shape a different end, but they prayed anyway—them who would—and made promises to God that they could not keep. Then they bent to the long miles, making ready, each man telling himself that surely he would see tomorrow.

The Ditch

❖ 9 ❖

ASS WAKEFIELD WOKE SHIVERING WITH ANGER AND dread, the usual residue of his dreams. He did not believe his dreams meant anything—their only purpose seemed to be to scare the shit out of him—and he cursed them in the same way he cursed the deep midnight. Both left him weak, unsure, cowardly even. Waking and midnight; everything seemed worse then, and the smallest tic of the universe seemed insurmountable.

He had no idea where he was—the hotel room looked like any of the hundreds he had been in—nor even if it were morning or evening, for the light in the window was pale and transient, preparing to slide into light or dark. He lurched from the bed and crossed to the window and banged his fist against the glass. He focused on the frosted rooftops below him, and the smoke from the chimneys, and decided it was morning. Then he remembered he was in Franklin, Tennessee.

At the washstand, he splashed water in his face and caught a glimpse of himself in the cloudy mirror. He looked like owl shit, he thought: unshaven, baggy under the eyes, in the same shirt he had worn for—how many days now? Well, no matter. A shirt was good for four days in the wintertime if he did no heavy work.

He had slept in his clothes, so dressing was only a matter of putting on his shoes and finding his hat and frock coat. He needed coffee. The world would look more manageable then. He wondered if Alison was awake. He hoped she was not, for she needed to rest. Besides, in his present humor, Cass would do better not to see her. At midnight, he had wanted her company; at waking, he didn't—unfair, but there it was.

He cracked the door and peered out to find the hall empty. He moved quickly to the stairs and in a moment was in the lobby of the Avalon, a dark-paneled room with tired wicker chairs arranged on a threadbare rug, newspapers littering the tables, a few struggling plants, and tall windows through which the winter sun slanted hopefully. The place had the weary, used-up smell that Cass associated with hotels: a compound of cigar smoke, newsprint, kerosene, furniture oil, and the indefinable scent of peregrine souls. Behind a pair of glass-paned doors was a dining room, but Cass could not bear the thought of the smell of frying meat. Then he beheld a great steaming samovar, polished and formidable, surrounded by heavy white cups. The sight elevated his spirits, and he allowed himself to observe the others gathered in the lobby.

The desk clerk, in shirtsleeves, was sliding mail into pigeonholes. A black porter leaned on his broom in a ray of sunlight, talking quietly to the bellman. Two fat drummers on a couch leafed through their order slips, valises opened beside them, and from the dining room came the clink of silverware and muted voices. Cass smiled at the familiar scene and felt comfortable in its midst. For a moment, he wished he were only on a selling trip, alone and anonymous in some northern city with his traveling case of pistols and order slips of his own, far away from memory and no business with the dead. The road was not so bad, he thought, and when he heard the sound of his name, he believed it must be some fellow traveler crossing his path again. He was still smiling when he turned and saw Lucian on the stairs.

For an instant, Cass was confused. Here was the kind of infernal jumbling that dreams delighted in: Lucian Wakefield, whom Cass knew to be far away in Cumberland, was descending the frayed carpet of the stairs in a rumpled frock coat and cravat all askew, unshaven, hair disarranged and greasy, looking like owl shit himself. "Lucian, for God's sake," said Cass sharply. The drummers looked up. Lucian stopped, his hand on the newel post. Cass said, "Do you . . . do you know where you *are*?"

Lucian's hands were shaking, his eyes red. He straightened his cravat and ran his fingers through his hair. "Well, hey, Cass," he said, and smiled. "We came in on the same train after all—funny, ain't it? Spring Hill, the switching woke me up, and I looked out and saw you and Alison at the depot, and I thought to find you then, but it was late, so I decided—"

"Listen to me," said Cass. He closed the distance between them. A telephone rang feebly behind the desk, and the front door opened and closed. Cass said, "You got no business here. I told you yesterday—"

"Roger wanted to come, too," said Lucian.

"I told you, boy—"

"God damn what you told me, sir," said Lucian, his own voice sharp now. He came off the stairs and poked his finger in Cass's chest. "I am not a boy. That is a mistake you make too often. And *you* wouldn't cross the Pontotoc Road."

"The Pontotoc—"

"Christmas night. You laid it off on me, but you wouldn't cross it your own self—you would of froze to death first."

"I was distracted!" said Cass. "Drunk, if the truth be known—but not so much as you."

"Hah," said Lucian. "You were afraid. You were *afraid* to cross it. So how do you expect to cross that ditch this mornin'?"

"What ditch?" said Cass, but the question and the answer came to him in the same instant. There was only one, after all, and he had put off thinking about it, and now here it was. Cass turned and walked to the window. Beyond the glass, the day was unfolding in its ordinary way. People were moving on the street. A man on horseback trotted by, his mount tossing her head in the joy of morning. All so ordinary, so regular, yet all distant and alien, as if the window glass were a bourne no traveler—at least no Wakefield—was allowed to cross.

Do you know where you are? Cass might as well have asked the question of himself. Somehow he had missed it in the blue hours of the night, on the hack ride from the depot with mist swirling around the lamps, in the dim lobby crowded with suitcases and cranky passengers. He was tired then, and only wanted to sleep, and the morning seemed far away. Now it had arrived, and with it, Lucian and another burden of truth.

Cass walked back to the stairs, the drummers watching him. "What is this about Roger?" he said. "I don't recall—"

"Oh, I told him myself," said Lucian. "Then I had to kick him off the train."

"You had no business inviting anybody!" said Cass, shouting now. "Not even yourself!"

"It ain't a question of God damned invitations!" said Lucian.

"Hey!" said one of the drummers. He slammed down his order book and rose from the couch—a big man with an extravagant beard and a fine silk waistcoat, a northern man by his speech. "Why don't you ladies take it outside?" he said. "We got business here."

"Damn, Charlie," said the other man, laughing. He closed his book and rose, too, pushing back his coat sleeves.

The desk clerk vanished into the office. The porter disappeared through the broom closet door, and the bellman eased to his podium. Cass Wakefield turned, slipping his hands deep into his pants pockets. He liked to go into a confrontation that way, for it made him seem unready, vulnerable—a man who could be talked down. Meanwhile, Lucian moved out into the lobby. He lifted a brass paperweight from a table and hefted it in his hand.

"The morn is just breaking," Cass said. "The whole day lies before us." He took a step, then another.

"So much work to do," said Lucian, circling to the desk.

Cass understood that the two drummers—men widely traveled, whose lives were spent in cheap hotels, in saloons and taverns—might well be dangerous in a fight. Indeed, if they knew the South, as well they must, they would not have picked one otherwise. However, Cass knew also that over these men he and Lucian held a great and insurmountable advantage: they did not give a shit.

The first drummer was about to speak again when the dining room door opened, and a swarm of women emerged into the lobby. They wore the sashes and pins and ribbons of the United Daughters of the Confederacy—a breakfast meeting, no doubt. Some were pretty and slim as whippets, though most were formidable Brunhildes who, given the chance, might fight the yankees all over again, and do it right this time.

The second drummer picked up his book and valise. "Aw, forget it, Charlie," he said. "We got a train to catch." And that was all.

The lobby was soon quiet again, the clerk at his desk once more, the porter sweeping the steps in a cloud of dust. Lucian poured a cup of coffee from the samovar, and from his pocket took a little amber bottle of laudanum. He shook it at Cass and said, "This is just the kind of thing that occurs when you leave home."

"Well," said Cass, "you was the one wanted something to happen."

They drank their coffee on the couch vacated by the drummers. Cass was stirred up by the excitement, and now he was impatient for Alison to appear. He remembered what L. W. Thomas said once: *Boys, they's only two things I cannot do. I can't travel with a woman, and I can't take a shit with my hat on.* Through experimentation, Cass had found the second anomaly to be true of himself as well. Now he was learning about the first, and not doing well with that, either. He had not traveled with a woman since he brought Janie upriver on the steamboat *Alonzo Child* at the beginning of the war. She was little trouble, though she did have a good many trunks. Then Cass thought how he should have left her with her people in New Orleans. If he had, maybe the typhoid wouldn't have taken her. *No, it would have been the yellow fever then,* he thought, *or the cholera.* He stood and paced the rug, up and down.

"What?" said Lucian. He was dipping a willow twig in his coffee.

"Nothing," said Cass. The electricity was sparking in his head, bouncing around. A chromo in a gaudy frame caught his attention, and he went to look at it: a broken column, like the ones in graveyards, shrouded in the old battle flag. The column sat atop a stone carved with the portentous date 1865. In the foreground lay all manner of warlike rubbish: shattered cannon, broken sword twined in laurel, a shield, more flags, a harp—the minstrel boy's wild harp, no doubt, or the one that sang in Tara's halls, the warrior-poet's harp, strings all loose as if the song were finished, the poet silenced forever. In the background, a grove of trees, a suggestion of smoke or mist—the ghostly legions, perhaps—and under all, the inscription *In Memoriam.*

The picture made him sick, and he turned away. He looked at Lucian, chewing on his willow twig. *The minstrel boy to the war has gone*—"What makes you think we'll go to the ditch, anyway?" Cass said.

"That's where we'll *have* to go if you want to find the place," said Lucian. "That's where we'll have to start."

Cass knew the boy was right. They would go to the cotton gin, where the ditch had been, and from there they should be able to follow the ground over which they bore the dead. That was the easy part.

"I got to move around," said Cass. "If I told you to wait for Alison—"

"I will wait for her," said Lucian, "though, if you ask me, we could get it done without troubling her."

"I didn't ask you," said Cass, and went out the door before Lucian could make reply.

✠

When the door of the hotel closed behind him, Cass was alone in the sunlight. He looked at the windows above. Somewhere up there, Alison was sleeping, or combing out her hair perhaps. What did women do in a hotel room? he wondered.

He was not much surprised to see Lucian. In fact, it was a wonder that a half-dozen others had not come with him. Perhaps they should have done it that way—engaged a whole railway car, draped it in bunting, made an excursion of it with wives and picnic lunches and the like, waving the old flag out the window, singing. . . .

Alison would not be sorry for Lucian's company. She had always favored the boy. *He is not a boy,* Cass chided himself. *He can stand it.*

Cass plucked at his watch chain and the buttons on his coat. He consulted his watch, then put it back, still without any idea what time it was. A whiskery old woman shuffled by, muttering to herself. When Cass lifted his hat, the old lady snarled at him.

The various churches of the town all seemed to be on this end. Cass had seen their steeples for the first time by the light of a dying sun twenty years gone, but he had not seen them up close until the next day, when the long column marched through Franklin, chasing the yankees, whom General Hood had promised were sorely whipped. By then, the town was no longer a thing to be gained, but to be left behind. It belonged to no army, no country—only to God, who had not surrendered, and to the dead still lying in rows and piles, and to the ruined ones. With these last, the churches, houses, public buildings, corncribs, everything with a roof was crammed and overflowing. The iron fences around the churchyards were hung with blankets and drying bandages; the sanctuaries echoed with cries, curses, pleadings. They were rife with smells that spilled out into the street. The soldiers hurried by, closing their minds against the knowledge that sooner or later it would be their cries and pleading, their blood on the sticky floors and thrice-used bandages—not here but somewhere. Soon or late, and somewhere.

Now the churches were peaceful, orderly, seemingly forgotten of all that had happened, though Cass knew they had not forgotten. The placid morning was only part of the air around him; not an illusion, exactly, but a gauzy curtain that would part with little effort, or none, if the watcher knew but to lift his hand. All that had happened was still there, just beyond the thin curtain of time.

A junction of five roads wandered off into the countryside. Of these, the heaviest traveled, besides Main Street itself, was the Columbia Pike, identified by a sign nailed to a telegraph pole. Cass looked down the Columbia Pike toward the little rise a half mile away, and the old sorrow and anger rose again, unbidden, from the stumbling track—he could almost see it in the mud of the street—that he had left behind twenty years ago on the retreat—and Roger's, and Lucian's, and the blood trail Ike Gatlin walked in. He knew that if he put out his hand, he could open the curtain, and there would be the long, ragged column passing—going out or returning, no matter, for it was all the same: thousands of men struggling in a dark that came from within themselves, that they would never outrun. And down the road, just over that rise yonder—oh, there they were again, in another fold of time, caught forever, like moths in a vain striving toward some light they did not understand. Cass knew they were there still, that he should feel connected to them, and not to the living people on the street. . . .

"Ah!" he said, and rubbed his eyes. Whatever happened down the pike was over, and only ghosts strove there now. And if they strove still, it was for no other purpose, apparently, than that an old man, standing in the sun, might remember and be afraid again. Cass felt like a fool—afraid, indeed! Afraid of what? There was nothing in this place he hadn't visited in memory a thousand times in the last twenty years, and memory was worse than anything he might encounter in the sunlight.

A block away was a brick church with a crenellated tower. Cass thought he would go and see what kind it was. On the way, he stopped at a grocery and bought a bottle of Tennessee whiskey. He filled his flask, then asked the clerk to take the rest to his room in the hotel.

The church tower belonged to the Episcopal Church of St.

Paul. A Negro youth in brogans and ragged breeches and an old sack coat was cleaning the walk with a broom and bucket of water. Cass scraped his shoes on the edge of the boards. "It'll be spring soon," said Cass, annoyed to find his voice shaking. In fact, spring was three months away, but at least it was closer than it was yesterday. "Then summer," said Cass, "and no more mud for a while."

"Yes, Cap'n," said the youth. "Then it'll be the dry dust."

Cass sat down on the church steps, took a drink, and watched the boy sweep. People were beginning to stir about. Some schoolboys came up the plank walk, swinging their tattered books and jostling one another, each trying to outtalk the others. They looked to be about Lucian's age when he came to the regiment. A little way behind, a trio of girls in poke bonnets walked primly, clutching their own books to their coats, pretending to take no notice of the lads. He saw the old woman again, on the other side of the street, coming back from wherever she had gone, still muttering. This time, she was swinging a chicken, its head lolling. Every few steps, she would give the bird a twirl, as though she were not convinced it was dead. Cass tried to connect himself to these people and found he could not, as though the window glass were still between them.

Then a young woman with a basket on her arm passed by. She was pretty, her cheeks rosy, her eyes bright with Tomorrow. Cass lifted his hat and this time got a smile in return. She would not have understood his presence here, most likely, this girl passing into the morning. She had not been born when Perry and the colonel met their violent ends and were shoveled under the earth in a grave too shallow. Yet, Cass realized, she was the very reason for it all. It occurred to Cass that, for all the times he'd been asked *how* they did it, he had seldom been asked *why*. Now here, all at once on the streets of Franklin, the girl offered an answer. Maybe they had done all that for her, believing that what they suffered, what they tried to accomplish, would somehow touch her down the long corridor of years. The idea was almost laughable now, for they had lost, and their vanity and striving had come to nothing. The child was perfectly carefree and content, though the old flag, and not the Stars and Bars, was floating over the courthouse. But the idea might not have been so absurd in that distant November when the army aligned itself at the foot of the hills.

The smell of the church embraced him, and he rose and went up the steps. The door was open, and he passed through, removing his hat. Here the weak winter sunlight was transformed. It spread across the Tiffany windows and lit in glorious illumination the faces of angels and apostles, shepherds and Magi. Then it crept aloft to the timbers of the ceiling, diffused to shadow, holy and calm. The sacristy candle, suspended by a golden chain, burned beside the altar. Cass walked up the aisle, the boards creaking under his feet, and sat in a pew. He shut his eyes and fixed his mind on the silence, trying to believe in what the candle told: the presence of a God who had not surrendered, who alone understood the Why and asked only that He be trusted with it. Cass wanted to believe that God had healed this place, had shriven it of blood and chloroform and filthy bandages and death, of dying men calling for their mothers. He listened a long time, thinking if he only listened well enough, if he only paid attention, he would feel, no matter how lightly, the touch that once sustained him. The candle gleamed, a rafter creaked; that was all.

Beside him on the pew lay a pair of women's gloves and a prayer book, ribbons tattered, the gold cross on the cover worn nearly away. The gloves smelled of leather and lavender. Cass picked up the book, and a scattering of scraps fell out: poems clipped from newspapers, memorable lines from sermons, a Confederate banknote. Cass replaced these carefully, closed the book and laid it by, then rose and made his way back down the aisle. A sparrow in the eaves cocked his head at Cass, then flew out the open door. Cass followed him into the sunlight.

❖ 10 ❖

LUCIAN DRANK HIS COFFEE SLOWLY. IT WARMED HIM, and the laudanum warmed him—Mister Leslie, the druggist, called it Black Draught—and time turned more easily. Lucian had not been in many hotels: the Colonial in Cumberland, where he took most of his meals in the lunch-room, the Gayoso in Memphis a few times, and one down in Baton Rouge when he went to a doctor there. Last night, he waited outside the Avalon until Cass and Alison cleared the lobby before he registered. His room was small and threadbare, and when he blew out the lamp, he could sense the travelers who had passed time there. He hardly slept at all in the unfamiliar bed, with strangers pacing the hall, muted voices, and, as dawn approached, the noises from the street. Once, he thought he might go walk around outside, but he was afraid he might find himself in some place he had been before, alone in the dark.

The first time Lucian saw the square in Cumberland—the place Cass said was home, the place they were supposed to go to when the war was over—it was all ashes, charred timbers, eyeless shells of buildings. Lucian was sick then, but when he was able to get up and walk around, he found ashes still, and the same blank walls, and the people tired and sick like himself. Cass walked with him, holding him by the arm, letting him rest when he needed to. Cass showed where the courthouse had been, and such-and-such a store, and here was where so-and-so lived, and they went out to the graveyard and walked among all the new graves, and Cass pointed to one and said, "That is Janie that I told you about." In the army, Cass told all the time about how Janie would care for them when they got home, but now she could not. A long time they sat in the dry grass by the grave, looking at the hard, new-mounded earth and the little slanted board: *Jane Spell Wakefield,* it said, and the dates that told she was twenty-five years old when she died. Cass took up some of the dirt and held it in his hand. He cried a little then, and Lucian thought he ought to cry, too, but he didn't. He could not feel anything to cry for.

They went inside Holy Cross church. It was empty and dark, the pews taken out, the windows boarded up. Wasps by the hundreds bumped against the arched ceiling and swooped around their heads. They walked up the middle, glass crunching under their feet, to the place Lucian didn't know to call the altar yet. There, a candle burned in a red glass suspended by a chain from the ceiling. Cass told him it was lit by the priest, and it meant that God was present in the sacraments.

"Right now?" said Lucian. "He's here right now?"

Cass touched him on the shoulder. When he spoke, his voice was unsteady. "Kneel and pray," he said.

"Pray for what?" said Lucian.

"Forgiveness," said Cass. "Remember how Mister Lewellyn taught you."

"Forgiveness for what?" Lucian asked. "I ain't done nothing."

Cass thought a moment. He said, "Well, then pray for grace in time of trouble."

Lucian remembered the look on Cass Wakefield's face as they sat by the grave. From that moment, he could think back as far as he wanted and find nothing but trouble: hard times, battle and death, sickness, lonesomeness, meanness. He said, "They's so much trouble, Cass. If God is here, then why don't He just go ahead and fix it—or at least some of it? Does He have to be asked ever time? Can't He see?"

"I don't know," Cass said. "I used to think—" He stopped then, his head tilted, and Lucian could see he was crying again, though he made no sound. Cass began to pace up and down, muttering to himself, wiping at his eyes. After a moment, he stopped and looked up toward the ceiling, where the light was showing through a big hole in the roof. "Fuck it," said Cass. "Fuck all that." He stepped forward then and opened his hand and let the dirt from Janie's grave pour out into the glass that held the candle. The flame disappeared, and Cass turned and walked back out into the hot sunlight.

Lucian was sick a long time after that. He had a little closet of a room in the house on Algiers Street, and for a whole year he hardly left it. Sometimes Alison Sansing would sit with him, and sometimes Morgan Harper. They read to him when he could stand it—histories, Shakespeare, Bulfinch, the Bible—for they knew he was short on education.

During that time, Sally Mae and Roger were finally married. Cass did not attend the affair, but Alison told later how the bride and groom were both still sick, and Sally Mae swooned at the altar and had to be revived. Whenever Sally Mae came to sit with Lucian, she would not read to him but talked about the visions she had in her fevers, which were as lively as anything the old Bible prophets had to tell, and Lucian would tell his in return. Such a lot of dragons and red horsemen and ghosts and death angels moved through the room then, when Lucian and Sally Mae were together.

By early autumn—he was about fourteen years old, maybe fifteen—he could walk, and walk he did, long journeys into the countryside that made his legs ache but made him stronger. Cass traded for a horse and a pony and some old, brittle tack, which they oiled up together. Cass taught Lucian how to ride the pony, and Lucian would push the little fellow even farther out in the county, riding hard, using muscles he never knew he had. He watched the leaves turn scarlet and gold, watched them fall from the trees and drift in the ditches. Sometimes the yankee cavalry would ride by, and Lucian hid among the trees or in the broomsage and watched them pass, holding the pony's muzzle so he wouldn't whicker, wishing he had one of those carbines that would shoot all day without reloading. (*Always take out the last man first,* Cass had told him once, during a skirmish on the retreat from Nashville.) He would ease up to soldiers lounging on the square and listen to them talk, and he would think, *They are not much men, after all.* Sometimes he went out to their camp and watched them drill, for he did not want to forget how it was: the long blue lines, drums beating, fixed bayonets gleaming. Sometimes he watched the fat men from Illinois and Indiana and Wisconsin who ran the Freedman's Bureau, who had never done any fighting but had reaped the harvest nevertheless.

At night, sometimes, Cass would saddle the old horse and leave, always telling Lucian to stay in the house. But Lucian wouldn't stay. He would saddle the pony and follow, and watch as the men rode around with torches to scare the poor niggers and get chased by the yankees. He did that until Cass caught him; after that, Cass traded the pony for a real horse, and Lucian was allowed to ride along. Cass gave him a pistol, too, and he used it once.

He and Cass spent an hour every day lifting a section of iron rail in the backyard, and after a while their arms grew knotty and hard, and they were not so easily tired. On the square, a new courthouse was going up—Cass and Lucian and Roger hauled bricks and hammered nails for ten cents a day—and new stores, and the people no longer looked weary and sick. Pretty soon, Tom Jenkins took Lucian to work in the hardware store and taught him about nails and harness and pipe and lumber, and how to cipher and make change. The store was new-built out of heart pine by Tom Jenkins's own hand, but it wasn't long before it took on the smells of time passing: oiled floors, grease, leather, iron, kerosene, and the sweat of the men who came there.

Meanwhile, Cass worked at odd jobs and passed his idle time stealing from the yankees. He drank a good deal and talked about Janie and about dead men and old battles. He no longer carried his rosary. At night, he would rage and curse and throw things around, and then he would talk *to* Janie as if she were still there among them. It was then that Lucian began to walk the streets at night. He could not reach Cass Wakefield in the place where he was, so Lucian went off alone, in spite of the yankees' curfew, and in time he met others who did the same. The little house where Janie had lived began to grow heavy with smoke and dust, the walls growing closer and closer and hardly ever a lamp or candle lit. The house became a place where no one cooked or washed, where visitors never called—a museum of immovable furniture and locked trunks, of vases and lamps and ivy bowls still setting where Janie had put them, and her clothes moldering in the wardrobe, breeding generations of moths. When Lucian's headaches came, he would lie in his darkened room and dream his laudanum dreams. When he was well, he worked in the store, and walked the back roads, and paced the streets at night watching out for soldiers, and time passed right along.

One winter afternoon, the priest of Holy Cross sent his card around. The next day, he came to call. Brennan was his name. He was a short, balding man with a wooden leg, who wore no collar and smoked fat cigars. His speech was not of Mississippi. Cass was in a bad humor that day, but tied on a cravat and made some coffee, and they all sat together in what used to be the parlor, with the blinds closed and dust all over everything and a meager fire on the hearth. On a table was a dried-up fishbowl with Janie's petrified goldfish still curled up on the bottom. Cass sat upright, stiff and wary.

They talked about the war for a while. (Once upon a time, people began with the weather, but now they always started off with the war.) The priest told how he had gone off soldiering and lost his leg for his trouble—on Culp's Hill at Gettysburg, he said. Lucian had never heard of the place. Finally they reached a quiet spell, as people will do, and Cass said, "Well, Mister Brennan, no doubt you are here to inquire after our souls. What profound truths, what miracles of grace and healing have you come to offer?"

The priest looked up sharply. His coffee cup clinked into the saucer. "I didn't come to offer you a damn thing," he said. "Is that what you thought?"

Cass was clearly taken aback by this. Lucian, who had no knowledge of priests, thought that if they were all like this one, they might be worth listening to.

"That is bold language to use in a man's house," said Cass stiffly.

The priest laughed without humor. "Don't speak to *me* about language in another's house," he said. "I was in the sacristy the day you did your trick with the candle. My first day in the parish, and to be greeted with that!"

Cass's face went as red as the candle's little glass. "I was just come from my wife's grave," he said. "Before that—"

The priest waved him silent. "I know your story," he said. "It is like a good many others, as for that. In any event, it has taken until now for me to summon the humility to call on you, and to be truthful, it is of little interest to me whether you come around the church or not—that is between God and you and this boy here. If you are having a crisis of faith, maybe I can help you. On the other hand, if you are merely being an ass, then I bid you good day."

Cass Wakefield looked at the priest and laughed. It was the first time in many months that Lucian had heard the sound. The priest, red-faced himself now, started to rise, but Cass beckoned him to stay. A wind rattled in the windowpanes and stirred the fire on the hearth. Such a cold day, and bleak, and the fires from the yankee camp drifting across the yard—but all at once both men were laughing.

Cass said, "You put me in mind of our old chaplain, Sam Hook. He used language like that to good effect in a homily."

"Hah," said the priest, and poured another cup of coffee. Lucian laughed to himself then, thinking how the coffee but lately belonged to the yankee soldiers, and what the priest would have to say about that.

Cass put his hands together. He said, "Mister Brennan, I have not lost my faith, and I do not presume to fault the Almighty for His apparent indifference. It is only that I am tired of making excuses for Him. I am tired of hearing about *His design this* and *His design that;* if He has one at all, 'tis a sorry one indeed and of no use to anybody. The facts bear it out, as you ought to know yourself."

The priest nodded. He sipped his coffee and this time placed the cup carefully back in its saucer. "Well, then," he said, "I see your God is a personal one. Perhaps you'd be more comfortable with a vague abstraction." He smiled then. "I won't worry too much about you, though I might throw out a prayer now and again."

"As you will, Mister Brennan," said Cass. "Perhaps one day, when I am capable of sympathy again, I'll come back to the church house."

"Worship does not require your sympathy, sir," said the priest. "That's why they call it worship."

"Yes, it does," said Cass, "else I could send my card, if I had a card, and leave the rest of me at home."

That is how the war did for some people, Lucian thought. It used up everything, stole everything, and what remained— memory, mostly—was just enough to keep the shape of a man, just enough to propel the flesh from one day to the next, only without feeling or interest or desire. Time itself ceased to mean anything; with the laudanum, Lucian could lose two or three days and be no worse off than he was. The dead were the lucky ones, maybe, who quit with the dream still in their heads, who could still believe in Possibility only because they would never have to lose it.

Roger said once that, after a battle, you had to try to put things back together according to the rules you knew, and the best you could come up with was still a lie. So it was, Lucian thought. Once, in the back of the store, he took an old clock apart, laid out the wheels and gears and springs, cleaned and studied them, and put them back in the same order. Sitting on the workbench, the thing looked just like the clock it had been, except that it would not run. Nothing Lucian did would induce it to run. That was what the war did to people.

When the priest rose to leave at last, Lucian was sorry to see him go. At the door, Cass touched the man's sleeve and said, "Now, regarding this Culp's Hill in Gettysburg that we never heard of—"

"Never heard of Culp's Hill?" said the priest, shrugging on his coat. "Well, you must read the histories when they come out."

"That is unlikely," said Cass. "Anyhow, I was going to ask who you were with."

"Ah, I failed to mention that detail," said the priest, and winked at Lucian. "Fifth Maine Artillery," he said, and Cass Wakefield laughed out loud again.

In time, the yankees folded their tents and went away, but still there was trouble, for the war had opened doors that could not be closed again so long as any lived who remembered it. A restlessness drove them in those days, and a good many went out to the territories, and some to Mexico or Brazil or Argentina, never to be heard from again. Those who remained went through the motions of rebuilding. They dedicated a new courthouse, made speeches, ran off the carpetbaggers, cleared new ground—knowing all the while it was a lie, for they could not rebuild themselves. Beneath the ordinary strain of life ran a dark current of memory and violence, and sometimes a crack broke open and the black water boiled out.

One day in August, a blistering hot afternoon, Sheriff Julian Bomar jailed a man named Back Stutts who was waving a pistol around and threatening the citizens. Stutts was turned loose next morning, after the way of such things, but he stood in the street before the new jail and called down perdition on Julian Bomar and all his kin. The next day, Sheriff Bomar was shot down in ambush away out in the country and left to die in the middle of the southerly road. His horse, still harnessed to the sheriff's yellow-wheeled hack, came back to the square and trotted around and around the courthouse until somebody caught it. When the people saw the bloody seat, they asked no questions; they did not summon the constable or consult an attorney. Before sundown, the Cumberland Rangers had caught Back Stutts after a wild chase on horseback and a running gunfight. The affair ended with an all-night siege of an abandoned cabin that left two citizens dead and Stutts shot full of holes but mean and dangerous to the last. Before he could die on them, the men took a door off its hinges and laid him out on it, then propped him up on the cabin gallery where Professor Brown took his picture. Then they hanged Back Stutts from the rafters—Cass and Roger and Lucian were among those who put their hands to the rope—and left him dangling for the birds.

It took only a week for the real killer—a man who had proven himself bold in the siege of the cabin—to get drunk enough to brag about his deed at the Citadel of Djibouti. That night, the Cumberland Rangers hanged him too, from the only big oak tree left on the yard of the new courthouse.

That was home, then, for Lucian Wakefield, who knew no other home. For a long time, he felt lightly tethered, but the people accepted him and looked out for him just as the soldiers had—and with less cause, he supposed.

Now he looked around in surprise. He was no longer in Cumberland but in a hotel lobby in Franklin, Tennessee, wondering where Cass Wakefield had gone. Lucian rose in a panic, trying to remember what he was supposed to do. *Find Cass Wakefield* was his first thought. That was always the best thing.

❖ 11 ❖

THE SUN WAS BRIGHT, HARD ON HIS EYES, AND LUCIAN
took his green sun-spectacles from his pocket and put
them on. They were useful for keeping the headaches
away, but Lucian had not worn them in a long time and had forgotten until now that they were in his coat pocket. Now he
marveled once more at the world transformed by the green
glass, as if everything were under water. He could feel time
moving past him as if it were water. He took out the amber bottle with its glass stopper, poured a little Black Draught in the
palm of his hand, and licked it, for he understood that this was
a place where time might get away from him, or he from it.

Across the street was a sign on a telegraph pole: Columbia

Pike. Lucian knew well that the gin house, where they had struck the yankee line, was still down that road. A generation had been raised up; kings and princes and presidents had come and gone; the worms had long since conquered the dead of Franklin. They might never find the place where the boys were buried, but no doubt they would discover the God damned gin house intact, and the ditch before it.

The morning after the battle, the gin house drew them as a suck hole draws the autumn's floating leaves, back down to the center of darkness from which there could be no rising. They went timidly, like insects, even the ones who pretended to be bold under the light of torches. Then the packed charnel of the ditch surprised them, and Cass stopped and knelt, and Lucian knelt beside, and together they looked at the gin house, where it rose like the skeleton of some ancient carnivore against the stars.

When daylight came, they saw it clearly. The enemy had pulled the boards off to use in his breastworks. The roof was a colander of bullet holes. Cass speculated it would fall over when the first good wind came along, and Ike Gatlin argued to burn it just for spite. But they didn't burn it. In fact, they walked quietly around it and talked in whispers, for even in that first daylight—when many of the men did not yet know the name of the town where they had fought—it was already becoming a landmark dark and sinister in their memory. By the time the army went into the works at Nashville, the gin had become the Cotton Gin and taken its place among the sacred groves of their mythology. Certainly the sight of its skeleton against the timid light of dawn was already a fixture in Lucian's dreams, and there it dwelled yet. Thus Lucian had no doubt it remained these twenty years gone, and would remain a thousand years hence.

The gin was immortal, sacred, and cursed all at once. Too much of violence and fear and courage had happened there, too many had died there for it to ever lose its place in the universe.

Too many, too much. Was it quantity alone that made the gin different from the farmhouse in Alabama, the muddy field in Decatur, any of a thousand lost, nameless places where men had fought and died? After all, those lads had been just as scared, and the dead were just as dead. No, the butcher's bill alone was not enough, Lucian thought. They remembered the gin because they needed a place like it, a single immortal shrine to which they might return, tragic enough and fatal enough to contain not only itself but all the lost places, too, as if the soldiers' violence and loss and pain had been given a single monument to stand forever. That was as it should be, Lucian thought, for they were unlikely to have a monument of any other kind.

Lucian shivered and squinted into the winter sun. Yesterday morning—was it only yesterday?—Cass was packing his bag. He looked up at Lucian and said, *Don't you even think of following us up there. You been there once—that is enough.*

I wish to hell you'd told me that twenty years ago, said Lucian.

I did tell you, Cass said. *Maybe you'll listen this time.*

Well, Cass *had* told him, and he didn't listen that time, and he hadn't listened this time either. Now here he was, about to go hunting Cass Wakefield again. *But it's not Cass this time,* he thought, and suddenly he remembered Alison.

When they hunted down Back Stutts, every man on the expedition had been a soldier once, or had been ruined by the war, or damaged by it, including Stutts himself. So the war did this, too: it put those who suffered by it all together in a glass jar like so many strange, dangerous insects, and they could crawl up and down the glass all they wanted, but they could never reach the other side. By the same token, no one else could enter, so inside the jar they created their own world out of memory and grief. Here they kept alive their anger and fed on it; they pledged their own troths, guarded their secrets—and from these things drew a perverse strength and the knowledge that they could depend on one another, no matter what madness presented itself. Alison Sansing, by virtue of her loss, was one of these. She belonged to them and depended on them. It was no mystery to Lucian why she had come to Franklin, why Cass had followed, why Lucian had followed himself—nor why Roger Lewellyn had to be forced from the train at the depot in Cumberland. That was home, too, in a way—a community, at least—a secret society open to all ages, races, sexes, where lifetime dues were paid at the door.

"Perry?"

Lucian turned, and there was Alison in a green cape with the hood thrown back, and her hair all in disarray—she had cut it since he saw her last. The skin under her eyes was dark, and her cheeks were hollow, and she blinked in the sunlight. "Perry?" she said.

"No," said Lucian. He snatched off his spectacles and tucked them away, thinking how far away her voice sounded, thinking, *Her hair*—"No," he said, "it's—"

A flock of pigeons clattered from a ledge above, startling them both. They watched the birds wheel aloft and disappear behind the roofline across the street. Lucian spoke her name, and she looked at him. "Why, Lucian Wakefield," she said. "Way off up here."

"You . . . ain't mad, are you?" said Lucian.

She opened her mouth to speak; Lucian saw the words

shape themselves, but no sound came to him. He remembered a close room smelling of camphor and a woman's face in the candlelight, blurred by the pain that seemed to have no end or bottom to it. She was all in black, bending over him. Her hand was cool on his forehead, but he shrank from the touch of it, afraid. Lucian wondered how the woman came to be there—and then he understood. She had come to carry him off to where Cass and Mister Lewellyn had gone, away from the smoke and flame and struggling men. A moth flew around the lantern, circling madly, its shadow dancing on the wall. The little flame of the candle speared through his head, and he cried out against it, wishing she would go on and carry him away. Instead, she leaned over and snuffed out the light. Darkness then, and the coolness of her hand, and her breathing, and her voice making words he could not understand.

Then all at once, her words came together, like drops of mercury swirled in a bowl, and Lucian was outside the hotel in Franklin again. A heavy wagon was struggling past, dry axles popping, horses straining against the mud.

"Hardly mad," she said, "and hardly surprised." She put her cool hand against his forehead. "You look pretty frayed this morning. Do you understand why we are here?"

"I know what we have come to do, Miss Alison," said Lucian. "The 'why' don't matter so much."

"Don't it?" she asked. "Well, let us cross the road then, and find Cass Wakefield, and see what we can see."

✛

They found Cass down the street. He was playing marbles with a black boy on the porch of a brick church. The two rose and pulled off their hats, and Cass said, "Well, Miss Alison."

She laughed. "You would not find people playing marbles at a *Presbyterian* church."

"Puritans," said Cass. He indicated the black boy, who had snatched up his broom again. "This here is Madison. He has taken me for six bits with his infernal glass shooter." He came down the steps and swatted Lucian with his hat. "I see the orphan found you—or did you have to run him down?"

Lucian heard Alison's voice in reply, then Cass's again, but the talk was far away and did not concern him. He was trying to remember something important out of time, something he saw once at the beginning of things. He let go of Alison's arm and went up the steps to where the black boy was standing with his broom. He saw a square of dirty canvas with a circle drawn in chalk, and the clay marbles inside the circle. Lucian knelt and picked one up and rolled it in the palm of his hand. He said, "If I was you and was goin' to play marbles, I'd get a table outen that house yonder."

The boy looked at him. "Say what, Cap'n?" he asked, and moved back against the porch rail.

Lucian felt a hand tighten on his coat collar. He dropped the marble and let Cass pull him up. Cass shook him gently and whispered at him. "We are going down the pike."

"All right, Cass," he said.

✣

They went down the Columbia Pike to the top of the ridge. Beside the road was a brick house, neatly made, with a modest front after the Federal style. An old gentleman was sitting on the front steps, shaving off slivers of a cedar limb with a pocket knife. When the visitors approached, the old man rose and bowed to Alison in an old-fashioned way. "It's a cane," he said, holding up his work. "I like a cedar cane."

Cass said it was the best wood for such when you rubbed it down with linseed oil. The old man agreed.

"We were passing," said Cass. "Looking for the gin house."

"A little late for ginning," said the gentleman.

"Yes, sir," said Cass. "We only want—"

"You don't have to explain," said the old man. "You come back sooner or later, both sides. I look out the window, and there you are, standing in the street, gazing around as if you had forgotten where you left your horse tied." He waved his cane at the yard. "The dead ones, too," he said.

"They are the ones we're looking for," said Alison.

"Oh, they are here in great numbers, madam," said the gentleman. "Late in the evening, all night, in the early hours, it's a perfect convocation out here in the yard." He looked at Cass. "Pray tell me who you were with, so I can adjust my lecture."

"Mississippi," said Cass. "Adams's Brigade. We struck the line at the gin house."

"Ah," said the other. He told how his house was the center of the Federal line. He used his cedar cane to point out where the two lines of breastworks, still plainly visible, had been dug in his backyard. The guns, he said, were there and there. He pointed out where the rebels came pouring over, and where a full brigade of northern men came like demons in a mad, howling counterattack that stopped the rebels cold.

Cass said, "I never knew what happened up here."

"Well, of course, you wouldn't," said the old man. "We

didn't either, till after. We were hid in the cellar, all of us—
neighbors, children, niggers—all scared, the women praying—"
He stopped and looked at the ground. "I never heard a sound
like that, before or since." He looked up at Cass. "Have you, sir?"

"No, sir," said Cass. "I have not."

"The gin's down yonder," said the old gentleman, pointing.
"Take your time. It's morning, there's nothing to harm now."

Cass and Lucian and Alison crossed the yard lying peaceful in
the sunlight and shadows. Red chickens strutted before them,
squirrels bounded away. Jaybirds and blackbirds argued in the
leafless walnut trees. Then they passed between the farm office
and a brick smokehouse and gazed out on the fields beyond, the
hills in the distance, and the gap between them where the army
had come in its long, ragged columns to array itself on the plain.
Cass thought about the yankee soldiers waiting here, crouching
among the shadows, the day growing colder, as the Army of Tennessee spread out upon the plain. *They must have heard us, even this
far away.* The notion gave him a shiver. *We could never have won
this fight,* Cass thought. *Even if we had all day and a hundred armies.*

Lucian had come up next to Cass. He glanced at Alison,
then whispered, "A wonder we are not all buried in somebody's
backyard."

Alison said, "It's so *far,*" and Cass knew she was thinking of
Perry and Colonel Sansing, of the last ground they trod.

Cass felt helpless and foolish. "We were there," he said,
pointing, though he couldn't be sure it was the right place.
"Then we went off that way and ended up over yonder."

"Why so far?" asked Alison.

Lucian stepped forward and put his foot on the mound of
the old breastworks. "It is how it was done," he said.

Cass turned toward the road then but stopped. "Look there," he said. Alison made a soft exclamation. The men stared in silence.

The southerly walls of the two outbuildings were sieved with holes, each the size of a man's thumb, each representing the passage of a .577- or .58-caliber minié ball fired by a charging rebel. There were hundreds of chips in the smokehouse brick and hundreds of perfect holes in the wooden wall of the office, representing the hurricane of lead that came howling over this ground, crowding the air over a span of time hardly long enough for a man to make contrition—all this in only one portion of a field, in only one eight-hour battle. Never mind Shiloh Church, Murfreesboro, Perryville, Chickamauga, Lookout Mountain, Nashville, never mind the massive engagements in the east, or the ten thousand skirmishes no one ever heard of, fought in thickets and farmyards and along the banks of streams. Multiply hundreds by thousands by thousands more of minié balls, round balls, buckshot, pistol balls—of artillery rounds: solid, bursting, canister—all that lead and iron, rammed and charged, sent on its way toward living men who had to stand it somehow, who trembled behind their works while it hummed overhead, or walked upright into it, or ran away with it pursuing—or who met it, felt the terrific impact, the snap of bone, disbelieving (Cass Wakefield never saw a man shot who believed it at first), then knowing it had come at last, that thing which happened only to others—bowels spilling out, curls of fat and ligament, dark blood spurting, brains leaking—but still not believing, still denying. *Is it bad?* they would ask, always. *How bad is it?* And a comrade, bending for a moment, would always say, *No, not bad—it's nothing, nothing a-tall*—before rising, driving forward into the storm again. Cass stepped forward and put his finger into one of the myriad wounds.

Alison said, "What does it mean, Cass?"

Lucian rocked on his heels. "Those are bullet holes," he said simply.

"Bullet holes," said Alison. She came and stood beside Cass and passed her fingers over the wall.

Cass thumbed his hat to the back of his head. "The rebels were attacking, uphill, shooting high," he said. "These rounds had little effect, I suppose, but . . . look here." He pointed to a hole in the corner of the building; the passage of the ball, entrance and exit, was clearly visible. "Can you see it?" he said. "Look through there. This one came from the yard. Look—you can see where the man was standing when he fired."

"A soldier was there," said Alison. She stood on tiptoe and sighted down the hole. "Right there."

"A yankee soldier," said Cass. "If you were a man standing here, it would of took the top of your head off."

Lucian laughed suddenly, then caught himself. He turned away. "You ought not to say that," he said.

Cass took Alison by the hand and led her back to the worn earthworks. He stood behind her, took her shoulders, and faced her toward the field. "This was the second line of works," he said. He tightened his grip on her shoulders and whispered in her ear. "Now, Alison, if you were a soldier waiting here, you would of had a capital view of our advance. Look out yonder—what do you see?"

Alison shaded her eyes. "I see . . . a broad field, the hills, the road—"

"No," whispered Cass. "You are a yankee soldier now, hungry, scared, wore out, and you know—you *know*—what's fixing to happen. It is evening, the sun setting, colder than it was a while ago—a November afternoon, Injun summer, twenty years past. What do you see?"

Lucian drove his foot into the earthworks. "Cass, for God's sake."

"Quiet," said Cass. "What do you see, Alison?"

"I don't know," said Alison. "How am I supposed to know?"

"You're not," said Cass, "so I will tell you, and you must try to imagine it." Cass pointed over her shoulder. "Right out there, along the base of the hills, thousands of men in terrible array, thousands of bayonets, colors breaking out—that's the Army of Tennessee in its last great show—the last time anybody will see such a sight in the earth. Just to look at them makes your heart beat to bursting—even if they wasn't coming for you, you'd be scared—"

"I don't want to imagine it," she said. "Why should I have to?"

"I will tell you why in a minute," said Cass. "Now, look—see how far they must come—it is impossible, but they must do it, even if it means death. Only you don't think about *their* death; *they* are immortal, invincible. They *are* death—your death—and there they come, flags opening out, bayonets all aglitter—even this far you can hear their tramp-tramp-tramp, the drums and bands, officers shouting. *You* can't make 'em stop, so you beg God to do it, but the hour is late, He can't stop it either. You say, 'Just this once, Lord,' but it's no good, and they keep on, *tramp-tramp-tramp,* and you feel the sound under your feet. You pray, 'Then please

don't let me die,' but God can't help you now, too late for
that, and the thought comes and closes its hand around your
heart: in a little while you will be gone from the earth, no
more sunlight, laughter, girls, no more apples in the fall, no
more home, never again—"

"No," said Alison. She made to move, but Cass caught
her arm.

"Now, listen," said Cass. "Hear the guns—that's your artillery. It shakes the ground and makes your ears bleed, and
you think, *The guns will stop them.* Sure enough, the smoke rolls
out, the rebels vanish, you feel a little nudge of hope—but, no,
there is the line again, still coming—only now, listen—hear
the old cry, like ghosts, like demons, like women wailing for
the dead. There's no sound like it in the earth—"

"Why?" said Alison.

"I'll tell you," said Cass, "and you must never forget it.
That's old Cass Wakefield out yonder, Alison. Me and Roger
Lewellyn, Ike Gatlin and Gawain Harper, your father, your
brother—and Lucian, too. He is just a boy, but the name they
gave him was Lucifer." Alison turned her head toward Lucian,
but Cass snatched her back. "*Don't* look at him. You have to see
him as he is out yonder where it's twilight, how he's scared and
sick, with the blood running out his ears. You got to make
yourself understand what he lost and won't ever find again, and
nothing anybody can do will bring it back. Not you, not anybody. *That's* why you got to imagine it. That was us, once upon
a time, death walking down to death—Jesus. . . . "

Cass stopped and wiped his eyes. Lucian stepped close and
took Cass by the arm. "By God, sir, that's enough—"

Cass shook him off. He took Alison by the shoulders again,

gripping hard. "Everybody has to learn what hell is like, Miss Alison—and there it is, and we are its instrument—"

She wrenched away from him then, stumbling. Lucian made to reach for her, but she waved him away and turned to Cass again. "I don't need you to tell me what hell is like," she said.

Cass took a step back. "I . . . I don't mean that. I—"

"You don't know what you mean," said Alison, and turned and walked off down the lane, pulling her cape around her.

"Let's go on down to the gin house," said Lucian. "Get it over with."

Cass was watching Alison as she walked away. "Yeah," he said, and spat upon the ground. "You know, we should of listened to Ike," he said. "Should of burned it when we had the chance. Should of burned the whole goddamned town."

The gin, unlike the buildings in the yard, bore no signs of the violence that had once howled around it. The breastworks to its front were still evident, however—worn and grassy now— and the ditch had not been filled in save by weeds and the wash of rains. The winter sun lay kindly upon it, and the visitors could smell the warm boards, the cotton lint, the grease of the machinery.

When Cass and Lucian arrived, Alison had already crossed over. The two men joined her in the field and regarded the ditch and the old breastworks behind it. In the works was a worn place bowed deep like a Mexican saddle. This had been a gun embrasure, and from its relationship to the gin house, the two companions discerned, as nearly as they could, the shore upon which they had dashed themselves twenty years before.

Lucian turned away from Alison and drank a little from his amber bottle and wiped his mouth. He pointed to the embrasure. "That's where that gun was, the one that—"

"I know which one it was," said Cass. "You are taking too much medicine."

"Would you like some?" said Lucian.

"I got my own," said Cass, patting his coat pocket.

For a moment they were silent, as if waiting for some dreadful thing to happen, but there was only the quiet morning, the meadowlarks, a dove cooing in the rafters of the gin. Nothing to hurt, just as the old man had said. Lucian went down into the ditch and sat in the dead grass, moving his hand over it as if searching for a lost coin. "Well, it is not what I expected somehow," he said.

"What *did* you expect?" said Cass.

"I don't know. A monument, maybe. It is only a farm now. Only a ditch."

Cass knelt down among the cotton stalks and looked about him. There was the roofline of the gin house against the sky, and the image settled perfectly into memory. Cass heard the groaning of winter trees, the rattle of their branches. Alison called his name, but Cass didn't answer. Lucian looked up from the ditch, his face gone pale. The dove had flown, and in its place a big crow lit on the roof of the gin and watched them. They had come a long way to this place the first time, and even longer now, but no matter. For all time's turning, nothing important had changed; they still could not move forward, and they could not run away.

Cass took out his flask and drank. *Here was I, once,* he thought. *Here am I, again.*

❖ 12 ❖

THE SUN WAS FALLING. LONG STREAKS OF PURPLE crossed the sky to the west, and the landscape was all red and amber. The soldiers had arranged themselves in long lines-of-battle, and Lucian sat on the porch of the great brick house and watched them move away. He watched until the last of them passed into the wood, then hopped off the edge of the porch and followed, though Cass had told him not to, saying, *Lad, you have come far enough for today. Go sit on the gallery yonder—you can help when the hurt men come back. Go on, now—and don't you move from this spot.* Cass had told him not to follow, but Lucian followed just the same. The drums were beating, and off to the left a band was playing—the first band Lucian had ever heard, so that he did not know to call it a band. He did not know to call it music even. He knew singing, but he had never heard sounds put together in such a metallic way as this.

Lucian made his way through the smoky wood, following the soldiers. When he emerged from the trees, he saw the lines moving across a broad field. He watched the soldiers' backs, their jackets, cartridge boxes and haversacks, blanket rolls, slouch hats, their shouldered muskets and gleaming bayonets bouncing in time to their long stride. They were crowded together, shoulders touching, a solid mass of gray and brown that clinked of tin cups, of frying pans and canteens. The soldiers' legs made a swishing in the tall broomsage. The lines stretched left and right; they were too long to get around, so Lucian pushed through the ranks, darting and running like a rabbit, ignoring the soldiers' surprised queries and the officers who shouted after him. At length, he quit running and found himself walking in a broad open space between two brigades; he could hear the men tramping ahead and behind, he could hear the band, the drums beating, could hear his own breeches legs swishing in the grass. Then, up ahead, he saw Cass Wakefield pacing back and forth behind their company—*That is our company,* he thought. Cass carried his rifle in the crook of his arm, and his hat was crammed down over his eyes. Lucian looked for Mister Lewellyn but couldn't pick him out. The colors were opened out over the regiment, unfurling red and crossed with stars, and this for the last time in all their lives, though Lucian didn't know it yet. In a moment, he couldn't tell where Cass was anymore; he was swallowed up in the smoke and the shapes of men walking. Lucian saw only the solid lines moving forward, the smoke closing and rolling around them like a living thing.

When Lucian lost sight of Cass Wakefield, he wanted to run back to the brick house and through the front door and up the stairs and find a bed to hide under, but he didn't, because Cass Wakefield had given him his name, and Lucian knew kinfolks stuck together. He'd heard people say that, though he'd never had any to stick to before, much less follow across the edge of time to the place where death was.

The Angel of Death was up there, and Lucian wondered what his country would be like. He was sure that this time the Angel would take Cass and Mister Lewellyn, and the knowledge made his insides lock up. His heart was pounding like a steam sawmill engine, but no matter; he was not about to sit back yonder on the porch and wonder, *What if Cass is dead? What if he don't come back across the yard looking for me?*

The smoke was thicker now, full of bright flashes and a noise like horseflies made when they came around your head. Lucian had heard that noise at Decatur; he knew what it was, but he went on walking upright, for it wasn't any use to duck. He wanted something in his hands, so he picked up a willowy branch like the suckers he used to pick for switches. Now he could slap his leg with it, and he did, and it stung his leg just as the switches had done.

For some reason, the lines all at once began to wheel to the left, swinging around like big turnstiles, and Lucian followed. Men were falling now, lots of them, and Lucian suddenly realized they were marching at a right angle to the enemy. The Angel of Death made his choices—here, there—and men fell into the brown twilight under the smoke—some flung up their hands, some staggered and fell, some merely dropped like a bag of clothes—dead ones and hurt ones, so many—they were all tangled accoutrements, reaching hands, crying voices, bearded faces. Lucian was careful not to walk upon the fallen men. He saw bodies opened with the fat, oily insides laid bare to the light. Nobody was supposed to see those things—that was another rule broken—or see blood in fountains, or a white bone where a hand used to be.

Oh, Lucifer! he thought. At the orphanage, when one of their number died—once or twice a month in the wintertime, more than that when the fever came—the children were made to pass before the lost one, as if by looking they would learn some lesson. They would file past the dead child, who always had its hair brushed, who was always calm and pale and propped on pillows—nothing like these men, or like the dead cavalry man back in Alabama whose scarf Lucian was wearing—and every time, old Pelt would take Lucifer by the ear and whisper harsh into it, *Look you well, bastard—here's what it comes to, all your vanity and pride.* This was the lesson, the boy supposed, though old Pelt never told it to anyone else. Then the dead one would be shut up in a little casket painted black, and Lucifer would look down from a high window at the casket borne down the steps and away up the lane. At first, he thought they were only going away for punishment. He expected them to come back, chastened, but they never did, and after a while, he figured out they never would. That was death: you went away; you didn't come back. Now Lucian thought that if he followed Cass—he would find him again, he knew that—maybe he could see where the children went when they died.

The lines were turning back to the right now, back toward the enemy. When the lines straightened out, the men began to move fast. The musket fire from the yankee works was a single

steady roar, and the soldiers' bayonets came down, and they began to run toward the yankee works. They were all packed together, a streaming mob struggling to get forward, and from
their throats rose the strange, wavering cry that Lucian had first
heard at Decatur. His ears were hurting from the noise, and the
cry was like a nail driven into his head. Then came a sound that
hurt Lucian even worse, that almost knocked him over, and a
long spear of flame jabbed out into the smoke—one of those
black cannon guns, Lucian thought—and he saw men fly into
the air and come apart, heard their bones crunching. Now Lucian got down on his hands and knees, down under the smoke,
and crawled among the fallen men. He saw the man who'd been
playing marbles in the yard back in Decatur, the thin man in
spectacles—Jack Bishop was his name—only now his glasses
were broken and twisted on his face, and he was dark, smeared
with blood.

The band had quit playing. Lucian couldn't hear the drummers either, only the shooting and the yelling—and the heavy
thump and roar of the black cannons again, the hum of musket
balls and of something bigger, heavier, that ripped men to
pieces. Smoke rolled and boiled over everything, even down
where he was now, so that he kept bumping into dead men and
hurt men, and the living stepped on him and tripped over him.
He saw a man crawling along with a ramrod through his skull,
another with both hands dangling by threads. He found a boy
no older than himself lying on his back, arms outflung, eyes
open. Lucian thought the boy was taking a rest. He said, "Get
up! We got to follow!" Then he saw a single neat hole, oozing
dark blood, in the breast of the checkered shirt, and Lucian
knew the boy had gone with the Death Angel. The boy wore a

gray jacket like Cass did, and Lucian remembered Cass's words, how they didn't mind if you took what you needed. Lucian needed the jacket. He straightened the boy's arms—*It's all right; I will be careful and fix you right*—and loosened the belt buckle—it had a star on it—and pulled the box and haversack and canteen straps over the boy's head and turned him over—

Lucian cried out and scuttled backward on his knees. The boy's back was laid open, grass sticking to the sodden, ruined jacket and the white rib cage and the secret things that still pulsed and glistened. "Cass!" cried Lucian. Then something struck him in the face; it was soft and wet, but it knocked him over. He couldn't see what it was, for he was blinded with blood. He wiped his eyes. A man staggered back from the line; he was trying to hold his secret parts in, but they kept slipping through his fingers. The man cried out at Lucian, then disappeared in the smoke. Another came and fell across the body of the dead boy, then another and another, until Lucian couldn't see the boy at all. Lucian crawled to the pile of bodies and hid behind it. He could hear the heavy splat of balls striking the bodies, like when you threw a ripe tomato against a brick wall. A man reached for him; Lucian took the hand but found it attached to nothing and dropped it. Blood spurted in a fountain over him, then subsided, leaving him drenched and hot. His throat was seared, aching; he found a man's canteen, pulled the cork, and took a deep swallow of foul water. He was crying now, and suddenly he could hear nothing but a painful ringing in his ears. *I am dead now!* he thought. He was dead and in hell just like old Pelt said he would be. This was death, then: a place where sound could not be heard but only felt, a place without time, inhabited by demon apparitions wandering in the smoke, by piles and windrows of dead men who squirmed and thrashed; hurt men who pulled at their clothes and cried for water and God and Mother; a region littered of muskets and shreds of cloth, gobbets of meat, brown cartridge paper, tufts of cotton lint, canteens, hats, rags and haversacks, torn earth, and trampled grass slick with blood—and Lucian wondered what he had done that could not be forgiven.

A long while he cowered behind the rampart of dead, sobbing and praying, asking again and again to be forgiven. At last he gave it up, for God didn't seem to be listening, or else He couldn't protect them, and the Death Angel had beat Him again. Lucian knew then he would not be delivered, and he struck the ground with his fist in anger and shame, for it was not fair. Then he thought, *Cass is in it, too,* and he knew he had to find him. He could stand it if only Cass were with him. Cass would know what to do—and Mister Lewellyn, maybe he could pray them out of it. He rose to his feet, heart pounding, so trembly he could hardly move. But he told himself that he couldn't be killed any more than he already was, so he went forward, staggering in his fear and weakness, following Cass Wakefield deeper into hell.

Just before the regiment stepped off, Cass Wakefield took note of the evening and the long shadows, the sun hovering as if reluctant to depart, a pale crescent moon rising eastward, pulling the night after it. Before them lay an oak grove, already in twilight, ribboned with smoke. Cass wished they didn't have to pass through the grove, for the line would break up among the trees, and everything would be out of order until they cleared

the woods where the falling sun would light their way to dusty
death.

The brigade battle line was long, and before it stretched another, and before that another. The fields were crowded with soldiers, and from their myriads rose voices, shouts, a whisper of
movement, the thud of horses' hooves. Firing spattered from the
grove as the skirmishers retired. To the west mounted the roar of
a battle already begun, to which they themselves must go in a
little while. They had come here under fire from the guns across
the river, and they were taking fire yet. The shells burst over the
woods or plowed great gobbets from the field, and some men
were killed. Cass wished the line would move so they could get
the thing over with. There was always too much standing
around, too much waiting, and the longer you waited, the taller
grew the stalks of fear to twine around the heart. Thousands of
hearts here in this open ground, all of them beating hard, and
Cass thought it a wonder you couldn't hear them. Maybe that
was part of the whisper that rose from the massed ranks pressed
shoulder to shoulder, waiting: the weary, the ragged, the hollow-
eyed, the dysenteric and fever-ridden, marched twenty miles
since daybreak without rest, without food, only to be set down at
last in the midst of a gathering, fatal dark.

The officers clustered in groups, broke up, clustered again.
Couriers galloped to and fro, their horses white with foam, and
foam at the steel bits, and the hooves scattering clots of mud.
Then General Adams drawing his sword, and the call passing
down the line: *Attention . . . Brigaaade!* Then: *Load, prime, and
come to shoulder arms!* The fumbling for cartridges, ramrods
ringing from their sockets, rattling down the bores of a thousand muskets; the *click-clack* of hammers drawn back, the fum-

bling for percussion caps—*Keep your muzzles up, keep 'em up there, goddammit*—and a *bang* down the line where somebody let his hammer slip. Finally the men straightening, one by one, muskets at the shoulder, eyes straight ahead. Officers striding up and down, their swords at the carry or pointing here, pointing there. *Silence in the ranks. Eyes front.* Then: *Fix . . . bayonets!* A portentous rattling and clattering as the long steel blades were fixed to the muzzles. *Right shoulder shift . . . Arms!* and up went the muskets in a rampart of steel that no power of man, it seemed, could resist or look upon without trembling. Finally the colors uncased, the old torn flags breaking out among the forest of bayonets: symbol not of any nation or cause, but of who they were and of all that they had endured; the outward and visible sign of their courage, their honor, and their pride.

The illusion of order and purpose occupied the minds of men who otherwise might yield to reason. Familiar tasks, drilled into them day after day for years, guided muscle and sinew that otherwise might stiffen from the long march, or lock up in fear, or answer to the individual will. Thought, memory, fear, these three: no greater enemies could a soldier have in that moment when he stood before the half-opened curtain of his fate. And war itself, feeding on its own mad necessity, could not exist without subjugation of the will.

Cass Wakefield knew it was all an illusion. He also believed in it, deeply. He abetted the illusion. He was its instrument, prowling up and down the portion of the line allotted him, poking and prodding, encouraging, cursing, suppressing the collective will that, were it allowed to flourish, would have them all running like hares from the task before them. Cass acted his part as best he could, struggling against the will of mortal men and struggling most of all against his own. He was sore afraid, and his ears drummed with the clamor of his soul and the fluttering of the Death Angel. He had to believe the illusion, for only by believing could he ever hope to move at all.

Across the sky to the west, against a tall pillar of cloud, a vee of geese passed southward. If the birds were sensible of the doings of men, seeing far below the long lines preparing for battle, they might well have asked, *Why all this?* In that moment, Cass could not have answered, but he would come to understand that, in fact, illusion alone could not have driven them, could not have overcome their will. In the end, only truth could do that: the truth of the cord that bound them. The soldiers knew the truth, and the truth sustained them even in the shadow of death. Courage. Honor. Pride. Comrades. It was imperative that they believe in these things, and they did believe. So it was that when the command was given, they stepped off smartly to the drums and to the band playing "Annie Laurie" as if on parade. They were all moving now, passing into the twilit woods and beyond into a country none of them could see, that some of them would never live to look upon.

They had not gone far when the line parted to reveal the body of a soldier kneeling in the broomsage. The back of his head was cracked and leaking, the hair sodden with blood, and Cass knew the face would be gone, and he didn't want to look but looked anyhow. Sure enough, all the features were erased, and Cass could not name the man. Then he saw the outstretched hands waving blindly, the fingers opening and closing. Wesley Norman had been bitten by a spider once, and the wound had left a crater in his hand, and there it was. Cass wanted to lay the man down, but there was no stopping now. Cass left him there, still kneeling. *Good-bye, Wesley.*

Cass peered through the crowded ranks ahead. The lead brigades were almost to the woods now, and he saw a company going in after the enemy skirmishers. Foolish, he thought—they would only end up shooting at one another in the gloom. At that moment, in spite of everything, Janie crossed his mind, and he wondered what she was doing in her own twilight so far away, and if she somehow knew what was about to happen. He could see her standing in the yard, her head cocked as if listening, her mouth shaping his name, *Cass? Cass?* The image sent a bolt of pain and yearning through him, and he fought it down as he had fought down his own will. Then he thought of the boy Lucian, whom he had ordered to wait at the house. Cass wished he had found the lad a jacket, for the night would be cold. He would never see the boy again, most likely. He was glad they had taught him to pray. He thought of God then and shut his eyes for an instant and prayed hard for forgiveness one last time—*All my sins and wickedness, no time to name them now, and let it be easy on little Janie, and may she find someone who*—but he couldn't finish that, would not think on that ever. Not ever. He could not suffer the thought of Janie in a universe without him.

The noise of the band intruded. Cass looked that way, astonished. The field music, the drummers, always went into a fight with the infantry, but the band had never followed them so far. Then his astonishment gave way to annoyance at the idea, and Cass was thinking he might send a round through one of the horns himself—why not?—when a shell exploded brightly just above the musicians and enveloped them in a cloud of smoke, and from the cloud spun a silver cornet and a

flutter of sheet music, and the bass drum went rolling, bouncing, over the field, and the men behind parted to make way for
it. When the smoke drifted away, the band was scattered, bells
of horns blooming over the grass like dented brass flowers, but
the survivors played on—in mad discord, but playing still,
scrambling to close ranks—and Cass saw the chief musician
marching backward, his baton raised, one hand still on his
hip—still marching, but something wrong in it, the tall figure
jerking like a marionette. Then the chief musician dropped his
baton, stopped, swayed a moment, and only then did Cass dis-
cern that the man had nothing above his chin but a red welter.

Time was all around, and the soldiers passed through it,
but it had no more meaning to them than water does to fishes
or grass to the serpent. In the woods, the line faltered as Cass
knew it would; men stumbled over vines and brush, the low
branches snatched at their bayonets. Gaps opened, widened,
closed again, the colors dipped—the smoke was thick and
burned the lungs and made Cass's eyes water—tree limbs
showered down, broken by shells, clipped by bullets—but the
drums never stopped, nor the urgent shouts and curses of the
officers—*Dress this line, God damn it*—*Dress on the colors*—*Close
it up, men*—and Cass shoved his musket butt against the backs
of his comrades until they were in the fields again.

They stopped briefly to realign, and men died for it and
were left behind like piles of discarded clothing. Cass walked
over them without looking or heeding, and without sorrow.
Some were men he had known for years, his comrades, his
pards. No matter now. Sorrow was for those who lived to remember it.

Beyond the field he saw the barren trees that marked the

river, and the logs and raw earth of the enemy's works shrouded with smoke and lit by flashes. Adams's Brigade followed the lead brigades into this fire. They walked at the common step, measured and steady, the men silent, leaning forward. Closer they came, and closer, and the sound of their passage made a tramping like a terrible great engine—hundreds of men crossing the earth in their long stride, in time to the beating of the drums. Cass readied himself, some part of him thinking *Now* and *Now* and *Surely now*. He wanted to charge, for once they charged, the thing would be decided quickly: live or die, hold or run. Closer to the enemy lines they came, still silent but for the tramping, and men dropped in the grass, spun, flung out their arms and cried out, disappeared—the colors went down and were raised again—*Come on, come on*—but something wrong, a hesitation. Cass kept his head down, saw nothing but the legs of the man ahead, but he felt a tremor run through the line—disconnected voices spoke of hedges, abatis, some obstruction they could not pass. It was all wrong, but it was always wrong. Then the command rose above the tramping, the fire and smoke, out of voices gone hoarse with shouting: *By the center . . . Left wheel . . . March!*

For some reason, they could go forward no longer but must wheel the lines around to the left. The long lines began the maneuver, the center marking time—men walking backward on the left, hurrying forward on the right, faces turned toward the brigade colors invisible in the smoke. The surviving bandsmen had ceased playing, but the drummers went on. Before the lines, officers walked backward with their swords horizontal— the line bowed and swayed and straightened again, raked lengthwise by fire from the right but still turning, offering its flank—madness, but no matter. Only this: execute the wheel—no thought, no complaint—and keep your dress. They would have to find another place to breach the yankee line.

Cass held his musket across his body and pushed from behind, cursing and cajoling. He looked for Roger and Ike and found them still alive. He spoke their names in his mind, and the names of others—Gawain, Paul, Bushrod, Craddock, Bloodworth, all still alive—but the first sergeant was gone, and Byron Sullivan, and the line was growing shorter and shorter as the men closed ranks. Colonel Sansing was in front of the regiment, his hat gone, face bloody, sword gleaming in the twilight, and Perry strolling along, dragging his sword point through the grass, looking at the sky. Then the wheel was complete and the officers cried, *Forward . . . Mar—*

Cut short, the last order Cass heard at the Battle of Franklin. Nothing could be heard now, every sound absorbed into a single great Sound, perfect and complete, that filled the ears in the same way silence would. They passed at a right angle along the front of the Federal line, but how long and how far Cass never knew. He saw everything now as through a red pane of glass, and sometimes he saw nothing but darkness. Red, black, red, black, and images like a broken strand of beads—a foot, a man's face, a clump of grass, a hat. No dressing now, and no keeping step, for the right guide was gone and the drummers were gone and the ground was thick with dead, slippery with blood. The earth itself seemed distant, as if it had fallen away under the weight of those who struggled over it and those who lay heaped upon it in filthy piles. Cass felt a sting of pain and looked down. His hands floated uselessly before him, streaked with blood, a nail peeled back, rifle gone. Then a flicker of deep black, and when he looked again, he held a different rifle, no idea where it came from, and no matter.

For an instant, the smoke swirled away to reveal the line still intact but drifting to the left, away from the relentless gnawing at its flank. Then a battery fired from the works and the smoke rolled over them again, and the canister cut and sliced and hummed through the air. Men emerged from the smoke, swam through the red haze, and disappeared. They collided with one another and trampled the dead and dying; they moved forward, faces grim or slack with terror, some laughing, muskets still at the shoulder—always forward, for there was no place to run.

Then, at the moment when it seemed they could bear no more, something—an order dimly perceived, an exhortation, a collective impulse perhaps—jolted through the cord that bound them, and the broken line, the streaming, tattered remnants of Adams's Brigade, wheeled right toward the enemy again. Cass sensed their turning and followed. He saw General Adams flailing his horse toward the bright flashes. Through the smoke he glimpsed the flag of the enemy, ragged like his own, and heard the enemy cheering. He saw the head-logs, the fresh-turned earth heaving and boiling. No, it was not the earth; it was men piled upon men in a great writhing mass and bristle of bayonets and ramrods, swords, flailing arms. There a roofline suspended over the smoke, there an officer firing his pistol. He heard Colonel Sansing: *Forward, brave rifles! Mississippians! Follow me down, boys!* And now, at last, they began to run toward the enemy. The phantom shapes stumbled forward in the smoke, bayonets leveled, and in them was loosed every demon of their hearts, and from them rose a terrible cry born of demons that swelled out of them and became them and consumed them. Cass Wakefield felt himself carried forward by the cry. He felt it rise from his own cracked and aching throat as all things—truth and illusion both—fled away, and in their place the overwhelming joy of death. The Death Angel spread his wings over the dying sun, and men and sun and Angel together fell through the dusk and into the unutterable dark.

Cass made the charge gamely through the red haze of his vision. The line broke up into a streaming mob, and Cass ran full tilt, racing Ike Gatlin on one side and Bushrod Carter on the other. The three of them struck for a place on the works where a knot of men were struggling in a bare-hands fight, a tavern brawl in the middle of all that shooting. Cass felt a ball strike his canteen, another snatch at his haversack. All at once, Ike and Bushrod disappeared in the smoke, and Cass found himself alone and running blind. He did not stop but plunged into the smoke, and in an instant he came to the ditch that lay in front of the works.

He blundered at full speed into a solid wall of his comrades and almost ran one through with his bayonet. The man, blind in his fury, cursed and swung at Cass with his musket butt. Cass dodged, lost his musket, lost his footing, was stuck a hard blow on the shoulder. He went down in the melee, landing on a soft carpet of dead men all shot to rags. Cass believed he must be shot too, and a profound sadness came over him. He spoke Janie's name. He thought of the boy Lucian, and of the friends he would see no more. Then he shut his eyes and waited for death, which he prayed would arrive before the pain. But neither pain nor death came for him, and after a few slow minutes dragged by, Cass decided he was not struck after all. He was still alive and so must rise and go forward. Yet he could not rise. The illusion was broken and could no longer sustain him. Awareness had taken its place, and with it the return of his will and a fear such as he had never known. Fear and will together pressed him into the earth, and not even shame could make him rise again.

He caught a glimpse of the sky, a deep amber riven with black. He was kicked and trampled and trod upon. An iron heel plate ground into his hand. The air seemed to rain blood. Cass drew his legs up and covered his face with his hands. The fight went on around him, but he couldn't look, for it was death to rise up. He lost track of how many times the rebels fell back, re-formed, attacked again. They had ceased their yelling; the enemy had stopped his cheering. Now a terrible roar swelled up from them all, even above the constant and unbearable fire, as they clubbed and slashed and stabbed and fired in each other's faces. In all his battles, Cass had never heard such a sound from mortal men—mad and primordial, more unearthly than the yelling ever was, rising wave after wave, louder and louder, as though a great stricken beast were tearing itself to pieces. In counterpoint rose pitiable cries and prayers and pleadings, the screams of the wounded, the coughing and gargling of men drowning in their own blood, the ravings of men gone insane. Cass thought he would go mad himself if it did not stop. He prayed for it to stop, at least pause long enough to let him breathe, to let him get away, but it went on and on. At last he quit thinking at all. Then someone was pulling at him—"Cass! Cass!"

He opened his eyes then. A hand was pulling at his cartridge box strap, and even under the solid weight of sound he heard his name again—"Cass!" A man had fallen across his legs; Cass pushed the body away and turned over. At first, he did not know the face inches from his own, white with terror, smeared with grime and blood, and blood running from the ears. When he saw who it was, the shock blinded him for an instant; when he could see again, he found his rage intact. He grabbed the white scarf and screamed in the boy's face, "What are you doing here! What! What! I told you to stay, God damn you—I told you!" Lucian put up his hands. He said, "Cass, I come all this way—" but Cass said, "Shut up!" He pulled the boy close, felt the scrawny backbone and thin shoulder blades. "God damn, you won't listen—we get out of this, I'm gone whip you for certain!" The boy said, "What? What?" Cass cuffed him once, then pulled him close again and spoke in his ear. "I will get you out of this, God damn you, Lucian—I will get you home, Lucian." He cuffed the boy again. With the end of the scarf, he wiped at the boy's face to see if the blood was his, but he found no wounds. "Cass! Cass!" said the boy. "Shut up!" said Cass, and struck the boy again.

Then Roger came crawling like a spider over the rubble of dead, his bared teeth white in his grimy face, long hair tangled and wet with sweat. His ears were running blood, too. He put his face next to Cass's and shouted, "What is that boy doing here?" and Cass said, "What is happening?" and Roger said, "We must get out of this! We can't stay here!" and Cass said, "We can't run either!" Roger shook his head like a dog. He jumped up and thrust his musket between the head-logs and pulled the trigger. A man rose suddenly from the pile of dead as if jerked aloft by a wire. He flung out his arms—wild was his face, and his beard a tangle—cried, "God damn the Papist bastards!" He snatched at Roger, seized him by the throat, pointed—"Look ye, man! See the cross! See the cross of Saint Andrew!" Roger said, "Get away from me! Get away!" Then the man was shot in the head, and Roger pushed the body away and began to reload. A cluster of dark shapes rose from behind the works and jabbed at Roger with their bayonets; Roger dropped his ramrod and parried and thrust against them. Now Cass stood up without thinking. He left the boy, snatched up a rifle, and fired into the men on the parapet. He threw away that musket, found another and fired again, then thrust the bayonet through a coatless man who looked like a schoolteacher. The man's eyes bulged, and he coughed blood in Cass's face and disappeared. The wild man rose again from the dead, crying, "See the cross! See—" but Cass fetched him a blow with the butt of his musket, and he went away again. The yankees were gone from the parapet now. Cass took Roger by his jacket sleeve, pulled him down. Lucian reached for Cass's hand. "Cass! Cass!" The black snout of the gun emerged from its embrasure and fired, and the canister ripped into the men and sent them sprawling end over end like cornhusk dolls, their bones snapping like sticks. Some men mounted the embrasure and disappeared inside; one fell back, a hatchet driven in his forehead. When the gun came into battery again, Cass saw T. J. Beckwith of Cumberland walk right up to it and lay his hand on the muzzle. "T. J.!" Cass screamed. The boy lifted his hand, looked at it in puzzlement, then at the patch of his flesh stuck to the blistering gun tube. Then the gun bellowed smoke and a long yellow streak of flame, and nothing was left of young Beckwith but his legs still erect and trembling and a fine red mist where the rest of him had been.

With that image, time vanished altogether. Cass never

could say how long they cowered in the ditch with the dead piled over them and the battle swirling madly above. At last, darkness came, and the fight at the cotton gin guttered out. Cass and Roger and Lucian huddled together. They did not speak, though other voices rose pleading, crying, babbling around them. In a whisper, Cass recited the rosary over and over, in the Latin the Ursulines had taught him. Remembering the Latin kept his mind distracted. *Ave Maria, plena gracia*— They could not stretch their aching legs, for the yankees fired at any movement. Lucian was hard to keep still. *Ora pro nobis pecatoribus*—So far as Cass could tell, no one was left on their side of the works but the dead and dying. They could hear the yankees talking on the other side; sometimes they laughed, shrill and hysterical, as men will do when suddenly released from peril. *Nunc et in hora mortis nostrae—Now and at the hour of our death. Pray for us, Mary.* Full dark had long since come, but the battle went on elsewhere, and the night was lit with flashes. Finally Cass had to risk a look. The smoke had drifted away, and the stars were out. By their light, Cass saw heaps and piles of men. They quivered and heaved and groaned, and now and then the yankees would fire into them. He saw a pale officer standing erect in the ditch, starlight gleaming off his coat buttons, and for an instant Cass wondered how such a thing could be. Then he understood that the man was dead, held up by the press of men around him. All these souls, and the stars and thin sickle moon to light their passage.

Then the firing swelled on the left, and with it the quavering yell, more terrible for the darkness. A night attack— impossible—you couldn't see to fight in the dark. Yet there it was, and no matter why or how, for if it was hell for the lads

over there, it was salvation for the living men in the ditch. As
the noise of battle grew, the enemy began to shift his line. Officers shouted orders. Cass heard the clinking of trace chains.
He shook Roger and whispered, "Let's get out of this." Roger
nodded. The boy made to speak, but Cass clapped a hand over
his mouth. They pushed and shoved the bodies away. Cass took
the boy by the collar of his shirt, and they began to crawl out of
the valley of death. They seemed to crawl forever over the soft
and yielding dead. When they stood at last, their cramped
muscles bent them nearly double, and they walked as though
they were dead themselves, all the way back to the brick house
where they had set off from that afternoon.

They returned to the cotton gin just before break of day. A
good many men had gathered there, and the dead, so ghastly
by the light of the torches and fires, were already being pulled
from the ditch and laid in rows. Cass bent down to Lucian,
putting his mouth against the boy's ear: "You wait. You don't
have to go any further. You can sit right here and watch us."
The boy must have heard, for he shook his head no and held
fast to Cass's jacket.

They went down among the dead, wading to their knees.
The regiments had gotten so mixed up that they had to look
closely to find their own; they must look at faces when the men
had faces, or trust to find some token to know them by. Many
were torn to pieces, gone beyond all recognition; these they
laid in a separate row. Lucian had to let go of Cass but stayed
close behind. After a time, he must have believed that Cass
would not leave him, for he went back to the edge of the ditch.

There Ike Gatlin taught him how to arrange the dead, heels together, hands crossed on the breast. The boy went about his work in brave silence, his hands gloved with blood.

Meanwhile, the dawn peered timidly over the ring of hills as if frightened by what it must see. The dawn came so slowly that Cass thought it might not venture at all but draw away again, leaving the world to the darkness it deserved. But the morning grew imperceptibly, and by its first good light, they came to the colonel and Perry. The older man was lying on his face, arms at his sides, one hand still holding a pistol, the other his sword. The back of his frock coat was shredded where at least a half dozen balls had made their exit. They didn't know they'd found him until they turned the body over, and then it was not the face, blurred in death and hidden behind a mask of yellow mud, but the two stars on his collar and the crescent-moon charm on his watch chain. It took Cass and Roger both to pry the weapons from his hand. Around the colonel was a layer of dead they had to unravel like a tangled pile of accoutrements and haul away before they got to Perry. The lad had been shot once in the forehead. He stared up at them as if surprised to see living men in this place.

They laid father and son apart from the rest, and the men of the regiment paused in their work and gathered around, silent, dragging their hats off; not many, for most of the boys were lying with their feet together, hands crossed on their breasts. They covered the colonel with a Federal blanket. Cass had closed Perry's eyes and put a handkerchief over the wound, but no one was inclined to remark that he seemed but sleeping. That would come later, when memory had fooled them; for now, Perry just looked dead, and whatever sentiment he inspired had to make its way through a fog of bone-weariness and despair. Yet the men gathered and looked down in silence, as if these two ruined, savaged corpses stood for all those lost, known and unknown—as if they could, in that brief moment, hear the unspoken thoughts of the living and carry them away to the dead. Then the boys turned away and set to work again, knowing that they had but a little while before they must take up arms once more and wind their long columns north. They owned no illusions about that. The enemy was out there somewhere, and they must pursue him, and tomorrow, no doubt, they would be the ones arranged in the mud, sightless, soon to be hid forever.

But not yet. Now, still quick, they labored on. Some swooned from exhaustion and lay curled among the dead as though in rehearsal, and Lucian had to be careful in his work lest he mistake one kind of sleep for another. Presently, Cass went over the breastworks to see what he could see. More rebels lay there, scattered among the rubbish, but the enemy dead were all gone. This side of the works was eerie in its own way, like an abandoned house where some shameful act lingered in the rooms. Cass stayed only long enough to find a jacket for Lucian, one that was but a little bloody, and a canvas tent fly. When he returned, he covered the colonel and Perry with the tent fly and gave the jacket to the boy, who took it without comment this time, having learned the hard lesson that the dead were no longer jealous of their belongings. Cass found Roger sitting on the edge of the ditch, his head in his hands; Cass sat down beside him, and there they remained until Sam Hook came along and found them sleeping.

❖ 13 ❖

ALISON WALKED ACROSS THE COTTON ROWS AND
stood beside Cass, who knelt upon the ground, moving
his hands like a man dreaming. Lucian, meanwhile, sat
cross-legged in the ditch. She wished she could reach her companions and see what they were seeing. *No,* she thought, *I don't
want to see.* "You-all come back here," she said at last.

Cass looked up in momentary confusion, then scrambled to
his feet. He stumbled against Alison and caught the faint odor
of rose water on her. "I am sorry," he said. "That's the second
time I almost knocked you down."

"Yes, it is," said Alison. She looked at the flask in his hand.
"Does that do any good?" she asked.

Cass shook the flask, then put it away. "Well, it can't hurt," he said.

"This is the place, then? Where they fell?"

Cass nodded. "How are you faring, then?"

"I can stand it," she said. "But then, I was not here."

Cass pointed to the ditch where Lucian sat. "This is where we struck the line," he said. "Next day, we found them here, close by the parapet."

"If I asked you what they looked like—"

Cass shook his head. "I would say . . . they looked like they were sleeping. That will have to suffice." He thought a moment, rubbing his forehead. " 'Nothing . . . Nothing in his life became him like the leaving of it.' That is for them both."

Alison turned to the ditch and wondered at how ordinary it seemed. She watched a field mouse dart along the top of the worn parapet, watched him stop and sniff about, then disappear. Snowbirds peeped in the branches of a walnut tree. She had pictured this gin like the one that lay on the edge of Cumberland: rambling, surrounded by a muddy yard and a cluster of houses, shaded of oaks, covered in sheets of rusty tin that creaked and banged in the wintertime, branches and telephone wires festooned with dingy gray scraps of cotton lint. That image left no room for a rampart and a ditch crowded with dead. Now she could begin to imagine it; now, at least, she had the proper landscape to carry away in memory. Whether that was a gain or a loss, she could not tell.

"Cass Wakefield," she said, "in all these years, I never thanked you for seeing to my kin. I never thanked you for that."

She waited for him to speak, to trace out the expected reply:

honor, comradeship, the least he could do, and so on. When he did speak, she was reminded of how easy it was to misjudge him.

"You were right not to thank me," he said. His look was that of a man who hoped he'd said enough, all the while knowing he hadn't. He took out his watch and stared at it, then replaced it. He patted his waistcoat pockets, then the pockets of his coat. "Well," he said at last, and raised his eyes to the gin house. "We were played out, you see."

"I know you were," said Alison. She felt a shiver then, the familiar signal of mortality, and she allowed herself to be defeated by grief for a little time—giving that much to grief anyway. She turned away then, looked southward, across the brown fields to the hills beyond whence the army came. In his way, Cass had tried to make her understand, but he could not. She could never understand what had happened here. She could never understand what honor meant beyond the word itself. She only understood that, after all the violence and waste and suffering, the word had to mean something, else they were all lost. That, too, would have to suffice.

⚜

Cass followed Alison's gaze across the fields so quiet and still in the sunlight, and he wondered what she saw out there. He thought how, in the end, memory was no more than a stubborn insistence by the living that what they had done was not in vain. Maybe that's what he was trying to tell himself every time he looked up the Pontotoc Road. Maybe that's why Alison had come here in the first place—not to do it, but to have it done, to have these hard hours to cling to and prove she had done all she could. Cass understood that. Trouble was, if memory were only woven out of living thread, then the earth would have no reason to hold on to it, nor houses, nor fencerows, nor any of the places that the past claimed for itself. There would be no reason to be afraid of crossing a road, no need to gaze so intently over fields gone quiet and where all the blood was long since soaked away.

Cass took off his hat and passed his sleeve across his brow. He heard a mule braying somewhere, and from somewhere a carpenter's hammer driving a nail, *tap-tap-tap*. Looking down, Cass saw the broken cotton stalks sharply defined, the shadows on them and the subtle play of colors—more than you would think in old cotton. He saw a line of ants marching column-of-twos up a stalk. Time was going along, carrying them all down the stream.

"Alison," he said, "I am sorry for what happened back in the yard. I only meant it for another story, but I suppose it is different, being on the ground again. I never meant it for you—I mean, for a lesson. I have no business—"

"Never mind," she said. "I've known you for half a century, and that was the first time you've been a rude and insufferable ass—well, at least to me."

"Ah," said Cass. "Half a century?"

"I am sure it will be the last time," said Alison.

"Yes," he said. He drew a deep breath and expelled it. "You know, Lucian and me can handle this. You don't have to—"

"Hah!" she said. She turned her back on the ditch and lowered her voice to a harsh whisper. "Lucian doping himself blind, you drinking at eight in the morning—is that how you *handle* it?"

"The boy is not *doping* himself," said Cass. "That is his medicine that he has to take."

"Yes, he is," she said. "But never mind—it's not for me to say one way or the other. You think I'm afraid, Cass? You think—"

"No, Alison," he said. "I don't think you're afraid." He smiled lamely and turned his hat in his hands. "I can't say the same for myself. I have buried the dead but never raised them."

"Cass Wakefield," she said, "you raise the dead all the time."

He smiled then and took her hand; it was small and cold, light as a leaf. "Alison, when we get back home, I should like to—"

"Cass," she said, interrupting, "I was unkind yesterday, on the train when you told about those awful things. Do you know what I was thinking a while ago? Calves and foals and fawns, how they can walk and get around in such a little time, and know to hide and be still? We are supposed to be smarter, but we never do figure out how to do much—what's important, I mean. Who ever knew how to love, or to hide and be still? Who ever learned how to quit remembering? Then, when we finally have enough mistakes to learn from, it's time to die."

"I guess we know how to do that well enough," said Cass.

"I can assure you we do not," she said. "We watch others do it, but we get no practice for ourselves, you might say."

"The colonel died well, and Perry—a good many others—"

She shook her head. "That's only what we say to help us bear it. They were afraid, same as you and me. They weren't ready, and they suffered—and when you found them, they did not look as if they were sleeping. I know that."

"Still, I do not believe you are afraid," said Cass.

"That's wrong," she said. "It's almost more than I can bear. I don't know what to do or even what I'm supposed to be feeling, and if they were here today, and you in the cold ground . . . if they were here, they wouldn't know either. I have required a good deal of you. I—"

"Now, don't be starting with that," said Cass. He looked eastward again. *We took them over there, that way, along the ditch, in front of the line, until we found the place. . . .*

Lucian was rising from the ditch, wiping his hands on his coat. Cass turned and saw the lean face, pale and wondering— not the man's face but the boy's, always the boy's, black with powder and sweat, bleeding at the ears, looking to Cass Wakefield for an answer he had no power, no wisdom, to provide. Yet somebody had an answer, Cass thought, for in spite of everything, they were delivered out of the dark night of the army's ruin. All these years, Cass had insisted it was luck only, and no purpose or design, that kept them breathing and drove them through time. Yet here they were, come around to a place they had sworn never to lay eyes on again.

Lucian said, "Cass, we need to get away from here."

Cass nodded. "Look to Miss Alison," he said. "Follow me."

He turned and walked eastward toward the distant houses, the cotton stalks rustling under his feet. He did not look to see if the others followed. The ground was soft under him, and in one place he tripped over the cotton rows and fell to his knees. He felt the blood coursing in his temples, and with it the old sensation of electric shock and a dizziness that unnerved him. For a moment, he forgot what he was about, was unsure how to go—forward or back, and to what? Yonder was a stone wall hung with dead vines. It had not been there when they came this way before. Cass got to his feet and stumbled to the wall. He clambered over, tearing his hand on a thorny vine. On the other side, he licked the blood from his hand, then set off again. He went away from the ditch and the cotton gin and the field of Franklin, and he did not look back.

The Judas Field

❖ 14 ❖

LUCIAN WATCHED CASS WAKEFIELD WALK AWAY OVER the ground they once crossed with the regiment's dead. Time, rain, the turning plow and harrow—these might have changed the ground, but no matter. Some things could never be hid, and some places could not be healed. The war had never left this place and never would, for all the generations to come, and the lost ones would remain even in the sunlight. Lucian felt them brush against him. He could feel them under his feet, restless, pushing against the weight of the earth. He knew that Cass felt them, too. Cass could hear them better than most—what they wanted, what they had to tell—and they would guide him.

Lucian passed through a black space, and when he emerged, he was teetering on the edge of the ditch. He supposed he had taken too much medicine, but that didn't scare him. He didn't worry about dying, because he already was, and death was easy. Enough medicine, and you would dig your own grave, and gladly. Time began to order itself like the leaves of a book, where you could look at some pictures and not others, or go back and look at some you skipped—over and over, as much as you wanted. The pages turned, the pictures opened out. Injun weed was different; it made everything go away—pain and memory both—so that Lucian didn't care whether he felt anything or not. But the Black Draught made him see things clearly even when he didn't want to. He had tried to tell that to Cass, but he wouldn't listen. Cass preferred his liquor, which, he said, only made the pages blank.

Lucian looked one last time at the works the yankees had built long ago. They had dug frantically in terrible expectation, all through the Indian-summer day, until the earth was piled chest-high, the ditch ready, the head-logs in place. They had dug a grave that day, though they didn't know it—one big enough to bury a whole army. Now the works were worn and soft and carpeted with brown grass, and Lucian thought how, in summer, the grass must grow rank and lush and green from the blood in the ground. He wondered how long blood could feed the grass, and if it would always. *The ditch will always be here,* he thought. *Like the gin house.*

He remembered the gentleman by the Columbia Pike, who said the old soldiers were always coming back. *Even the dead ones,* the man had said, all the while carving his cedar cane, sitting in the sunshine as if nothing had ever happened on the ground around him. If Lucian saw the man again, he would ask him what his secret was. He would ask how anyone could live among all this memory.

A little while ago, Lucian had knelt there in the ditch, spreading his hands over the grass. In that moment, the leaves of time turned back, and Lucian saw once more the long lines-of-battle walking into the smoke. He saw Cass prowling up and down behind the regiment, his musket slanted on his shoulder, his fixed bayonet gleaming by the setting sun, the rising moon. Lucian had turned the leaves and seen it all the way to the end.

✢

The great Battle of Franklin had sputtered out before daylight. Cass and Lucian and Roger crawled out of the ditch, careful to make no noise lest the yankees discover them. When they could stand at last, they traveled a long time through a fearsome landscape lit by fires until they found themselves at McGavock's house again, where Lucian was supposed to wait on the gallery—a long time ago, it seemed now. That afternoon, the house—long gallery, old brick soft in the twilight, gardens gone to winter sleep—seemed immune to the terrible thing taking shape around it. Now, in the dark hour before dawn, it was immune no longer, but a part of all that must happen here. The house and yard had caught the wreckage washed out of the battle—a myriad of stragglers and broken men, crying out in pain, in grief, lying in heaps and piles or wandering aimlessly through the yard like ghosts. In the midst of such company, the house no longer seemed aloof.

Lucian was stone deaf from the noise of the battle, and he was glad of it, for he knew the air was full of terrible noises. He wished he could surrender all his other senses, too, just for that little while, so that he would not have to see the look on men's faces or the slithery pile of arms and legs and feet growing outside a downstairs window, nor have to smell the chloroform, the blood, the unwashed bodies. They sought no farther than the yard and at last found a place in a fence corner and stayed there until daylight, when Cass and Roger decided to go back to where the ditch was.

Lucian could not understand why they wanted to go back there, but if they went, he would go, too. Once more they crossed the fields among the dark figures of men, all fearful and mad, calling out the names of those who were lost. Lucian's clothes were stiff with dried blood not his own. He held to the skirt of Cass's jacket so he wouldn't be lost in the dark. He stumbled and floundered, but whenever he fell, Cass reached for him, caught his hand and spoke kindly, and never scolded. All the time Lucian was a boy, Cass never again scolded, never again struck him as he had when they lay fearful in the ditch.

Lucian knew Cass spoke to him, but he was still deaf and couldn't hear his voice, only felt it. He couldn't hear, but he could see, and he could smell the odor that hung over the battlefield as if the earth itself were bleeding. The smell clung to him, and the stink of fear that was like no other smell but closer to death than any. Torches and lanterns flickered in the gray dawn and cast a bitter yellow light, and what Lucian beheld by their lumination was more terrible than anything old Pelt had ever told of hell. He remembered how the little ones of the orphanage had listened to old Pelt. They cowered and were silent, and later in their dreams they saw once more the torn and blistered souls consumed in flame, burned and swollen to bursting, only to be made whole again, to burn again. Still, that was only imagination. Now, at Franklin, the boy once called Lucifer had come to that place old Pelt had spoken of, and he knew Mister Lewellyn was right: God, if He loved as He was said to love, could not be blamed for this, could not have planned this back when the planets were still being flung across the sky. Something else—vanity, madness, illusion, he would never know—had risen from the will of Man and laid all this under the moon. God grieved among them, as bent and helpless and alone as any, while each prayer of the dying pierced Him like a nail. God suffered more than any, for He had seen this countless times before and knew He would see it again and again, and the hammer would ring again and again. God was greater than them all and must suffer more than any, and suffer for them all.

Now Lucian watched Cass make his way toward the distant houses, watched him stumble once in the field, then rise again, then cross a stone wall. After that, Lucian couldn't see him anymore, though it was easy enough to see, across all this time, the solemn procession of men bearing their dead—the soldiers in gray and brown, or in the dingy white of their cotton shirts, all soaked with the cold rain, all pulling hard against the mud under a sky that held almost no light at all.

The sky was bright now, and Lucian put on his green spectacles and squinted at the light. The new moon was setting to the west, a pale crescent over the hills. The world was silent save for the crows down by the river and a meadowlark in the field.

Alison came and stood beside him. Lucian had forgotten all about her, but now he thought she looked beautiful in her green cape with the bright winter sun shining down. Her face was in shadow, though, and Lucian found that troubling, as if she were dissolving in the light. She was watching after Cass. She said, "He is forever going off somewhere."

Lucian took off his spectacles and tucked them away. "He is going to find the . . . the place. He wants us to follow him."

She looked at him a moment. "Lucian," she said softly, "how long have you had those green glasses?"

He didn't want to answer, though he couldn't say why. He stood blinking in the sunlight a moment, then remembered what Cass had said. "Cass told me to look after you. We need to get away from here."

Alison took his arm, but her eyes were still on his face. "Lucian," she began, but she stopped and shook her head. "Never mind," she said.

Lucian had already forgotten what they were talking about. He tried to remember, but he couldn't. "We need to follow Cass," he said.

They found him in a narrow, muddy lane that ran behind a half dozen houses. Lucian didn't remember the lane, and the houses didn't look right, but twenty years must bring a good many changes in the scenery: more trees, and taller, in the yards; fences intact, some whitewashed. No pall of smoke hung over the scene, of course, save that which drifted from the peaceful chimneys. The yards and fields were empty of soldiers, and down at this end, near the river, the old Federal works had

grown up with vines and mulberry thickets and so had lost all
their menace. Time had been working right along since the day
the army maneuvered under fire out there in the field.

This house was neat and orderly, the fence whitewashed,
the gate hung properly on its hinges. The yard showed the re-
mains of last summer's garden, and laundry—white sheets and
a counterpane—hung on a length of plow line propped up by a
forked stick. Muddy white chickens pecked at the dirt, and a
white rooster strutted among them. A goat, also white, was
tethered by the back steps. From the half door of a shed, a
brown mule, head and neck caked with mud, watched the visitors with mild interest. A bottle tree stood just inside the gate.
The bottles, of blue and brown and pale green glass, once held
ink and elixir; now they were thrust over the stobs of a cedar
post to catch wandering ghosts. Lucian was about to remark on
the bottle tree when Cass opened the gate and plucked off one
of the blue bottles and put it to his ear.

Alison said, "What can you hear, Cass?"

Cass was startled by her voice. He turned, and Lucian saw
that he was embarrassed. "There's a spider in this one," said
Cass, and slipped the bottle back on its stob.

Lucian crossed the lane, mud pulling at his shoes. He
gripped the fence palings and peered at the house, trying to remember. "This is not the place," he said finally. He shook the
fence. A rabbit shot out of the dead grass and darted away. Lucian said, "This is not the one. It was further down the line."

Cass was frowning. "I think it was," he said.

All at once, Lucian had a thought. "It'd be better if it was
raining," he said. He turned to Alison, who was hanging back
in the center of the lane where the mud was deepest. "It was a

cold rain," Lucian said. "We carried them through the field—I mean, *they* did—I only walked behind. I couldn't hear a God damned thing."

"Mind your tongue, lad," said Cass.

"It's all right," said Alison.

The mule snorted in his stall, and the goat bleated, and they all looked that way. A boy, carrying a bucket of corn, appeared around the corner of the barn. He looked to be about thirteen; he had red hair, and his face was all befreckled, and he wore jeans trousers and a shirt too big for him. For an instant, Lucian thought he was looking at himself.

When the boy noticed the visitors, he set the bucket down and stood questioning, hands at his side. "Hidy," he said.

Cass said, "Hidy, yourself." He indicated the bottle tree. "You-all troubled by spirits?" he asked.

"A right smart of 'em, sir," said the boy. "Daddy keeps hoping to catch 'em, but they are wily."

Cass said, "Well, what kind are they, mostly?"

"Well, sir, they are spirits from the battle," the boy replied. He smiled and added, "Like yourself."

"Hah!" said Lucian. He shook the fence again, but it was sturdy and stood fast. He said, "The boy knows what you are, Cass."

Alison said, "No!" She crossed the lane. "Come here, boy," she said, and crooked her finger.

The boy looked toward the house, then came and stood with his thumbs hooked in his galluses. Alison took the boy by the shoulders and searched his face. "What is your name?" she said.

"Peter," said the boy.

"Peter, where's your folks?"

"Mama run off, ma'am," said the boy. "Daddy's been out on the railroad since two days."

"Ah," said Alison. She looked away for an instant, then tightened her grip on the boy's shoulders. "Why would you say such a thing about spirits?" she said.

"I seen 'em," said the boy. "I seen shadows out in the field, nights, in the fog, and things like lanterns moving back and forth—that's the rebel soldiers searching for the dead. I told Daddy, it ain't no bottles going to hold 'em, but he is from way down south where they believe in such foolishness. I seen one this morning, early, but he wouldn't of fit in no bottle I ever saw. I wasn't scared, though."

"This morning?" said Cass. "You saw a spirit this morning?"

"Yes, sir. He was dressed like you-all, beg pardon, not fit for any work. I always thought, if I seen one in the flesh, he'd be dressed like a soldier; but when I seen this one, I thought, *I don't know what a soldier looks like,* so maybe that's why. Anyhow, he wanted to borrow of a shovel, so I leant him one. He said I should look for others to follow behind, and"—he made a little bow to Alison—"and a lady with 'em." He pointed down the row of houses. "Said he was going to dig up some men you-all buried after the battle. Them was his very words. I told him—"

"No," said Alison, and shook the boy. "Why do you say he was a spirit? Why?"

The boy seemed about to cry now. "He come across the field, same as you. I was looking to my rabbit snares, and he come up sudden, out of the fog. He walked past me, looking at the house, and I said, 'Hey,' and that's when he turned, and—"

The boy stopped and ducked his head and jammed his hands deeper into his pockets. Alison let go of his shoulders and touched the back of his neck. "And what, Peter?" she said, soft now.

The boy cried out. "I could see right through him!" he said.

"No!" said Alison. She grabbed the boy again and shook him hard. "No, you couldn't!"

"Easy," said Cass. "Sometimes the fog plays tricks."

The voices went on, but Lucian had quit listening. A leaf had turned, and he was no longer in the lane at all, but back in the mean woman's yard in Decatur, Alabama, talking to a man he thought was a general, that he didn't know yet was only Cass Wakefield. Then some other men came that he didn't know yet. One of them said, *He doesn't look like much,* and they all laughed because that's what men did. Then another leaf turned, and the same men were burning a house because of what the people had done to the boy Lucifer; and another leaf turned, and the snow was drifting through the trees, falling white and silent, and Mister Lewellyn said, *You can ask the dead ones. They know better than us.*

It wasn't the fog playing tricks, Lucian thought, and it was no spider Cass heard in the bottle. Lucian felt light and airy, like he might rise up into the branches of the trees. He held tight to the fence and studied the backyard. The mule was banging around in the shed, the chickens pecked and scratched in the dirt, the laundry hung limp in the still air. It was all so ordinary and peaceful, and Lucian thought he wouldn't mind being down under the earth with the years turning over him and the generations passing. But it was no good because even then he would dream of what happened here, and he would have to rise and walk the fields again, looking for lost comrades in the dark. He thought, *Maybe Cass is right—maybe the pages are better if they are empty.* Trouble was, Lucian didn't know how to make them empty, and he didn't think Cass or Roger did, either.

The pages went on turning back and forth in time, colors fading year by year but the pictures still sharp as if they were drawn yesterday: snow falling, a ditch crowded with dead men, the long walk through the dark, a great brick house where God Himself was mourning—*Too much hurting,* Lucian thought. *It was too much pain there*—and in the fence corner, Roger Lewellyn's face in the firelight, his hand reaching down—*Get up, lad. Get up. We have to go now*—Then another house, one that still smelled of Janie Wakefield that he never knew, that Cass had promised would take care of him, and again Roger Lewellyn's face, lit by the twilight this time. He sat in a rocking chair with a cup of tea beside him, reading *Hamlet* aloud so Lucian could hear.

Another leaf turned. It was yesterday, and Lucian was at the depot in Cumberland, about to board the northbound train. He heard his name, and turned, and there was Roger Lewellyn, wrapped in an opera cloak, his face red from the cold wind. *You shouldn't have told me,* Roger said. *If you didn't want me to go, you shouldn't have told me.*

You're right, said Lucian. The train was about to leave, the air brakes groaning as they went slack. *I shouldn't have told you. Cass shouldn't have told me either.* Lucian jumped on the bottom step as the train began to move. Roger made to follow, but Lucian pushed him away. It was easy; Roger was like a bundle of sticks. *You can't do no good,* said Lucian. He leaned out from the bottom step and watched as Roger Lewellyn stood by himself on the platform, growing smaller and smaller until he was gone.

Now the voices came from someplace outside, demanding that he listen, and Lucian found himself in the lane again with Alison's face close to his own. She said, "Why did you tell Roger! What was the use in it!"

"Easy," said Cass.

Lucian tried to pull himself into the light. He said, "I told him he couldn't do no good."

"Never mind all that," Cass said. "Roger is come, and we got to find him." Then, to the boy, "Now, listen here, we are not spirits—you understand? That was a man you saw. His name is Roger Lewellyn."

"Don't let him fool you, Peter," said Lucian. "We been dead a long time," he said. "I am still a boy like you, Cass is still a soldier, and Miss Alison"—he waved his hand toward her—"Miss Alison is still young, still wearing her green and yellow dresses, waiting to hear—"

"Be quiet," said Cass.

"Everything stopped right here," said Lucian to the boy. "Right here at the great Battle of Franklin. Oh, there's plenty happened since then, but no matter. We are froze right here in this field, boy. That's us you see in the fog at night—me and him and Roger—"

"Shut up, Lucian," said Cass.

"I won't! You said it your own self—'That's us out there,' you said. Death and hell and grief—that's us, every time!" He took out his bottle of Black Draught and waved it in Cass's face. "You want some of this? No—you got your own medicine. I forgot." He pulled out the glass stopper and dropped it in the grass. "Let's see what happens."

Cass reached for the bottle, but Lucian ducked away and drained it in a single swallow.

"Drank it all!" he said. "Just let's see what happens." He slid the empty bottle over a stob on the cedar bolt. "Now, that ought to fetch 'em," he said. "If they don't like that—" He stopped, and laughed at the idea of spirits on laudanum, like the time Cass gave some whiskey to a squirrel. That was pretty funny for a while, until the squirrel passed out and died. Lucian looked at his companions, but they were not laughing. "What's the matter?" he said.

Cass moved close and took hold of Lucian's collar. "Do you know what you're doing?" he whispered. "We got no time for this."

"I want to be ready," said Lucian, pulling away. "I want to help Roger dig up that whole God damned yard. I want to see all them skeletons laid out, feet together, hands folded, just the way Ike taught me, and I want to say to 'em, 'Why, boys, you just don't *know* what you been missing all these years—'"

"But it *ain't* no skeletons," said the boy. "I told the other feller that, but he wouldn't pay any mind."

Cass turned suddenly away, and Lucian was left wavering, holding tight to the fence. Cass said, "What you mean, boy?"

Peter seemed about to cry again. "It's a good many *spirits,* but—see, Daddy told me it's all what's left behind. He told me Miz Caroline McGavock took them poor fellows over to her own graveyard afore I was born."

"You mean the men are gone?" Alison demanded.

"They been gone for ages," the boy said. He was talking quickly now, waving his hands. "Daddy told how Miz Caroline McGavock had gangs of niggers going all over town, out in the fields, digging any place a soldier was laid. She couldn't find all of 'em, but them she did find is in her cemetery over to the big house where she lives. I seen it once—rows and rows of little wood markers, and every one with a number. It's mighty peaceful. She wouldn't let the soldiers lie forgotten, and the names are all wrote down in a little book—"

McGavock, thought Lucian. He remembered a kind woman there. She wore a dress bloodstained to the knees, and she gave him a drink of water. Her place wasn't peaceful then. Maybe it was now, and maybe the soldiers were all written down in a book, but it was unlikely they rested quiet.

Alison stood up and leaned against the gate post. "How come I never knew this?" she said.

Lucian could tell the disbelief in her voice. What would they do now? Search forever, wandering from cemetery to cemetery until Resurrection Day, seeking the particular dead. Lucian thought that made sense. He was ready. But no—they would only have to hunt in one place. Lucian thought, *The Book of the Dead.* That was where he was written down—him and Cass and Roger, all of them.

"How come I never knew this?" Alison said again, and this time Lucian heard not just disbelief but disappointment.

Cass touched her arm. He said, "But now you *do* know. Now you can rest easy. We can go see them anytime you want."

"No!" she said. "I want to see the place where they lie!" She was crying now and pushed away from the gate. She stumbled, shaking the bottle tree, and Cass took her by the arms as if she, too, might rise into the branches.

"It's not here," he said. "Not anymore." He looked at Lucian. "You-all stay here, and I will fetch Roger."

"You believe this boy?" said Alison, her voice drawn tight. "What does he know?" She pulled her arms away and struck Cass in the chest with her fists. "What does a boy know!"

"We got to find Roger," said Lucian. He was worried now. "We got to go back to the ditch and find him, Cass."

The boy said, "That Roger knows something by now, I guess, if old Ambrose is home."

Cass turned on the boy. "What the hell does that mean?" he said. "Be quick!"

Roger knows, thought Lucian. *We got to get back to*—Then all at once the ground swept up around him, and he was on his hands and knees in the mud. Time left him altogether then, and he was in a black, empty place like a cave. Away off, the boy Peter was speaking, his words falling one by one through the dark: *Mister Ambrose is a bad man. I ain't allowed to go down there.* Then Cass's voice: *You tell me, boy. You tell me.* And the boy again: *He was a fierce Union man and went off with the yankee army. He come home from the fighting, and when Miz Caroline McGavock told him they was rebels in his yard, he wouldn't let the niggers dig. He dug up all them boys hisself and flung the bones all over, what Daddy said. Old Ambrose ain't nobody to trifle with, and he don't let nobody come in his yard. I told that feller, but he wouldn't listen*—

That's enough! said Alison.

What happened to them? said Cass. *What happened to the bones?*

Miz Caroline came and got 'em, said the boy. *She brung the sheriff—*

The voices got all jumbled up then, and Lucian couldn't tell what was happening, only that Cass's voice was louder than the rest. Pretty soon, he forgot about it and was on the square in Cumberland again, going down to the hotel for dinner, glad to be home. But Cass ruined it. Cass snatched him by the collar and pulled him up. "You stay here," said Cass, his voice tight with anger. He jabbed his finger at the ground. "Don't you move from this spot till I come and get you."

Lucian thought he said no, but he couldn't be sure. He rubbed at the mud on his palms and stood unsteadily in the lane. It was hard to keep a balance. The boy was running for his own back porch, and Cass and Alison were moving down the lane. Lucian let them get a little way ahead, then followed behind, listening to their sharp voices.

"That boy was wrong," said Alison.

"I am tired of this," said Cass. "I wish you-all would stay here, but you won't, so I will show you the place and dig up the whole yard if you want. I guess Roger has a head start anyhow."

"Father is still there," said Alison. "Perry is still there."

"All right," said Cass.

They came to a house at the end of the row and stopped. Lucian saw the house all at once, clearly, and knew it was the right place, though it was almost hidden by chinaberry trees now. An old dogtrot, piled with firewood and scrap lumber, still ran down the middle—through it, Lucian could see the trees by the river beyond—but the place had accumulated a second story on one end, and an ell on the other, and various chimneys here and there. All these accretions seemed to argue with one another, and all needed paint and repair, hardly un-usual in the South. But even the poorest house could possess a quality that gave it life, even an air of contentment, even hap-piness, like an old person who had seen too much but was stronger for it. This house gave only of sorrow and defeat; it huddled among the chinaberries as a beaten old woman might hide behind the bed.

Gray rags of curtains hung in the open windows, some draping over the sills, some moving in the little breeze. Beyond the curtains was only darkness. A thin finger of smoke rose from one of the chimneys. The gallery sagged, the steps had long been rotted away, and a great stone rolled in their place. The yard, littered with junk, lay beyond the leaning ruins of a fence.

It is not the Garden of Eden, thought Lucian.

"Well, boys, this ain't the Garden of Eden." Cass had left his hat and coat at the ditch, and the rain was running down his face. He had unbuttoned his waistcoat, and his watch chain was caked in mud, and his shirt was a gray rag stained with mud. Lucian watched as Cass pulled a picket from the fence, the nails squawking. Other soldiers had done the same, and there was a line of them waiting to get theirs painted, and Cass fell asleep in the line and would have lost his place if Lucian had not punched him awake. Finally, they were next. A man named S. Cragin Knox was sitting in the dogtrot in a cane-bottom chair, painting the names. Knox was one of those who were playing marbles back in Decatur. He was in a daze from the battle and was suffering a bad cold besides. He was hud-dled inside a civilian frock coat too big for him, which seemed to anchor him to the boards. Knox wore a cap; the bill was creased and cracked, the strap gone, the faded crown adorned with a little brass star. At the moment, he had the cap turned backward, and his curly hair stuck out in all directions. When Cass and Lucian approached, Knox looked up, peering over his spectacles with red, watery eyes. "Hey, boys," he said, and sneezed, and wiped his nose on his coat sleeve. " 'Scuse me," he said. "I wish I'd get better so's I could die."

Lucian was getting his hearing back. He heard Cass: "Don't be sayin' that. Not today." Cass sounded like he was under water.

Knox took the fence picket from Cass's hand. "Who's this for?"

Lucian was so tired that he sat down on the steps, and as soon as he did, he fell half asleep. He heard Cass say, "For the colonel and Perry. We'll bury them together, I guess."

Knox said, "Perry is dead, too?"

"Well, I thought you knew that," said Cass.

"I should of knowed it," said Knox. He sneezed again. The sound was so odd that it startled Lucian, and he looked up to see Knox wipe his nose as before. He laid the picket across his lap like a dulcimer and brushed absently at it with a rag. After a while, he asked, "Who'd you say this one is for?"

Cass told him again.

Knox took off his spectacles and rubbed his eyes. "Ah, me. Cass, I wish I didn't have to make one for them. It's too hard."

Cass sat down on the steps beside Lucian. "I know, Sam," he said.

Lucian looked up at the sky. It was low and gray, bleared of smoke, and mist shrouded the hills about. Mister Lewellyn said falling weather seemed to always follow a battle, as if the sky grieved at what it had to look upon. Way aloft, circling and patient, the carrion birds balanced on their pinions.

Cass said, "I wish we had some coffee." He said it to no one. Lucian watched S. Cragin Knox twist his spectacles in two. "Sam?" said Cass, looking around.

"It's too many," said the other. He wiped at his eyes. "I could paint all day for ten years and never get to the end of 'em."

"It's all right," said Cass, rising. "You don't have to paint 'em all; just the ones in the yard."

"Sure—just the ones in the yard," said Knox. He began to rock his body back and forth in the cane-bottom chair.

"You don't have to paint any more a-tall if you don't want to," said Cass. He put his hand on the man's shoulder.

Knox looked at his ruined spectacles, then stuffed them under his coat. "It ain't I don't want to," he said, and stood up quickly. The picket clattered to the porch. "God is tryin' to learn us a lesson, Cass," he said. "I just don't know what." He looked at Cass and wiped his eyes yet again. "What do you reckon it is?"

"He is not," said Cass. "It ain't His way. You are tired, is all."

"Yes, He is," said Knox. "We gone too far this time, and He's held off His judgment till now." He stood unsteadily, his hand on the back of the chair. "See them birds up there? They are His messengers."

"Sam, they are only birds," insisted Cass. Lucian looked at the sky again. He had been told how buzzards always followed the army and always descended in their eager myriads after a fight, as regular as the rain. Sometimes, the soldiers had to beat them off the dead with ramrods. "Messengers they may be," said Cass, "but not from God." He spoke only to himself now, for Knox was across the yard and gone.

So it was that Cass Wakefield painted the board that would mark the grave of Perry and the colonel. He made a clumsy job of it, for his hand was unsteady. When he was done, he rose, and Lucian followed, holding to his jacket. Cass carried the fence pale to the open grave, where his comrades waited patiently in the rain. Their faces were gray, smeared, deeply lined, like those of old men. They were sitting or kneeling in silence, some of them nodding, but they stood up when Cass and Lucian approached. The rain pattered on the canvas that shrouded the bodies; it ran in rivulets down the mound of earth beside the hole. "Well, boys," said Cass.

Lucian heard the rustling of the tent fly as they wrapped the bodies. Down, down, down into the mud they went. The day was already falling colder, and Ike Gatlin said, "It'll be rough in Nashville. We ought to keep that fly." The men talked it over and decided Ike was right, but they left the fly anyhow, for the earth was cold, too, and none of them wanted to shovel dirt in their comrades' faces. Lucian would learn how that was the way of it sometimes: you couldn't let go, could never convince yourself that the newly dead had surrendered everything that touched them in life. Wherever they had gone, they might still be cold or hot, hungry or lonesome. Their names were still alive, after all, and men could still hear their voices—a minute ago, an hour, yesterday—and the meal you had cooked together was still in your stomach, and theirs, and you still carried the dollar lent or the letter given for safekeeping, the chess game sketched on an envelope to be taken up again when there was time. Only the time would never come now, the game never played out, the castle, king, queen, pawns all frozen in place forever, the knight paused for a check that might have won it all. No one wanted to shovel dirt in their faces. Sleep, comrades, and wait for us.

The burying didn't take long, and when it was done, they stepped back and looked at the grave. All over the yard the graves were mounded, but this one was nearly level as if nothing was down there at all. Lucian tried to think about why that was, but he was too tired. At last, they drove in the fence picket with a musket butt, and Gawain Harper went to fetch the chaplain.

Cass knelt beside Lucian, who was sitting cross-legged in the mud. "You still deaf?" he asked. The boy shook his head. Cass leaned closer. "Hey—how you like that new jacket?" he said.

Lucian plucked at the tarnished buttons of his coat. "Can we go home now?" he said.

✛

Lucian wore a frock coat now, and he plucked at the buttons and moved his hand across the front of his waistcoat and felt the chain for the watch Cass had given him once. He could hear the watch ticking and feel the weight of the pistol in his coat pocket. He fumbled in his pockets for the Black Draught, then remembered he had taken it all. He was tired and wanted to sit down, but Cass and Alison were going into the yard, and Lucian followed. He could hear his feet in the long grass and felt the dampness. A yellow hound ran out from under the porch, snarling, and Cass stepped between the dog and Alison. Cass snarled back at the dog, and cursed, and fetched the dog a kick in the head, and it howled and ran away.

Lucian looked around, thinking he should see Roger, but the yard was empty. Cass called out, "Roger!" He walked back and forth in the grass, calling out, but no one answered. Lucian thought he saw a face in a window, behind the gray curtains, but he couldn't be sure if it was this time or another. Lucian remembered how, at McGavock's, faces were in all the windows, pale and round like owls' faces. The curtains there were heavy and brocaded, and a man with scissors was cutting them up for bandages.

Cass walked back and forth. He was talking to Alison now, pointing to a sunken place in the yard. "This is the place," he said. "I stood right there, and Tom Jenkins there, and Sam Hook—does that satisfy you?"

Lucian quit listening. That was not the place, and Cass knew it. He was only trying to mollify Alison. *Well, never mind,* Lucian thought, *one place or another, it doesn't matter now.*

Lucian moved away, and the grass brushed his pants legs as the broomsage had done once. *Nothing good has ever happened here,* he thought, *and it is our fault: we put a curse on this ground years ago.* Lucian looked back toward the gin and saw the roofline across the field. How many men were carried across the mud to this yard—and why? Lucian wondered why this place had been chosen. Well, he thought, the answer was left behind in the cold rain among men too tired and sick to know why they did anything.

Lucian moved through the yard. To his right, the house sat brooding among the chinaberries. It was being pulled slowly down into the earth like an old bee-stump, but Lucian knew that the house, like the gin, would outlast them all. Still, the gin was what you made of it, and only those who had been there could make anything of it at all. This house was different. Anyone who came here could feel the malice in the paintless boards, the windows with their gray curtains, the shadowy tunnel of the dogtrot. It wasn't like that the first time—it was only a house then. *Maybe it isn't our fault after all,* thought Lucian, and he remembered what the boy said. If the man who lived here was a Union man, then he must suffer the very defeat he helped create, and be reminded every day of a victory that had left him behind.

Lucian knew the war was still with them, that it would not be over until they were all gone: yankee and rebel, white and colored, men and women—all those who had suffered by it. That's what this house was, Lucian thought: a place where the war had never quit, where it lived still. In that way, the house was like the men themselves, the dead and living both. Now the house had drawn them back to stand once more in the yard, in the little square field of blood where they had laid their comrades uneasy into the ground.

Lucian stumbled across the yard. He looked to the sky where the carrion birds once hovered. He remembered how graceful they looked, their heads turning this way and that as they sailed overhead; but they were gone now. There was only the deep blue sky of winter, and a little flag of a cloud drifting by.

Then all at once, he was falling. It seemed to go on a long time before he felt himself strike hard. It didn't hurt much but jarred him and made a buzzing in the back of his head. He was lying on his face, smelling the fresh-turned earth, which was wet and clotted. When he turned over, he could see the sky and the branches of trees and the handle of a shovel. Somebody had dug a shallow grave, and he was in it.

He heard his name, but it was a long way off. He remembered how Chaplain Sam Hook said the dead could rest now, how they could dream in peace, and how they would be waiting. Well, Lucian thought, they would be waiting anyway; that much was true.

They think I am dead, Lucian told himself. *Now they will throw dirt in my face.* It seemed unfair, and he cried out. He saw Cass Wakefield above him. "I am not dead, Cass!" he cried.

"I know," said Cass. "You stay right there and rest."

Alison's voice: "Is he hurt?"

"He is not hurt," said Cass. "Roger has been here—been digging. Where the hell is he?"

"Don't let them shovel the dirt in my face!" Lucian cried.

"I won't," said Cass. "That's a good place for you; just rest, and I'll come and fetch you after a while."

Cass went away, but voices tangled in the air where he had been, going farther and farther away, Alison and Cass.

What is this? You can't leave him here—in a hole!

He is out of his head. He took too much medicine. He needs to go to sleep. I got to find Roger.

The voices went away. Lucian wanted to follow. He tried to move his arms, but they seemed to weigh a hundred pounds, and his hands a hundred more. He was in a black place for a while, then out of it again, and a dog was barking somewhere, and voices—a stranger's voice now, angry: *I told ye once, I ain't goin to tell ye agin!* And Cass: *By God, sir, where is he!*

Something was happening, but it was all far away. Lucian smelled the cold, damp ground. He thought, *Well, this is the way being dead is.* He had seen a good many dead men, and now he knew how it was for them: looking out at the living, wanting to help, trying to speak and move, refusing to believe. Pictures came to him: the cavalry man in Alabama, and Colonel Sansing when they turned him over in the ditch, and Perry when they found him. In Alabama, Lucian was afraid and sorrowful; after Franklin, there was only a gray, empty place where feeling used to be. In memory, none of the dead men had faces, and Lucian wondered if he had a face now, and if he only had his old shawl, he would cover his face, if he had one, so the dirt—

Lucian.

A woman was in the grave with him. It was like a long cavern now, and the woman was dressed in clothes he remembered, which hung in the wardrobe in the shape of her. When he first came to the house on Algiers Street, he would press his face against her clothes and smell her, because that's all he would ever have. Then the moths came, and the mildew, and the smell of her was gone, and the shape of her lost in time. Now she was here with him. Lucian marveled at her face and the fall of her hair.

Lucian said, *I know you.* She seemed at peace, calm and graceful. The sight of him made Lucian feel sorrowful, and he wished Cass could see her.

She said, *Rise up, Lucian Wakefield.* She put her cool hand against his forehead and said, *Don't be grieving. It is like Roger said—they are always close.*

Who is close, ma'am? asked Lucian, though he knew very well.

All of them, in the air and leaves and earth. Alison will know that, too, if you tell her.

I will tell her, said Lucian.

The woman smiled. *I know,* she said. *But right now, you have to rise up. You need to help Cass.*

Then she was gone. Lucian was alone and somehow standing in the yard again, risen up from the grave. It was hard to move, and he couldn't keep his balance. He fell once, fell again. The dead grass and the sky and trees wheeled about him, and he was sick and vomited. When he looked up, he saw S. Cragin Knox sitting in the yard in a cane-bottom chair with his cap turned backward. Knox was making letters in white paint on a fence picket, and he turned the picket so Lucian could see what he had written,

Lucian Wakefield

A Good Boy

and Knox wiped his nose and said, *Well, this is the last one.*

So it was all right. Lucian was in good company, had been since the day he saw Cass Wakefield sitting by the fence. It was something to have been one of them, one of the boys, and if that was all his life came to, it was enough.

Lucian began to cry then, for the first time since the farmyard in Alabama. He didn't want to, but he couldn't stop. A woman came to him, and Lucian blinked at her and wiped his eyes, trying to remember. This was not the one in the grave, but another, her face wet with crying, not a spirit or vision this time. She put her hands flat against his chest and said, "Lucian, Lucian!"

"Why, Miss Alison," said Lucian, remembering. "What are you doing here?"

"I don't know what's happening," she said. "Cass is in yonder, with . . . with that man, and he has a gun, Lucian. He is
crazy—"

"Oh, Cass has always been crazy," said Lucian.

"Listen to me!" she said, and slapped him hard across the
face, and again. "Wake up!" she said. "God damn you, wake up!"

The blows stung him. Lucian shook himself, trying to clear
his head. *You need to help Cass,* the other woman had said, and
now Alison was telling him the same thing. "All right," said
Lucian. "Where?"

"In the house," she said, and stroked his face where she had
hit him. "I'm sorry. I'm sorry, Lucian."

"It's all right," he said. "It's what I come for." He put his
foot on the stone where the steps used to be. He was in the
dogtrot then and chose a door and kicked it open. The room
was smoky and dank, and an old crone cowered by the hearth.
She cried out and pointed a long finger at Lucian and said,
"Hit's a jedgment on all you goddamned rebels!"

Lucian wanted to reply, but he fell into a black place, and
when he came out, he was across the dogtrot, stumbling
through the door into the other room. The walls were lined of
newspaper; a fire lay on the hearth; a lamp was burning on a
trestle table. Roger Lewellyn sat against the wall, his face running blood, and Cass kneeling beside him. A man—blue-
jowled, long of hair, in an old ragged greatcoat and canvas
breeches—was yelling and cursing and waving a shotgun.
"Here, now!" said Lucian, and lurched forward. He almost fell
but caught himself.

"Get away!" said the man. "I won't suffer it!"

Lucian drove his hand into his pocket where the pistol was.

He saw Cass rise, hand darting inside his coat. The man swung the shotgun around, and Lucian heard the hammers pulling back. Cass said, "No! Don't do it!" and everything was moving slow and graceful so Lucian had time to think, *You ought not to of done that, God damn you.*

Then a sound filled the room and drove all the air out of it, and flame was everywhere, and Lucian felt a blow in his stomach like somebody had swung a sledge hammer. He hit the wall just as Cass drew and fired his pistol, and before the black place came again, Lucian thought, *You can beat me, you son bitch, but you can't beat Cass Wakefield.*

⚔ 15 ⚔

LUCIAN HEARD THE COURTHOUSE BELL RING OUT dinnertime across the square. The clamor sent the courthouse pigeons flapping and clattering from the cupola as they did every hour in daylight, year in and year out, generation after generation. The bell did not seem to disturb them at night, nor would they stir from their roosts on Sunday, and when Lucian was a boy, he had asked why that was so. Cass said the pigeons had a job like everybody else, and they should not be expected to work nights and Sundays, too. That made as much sense as anything, Lucian decided. In any event, he was glad for the birds' hourly eruptions, for it always made him laugh.

It was high summertime, and he was in his shirtsleeves, leaning against the wall of Tom Jenkins's store, in the shade under the striped cotton awning. Behind the tall framed windows, barely visible through the murky glass, kerosene cans and harness and coffeepots and bolts of cloth faded by the sun were laid out in a display that had not changed since Reconstruction. The smell of the dim interior—that distinctive compound of seed, leather, and old wood that grew richer and more eradicable every year—was drawn through the open doors and spread out upon the air.

At noon, everyone emerged into the bright sunlight. Lawyers and merchants struck homeward for dinner, pulling on their coats. Country people ambled off to their wagons or to Fudge's Grocery, where they would buy potted meat and hoop cheese and sardines, to be eaten in the shade of this gallery or that, or under the oaks around the courthouse. From the grocery, too, came women, white and black, with baskets draped in dishtowels to keep the flies away. The bailiff announced recess from the courthouse gallery, while, beneath him, judges and lawyers and defendants and plaintiffs made their way to the Colonial Hotel, and the jailer went off to get dinner for the prisoners. Mothers and colored nurses called up their children, and the children called back in return, complaining. At the depot, the noon passenger train blew for the first crossing, and everywhere men were pulling out their watches and setting them. Down the southerly road, Queenolia Divine was still ringing the dinner bell at the Citadel of Djibouti long after the courthouse had ceased and the pigeons settled in again.

A black boy skipped along with his shoeshine box. Mister George Boswell, hands in his pockets, passed by whistling

"Old Gray Mare Came Storming out the Wilderness"—whistling badly between his teeth stained of tobacco—and Mister Johnny Cross and Mister Audley Brummett with him, just come from the horse lot. "Say, hey, there," said Mister Cross, and shook Lucian's hand and held on to it while he asked about Cass and Tom Jenkins and Miz Margaret Jenkins, and told a long story about a fellow he knew once who hunted rabbits with a pack of tomcats.

It was a breezeless noon, and dust rose from the square. The courthouse oaks were deep green, and the shaded ground beneath them trodden grassless and gray, littered with cedar shavings and tobacco spit. Tethered mules and horses bowed their heads and swished their tails at the flies, and some were led to the long cedar troughs for drinking. The sky was piled high with clouds, but no one thought they held any rain, and people talked about the cotton and how it might be good this year.

Lucian knew every person and nearly every horse and mule in sight, and who belonged to every dog. He knew what lay behind every window in the buildings of the square—knew that right now a noontime dice game was going on at the lumberyard, and Gawain Harper was working on the noon train, and L. W. Thomas was practicing his mandolin under a hackberry tree behind the Citadel. Time was going along, and Lucian with it, and all the elements of his universe in place. He felt at home, and it was something like he imagined true love might be, when you were comfortable with a person, and you moved together in time and harmony for all your flaws and strife. It was good to feel that, good to feel anything after so long a time.

Then someone called him from inside the store. He was

about to turn back when he noticed that time, and all things in it save himself, seemed to be slowing. He watched, puzzled, as the people and horses and dogs slowed down, and the leaves on the trees grew still, and sounds lost their resonance and stretched out long and solemn until there was no sound at all, and no movement—only a flat plane in gray and white, like an illustration.

He heard his name again. It seemed to come from the air this time.

⁜

Alison was leaning over him, stroking his hair, and crying. "Lucian," she said.

He was laid out on the ground, and above him was the deep blue sky. He felt cold all over, but he was sweating, too, and he could feel heat from somewhere, so he thought the cold must be inside him.

Then Alison lifted his head and cradled it, and he could see they were in a field, and a scrap of old canvas was pulled up to his chest. The heat was coming from a burning house. The flames had eaten through the roof, and a black plume of smoke rose toward the sky, and the stink was awful. He saw Roger Lewellyn sitting against a fence post, holding his head, and Cass kneeling beside. Lucian knew that all this had something to do with him, but he couldn't remember what. He looked up at Alison. He said, "It's all right. Whatever it is will be all right."

"I know," she said. "Hush now."

"I was just home," he said. "Just now." He thought the fact might comfort her, but it only made her cry again.

"How did it look?" she said. "How is it at home?"

"It was summer," said Lucian. He tried to look around. "Are we on an excursion?" he asked.

Cass was there then, in shirtsleeves, without his hat, and his face was drawn and streaked with soot. "Lucian," he said. "Hold on. Don't go drifting off."

Lucian tried to sit up, but Cass said no and held him down; it didn't take much, for Lucian had no strength in him. He knew something was wrong, for a thing heavy and wet, like a full wineskin, was lying on his stomach. He fumbled at the canvas, said, "I want to see—"

But Cass took his hands and held on to them. "No, you don't want to look under there," he said, and his voice was shaking. "You been shot up, Lucian," he said. "A man in there shot you."

"Is it bad, Cass?"

"Oh, no," said Cass. He hunched his shoulder and wiped his eyes on his shirtsleeve, but he didn't let go of Lucian's hands. "No, no," he said. "It ain't so bad."

Lucian remembered some of it then. He remembered the close room, the terrible noise, and the flame, remembered being struck in the belly with something like a sheep-nose hammer. All at once, he knew what was hidden under the canvas: secret things spilling from his insides that Cass didn't want him to see, that nobody should have to see. He thought, *I should be afraid,* but he wasn't afraid. Everything would be all right. He felt no pain, so it must be all right, like Cass said. Lucian recognized the lie, of course; he had heard it told to other men. Still, he would believe it so long as there was no pain.

"A doctor will come," said Alison. "We sent Peter to fetch him."

"I'm sorry about Roger," said Lucian. "I never should of told him."

"It's all right," said Alison. She tried to laugh. "He just *had* to come, same as you. Now we're all here together."

"The house caught afire," said Cass. He looked at Alison. "It was the lamp. An accident."

"An accident," said Alison. She began to tremble. "If I hadn't brought you here—"

"None of that," said Cass. He touched her shoulder, then her face. "It don't work that way," he said. "It's like you said: nobody came that didn't have to. Now, why don't you look to Roger for a minute."

She was gone then, and Cass was kneeling there, grinding his fists together.

"Goddammit," he said. "Goddammit, Lucian."

"What happened?"

Cass shook his head. "That old man, Ambrose—I don't know. Roger found the place—the right place—and he was digging, and the old man bushwhacked him. Beat him up pretty bad, dragged him in the house—told me Roger was his prisoner, he was holding him for the provost—" Cass stopped and looked at his hands. "An old soldier," he said. "He wouldn't give it up. Then you come in, and before I knew it—" Cass stopped again and drew the heel of his hand across his eyes. "I'm sorry. I should have seen it coming."

"No," began Lucian, but all at once he was choking. He coughed and felt the hot blood on his chin. Cass wiped it away. For a moment, Lucian couldn't speak for coughing and spitting out blood, and Cass wiping it off with his hand. He wanted to tell Cass that nobody could have stopped it, that it was nobody's fault because all this started long ago, and all of them a part of it, and they would never be free. Never. But the thought was a jumble in his mind, like a gray cloud rising out of time, and he couldn't say it because he was starting to be afraid.

"So I killed him," said Cass. "Too late, but I killed him." He looked toward where Alison had gone, where she was sitting by the fence with Roger. "The house was no accident," said Cass. "Alison knows, but she won't say it. We laid you out here and made her stay with you, then Roger and me set fire to it. We burned it, and him in it, the son of a bitch."

Lucian felt sorrow at that. Seemed like they had come so far, just to get to the starting place again. Then a thought jarred him. "The old woman," he said. It was getting hard to talk at all now. "There's an old woman in there."

"No, there was nobody else," said Cass, and smiled a little. "We always make sure when we burn a house, don't we?"

Lucian shook his head, wanting to argue, but he couldn't make the words. He cleared his throat and spat, but he had forgotten what they were talking about. Then he thought of something he needed to tell. He said, "Cass, I saw Janie. She came to me in the grave yonder."

Cass put his hand on Lucian's chest and bent down close. "What?"

"Janie," said Lucian, and Cass looked away as if he had not heard, but Lucian saw in his face that he had heard. Lucian said, "It was not a bad thing. She was beautiful. She said not to worry, not to grieve."

"She said that?"

"She said it don't matter where they lie, Cass. They are all around us. Will you tell Alison that?"

"You can tell her yourself," said Cass.

But Lucian couldn't talk anymore. He laid his head back and began to turn loose of things—so much trouble and worry, and maybe he would rest now. He was scared a while ago, but he wasn't now. Alison was come again, and Mister Lewellyn with her, and Cass was there—all together, just like Alison said, in the little room on Algiers Street, and nothing to be afraid of now. The window was streaked with rain, and Lucian could hear it pounding on the roof as it did on summer afternoons—hard and violent, then gone all at once, then the sun again, and the steam rising. Lucian's head was hurting, but no matter. Pretty soon he would be well once more, and he would get up and walk in the yard among the old privet and the bright marigolds that came every year without anybody planting them. Then, when he was strong enough, maybe they would all go down to Leaf River and fish awhile, and make a picnic on a gravel bar. They would be able to hear the courthouse bell from there, ringing the hour across the slow afternoon.

Others came then: Colonel Sansing and Perry, Bushrod Carter, Jack Bishop, Cragin Knox, good Captain Byron Sullivan, all crowded into the little room. Lucian heard their voices from far away, and he took comfort in them. He thought how, when Sally Mae came, he would have a long dream to tell her. The laudanum warmed him. It was time to sleep. He would sleep a little while, and they would be there, all the time, and when he woke, they would be there still.

❖ 16 ❖

ALISON SANSING SETTLED HER AFFAIRS IN CUMBER-
land. Then she waited, and early in February the pain
arrived. She knew a good deal of it, and for a week or
more Cass Wakefield could not bear to enter the room where
she lay. Finally, Alison gave it up. She sent Morgan Harper to
the attic for the Black Draught and drank a cupful and fell
asleep. Only then did Cass come to sit with her. The Death Angel followed close behind, and on St. Valentine's eve, he took
her at last. So deep in dreams was she, and so quiet and peaceful her passing, that the watchers never noticed when she
crossed.

Cass knew she was sick on the journey, but he had supposed

it was the journey itself that troubled her—that long traveling into a past she could never understand. He only learned how sick she really was on the day after Lucian died, when they were sitting on the hotel gallery after dinner. Lucian was at the undertaker's; Roger was upstairs, his head swathed in bandages, full of morphine and sleeping like the dead. Alison sat in a rocking chair, wrapped in a shawl. Cass was trifling drunk and pacing, pacing, over the hollow boards of the gallery.

I will rent a hack, said Cass. *We'll go out to McGavock's, and you can see them, where they're buried.*

She was rocking slowly, the boards creaking under her. She smiled a little and said, *No, Cass, I won't have you go out there. You have seen sufficient old places for one trip.*

I don't mind it, said Cass. *It might ease your mind. Did I ever tell you how I made Lucian wait on the porch? Only he wouldn't—he just had to follow—*

Cass choked up, unable to speak, and Alison looked at him, her eyes liquid and soft. She reached and took his hand. *You told me that,* she said. *My mind is eased. I am satisfied, and anyhow, I'll see 'em soon enough, and Lucian, too.*

Cass knelt beside her. *That's a good while yet,* he said.

No, Cass, she said. Then she told him of all that Doctor Craddock said, and Cass had the truth at last. Later, when Alison fell asleep in her chair, Cass left the gallery and carried her truth out into the sunlight, took it with him on an aimless wandering through the quiet streets, down into Freedman's town, where he sat on a bench under an oak tree. A yellow dog with drooping ears and a sad face came and lay beside him, and Cass talked with him awhile. Finally, he rose and went back to the hotel, for he did not want Alison to wake alone.

The police made inquiries, but none that Cass could not lie his way out of. The law seemed ready to accept his tale of an accidental shooting, an overturned lamp, a tragic fire from which old Ambrose, in his perversity, refused to be saved. No one mentioned that the burned corpse had a .38 round in him. Alison said little to the police, speaking only when they addressed her directly, which they did deferentially, with exaggerated courtesy. They never questioned Roger at all, who remained hors de combat in his room. The next day, they were on a southbound train with Lucian's casket in the baggage car. Alison slept most of the trip, and while she slept, Roger and Cass took turns riding with Lucian. They would not go together. One of them needed to be there should Alison awake.

Now Alison was in a long sleep from which there would be no waking. For the first time in many years, Colonel Sansing's old house was filled with people. The women washed and dressed her body, and the coffin was brought, and the women allowed Cass and Roger to lay her in it. Then, in due season, the casket was taken away to the church, the mourners walking behind the plumed hearse with its plumed and black-clad horses. Cass stood on the porch and watched until Alison and all who loved her were vanished into the short winter twilight. He could not follow yet. Not yet. Cass knew that the house still held her, that some part of her lingered in the darkening rooms, reluctant to pass. It would never pass, of course, but neither would it be as strong as it was now.

Cass walked down the porch, his steps ringing hollow on the paintless boards. He leaned on the balustrade and looked down at the rusty azaleas in their leaf-choked bed. Among them, a single Cape Jessamine bush was green still. No birds sang, but somewhere a cricket, sleepy in the cold, made a thin, monotonous chirping.

The parlor was cold when Cass entered, the fire dying on the hearth. The room smelled of snuffed candles, and the branches outside made thin shadows on the windowpanes. Cass opened the piano and touched a single key; the note hung in the cold air like the blade of a wind chime turning, and as it faded, Cass believed he heard voices just discernible—no words he could tell, but voices still, such as murmured sometimes on the edge of sleep. In that moment, Cass was sure that sorrow would defeat him, that there could be no rising from the place where he had gone. Then, all at once, the falling sun drove a spear of pale light through a grimed window. One fragment pierced the crystal pendant of a candlestick and broke in colored ribbons across the floor, but the balance spread in a pool of momentary gold over Alison's desk, as though a lamp had been lighted there. Cass knew then that the voices would be there always; that they came from the room itself, from the furniture, the faded curtains, the dark wood and plaster walls that spoke of all the hours they had seen unfold—not beginnings or endings, but time in passage, the quiet unreeling of one unremarkable moment to the next that made up the sum of life. Cass listened and watched until the light was gone and the room was occupied by darkness and the voices ceased. Only then did he leave, down the quiet street under the quiet winter trees, already too late for the funeral.

✛

Time passed along, carrying them all together down the stream. March brought the martin scouts and filled the yards with yellow daffodils, and daffodils marked old buried walks on the sites of houses the yankees had burned long ago. Good, slow rains fell for days at a time, promising tall cotton and corn. In the last week of April, Leaf River stepped out of its muddy banks and walked over the land just to prove that it could. A few days later, the chimney swifts arrived in their myriads. One day they were nowhere to be seen; the next, the evening sky was filled with their darting and chattering, and that night the Flower Moon rose full and red.

Other signs arrived in season: the blue iris, poke salad, swarms of lightning bugs all at once twinkling under the trees. Morning glories twined on porches and opened their bells to the sun, and the cow-itch vine lifted its red trumpets. The leaves settled to a deeper green; the grass grew rank in the ditches. Finally the cicadas began their drowsy afternoon chirring, and with that, high summertime lay upon the land.

On a morning in early September, Queenolia Divine came in to light the stove in the Citadel of Djibouti. She fussed around in the kitchen for a good long while, putting things right, muttering to herself of the many injustices laid upon her in the course of her days. Finally, when everything was right and a fresh gob of lard was laid in the big frying pan, Queenolia smoothed her apron and passed through the greasy curtain. The tavern was gloomy dark, as it always was, and she took a moment to let her eyes adjust to the dim light. Shapes began to emerge: tables, scattered chairs, a hat rack, the forlorn mounted head of a deer. L. W. Thomas was sitting in a corner, feet propped on a table, his mandolin in his lap. Queenolia spoke, and when she got no answer, she crept near. His eyes were open and fixed on the spot over the bar where once, in the

first Citadel before the fire took it, hung the mysterious portrait of a reclining woman. Queenolia stood quietly for a while,
remembering, then closed L.W.'s eyes and crossed his hands
over the mandolin and went to fetch Doctor Craddock. In a little while, when the body had been borne away, Queenolia
swept the tavern clean and stopped the clock and turned the
grimy bar mirror to the wall. She stood a long time in the
smoky light, listening, then went back to her cabin and got in
bed and never left it until the time came to carry her to the
grave.

Cass Wakefield sat with her as the twilight closed down.
Toward the end, she rallied and wanted to tell Cass once again
of how she had saved him. The telling occupied the last hour of
her long life, and was mixed in with other tales, and many a
ghost rose in her voice and walked through the room, and
those who had come for the vigil—a goodly number—could
see them plain, as if the old times had come again. When her
voice failed at last, Cass took her hand. *Do you hear the angels?*
he said, and she nodded. The tears ran down her face, but no
one wiped them away, for they all knew her tears were not from
sorrow. She petted and stroked Cass's hand for a little while
yet, but her eyes were looking past him at the window. When
the September moon rose, lifting its lantern behind the trees,
she seemed to be satisfied, and her eyes closed, and her soul
went off into the moonlight, dancing like a girl.

She was buried in the colored section of Holy Cross Cemetery, among wooden markers and markers hand-carved of sand-
stone, the names slowly leaching away, and graves decorated
with bits of colored glass. The air that day was hot and full of
dust and almost palpable, and the voice of the black minister

rose against the hypnotic cicadas' chant that L. W. Thomas always said was the finest sound in the world.

Cass and Roger watched the funeral from the shade of an oak tree on the hill. When it was done, when the people had dropped their handfuls of earth into the grave and departed, the two men walked back through the cemetery together and sat on an iron bench in the dusk. The day, like the mourners, departed slowly, reluctantly, for even in September the light was master and would have no sudden falling toward the dark. In that season, the day released its hold little by little, sometimes painting with yellow twilight; sometimes, like today, merely softening, but holding on long after the sun had passed below the trees and western ridges.

The cemetery plot before them was ringed with cedars that were already gathering evening. The grass would hardly grow beneath them, but a thick crop of sweet william and four-o'clocks—yellow and tired, but still blooming—flourished around the fence where the sun could reach. The fence itself was twined with iron vines and berries and surrounded a pedestal crowned by a weeping angel. Close beside was another stone, the kind that the government provided for its former enemies, an upright stone, dignified in its simplicity:

Lucian Wakefield

Pvt Co C

21 Regt Miss Inf

Once they were settled on the bench, Cass and Roger lit cigars to keep the mosquitoes off and talked awhile. Cass told once more of how Queenolia had birthed him, then kept him from being thrown out with the bedclothes. He remembered the Citadel and things that had happened there, then went on to tell other stories Roger already knew, but Cass told them anyhow, and Roger listened, for by such means do men anchor themselves in the stream of time. Surely this was the best time of day for stories, and the best season, in a fragile, melancholy twilight as the world tilted toward autumn and night. At such a time, everything seemed to pause, and the old hours rose like fireflies or the smoke from chimneys, or like shades whispering to be heard.

A thunderstorm was growling to westward, coming fast, pushing a wind before it. The stone angel's face glowed pink in the failing light. After a moment, Roger pointed his cane at Lucian's marker and said, "We were not in Company C."

"You have mentioned that before," said Cass. "Several times."

"Yes," said Roger. After a moment, he said, "If she hadn't asked, would you have put him beside her?"

Cass shrugged. "I guess I wouldn't have known to. I guess I'd have put him over there with Janie and Mama."

"No," said Roger. "No, you wouldn't have. You'd have put him with Alison anyhow."

Cass spat between his feet. "Well, if you already knew that, what did you ask *me* for?"

"Just making conversation," said Roger. He leaned forward and tapped his cane on the hard, dry ground. "I don't remember much of what happened up at that house. Have I mentioned that?"

"No," said Cass. He watched his comrade's face. On this subject they had hardly talked at all, each assuming, as men will do, that the other would speak in his own good time—or never, if that suited him. Cass said, "It's no wonder you were knocked in the head pretty bad."

"Not so bad," said Roger. "You know, I followed you all because—well, I guess I was mad at being left out. If I hadn't come . . ."

"It's no use thinking like that," said Cass. "Anyhow, I'd of done the same. So would Lucian."

"I know," said Roger. "I remember we shot a man, then we burned his house down and got away with it."

"Are you sorry we did?"

"Which one?" asked Roger.

"All of them," said Cass.

"No," said Roger, "not in the least. Only—" He thought a moment, moving his cane back and forth in the dry grass. "Only that's the trouble. It was all so easy. That seems a thing one ought to forget how to do, or even want to do."

An image drifted through Cass's mind: Roger Lewellyn clawing his way through the ditch at the cotton gin. A leaf turned, and there was Roger again, bayoneting the dead at Shiloh. Cass said, "I guess some things you learn, you're not allowed to forget."

Roger laughed. "All I ever wanted to do was play the piano."

"I know," said Cass.

The sun was gone now, save for a single bright ray lancing through the clouds, and the air was cooler and smelled of rain. Roger stood up and pointed once more at the graves. "You did the right thing, Cass. They are in good company."

"The best company," said Cass.

The two men were quiet for a moment, then Roger looked

to the west and said, "Storm coming. I should go home and see what the cook has for supper." He turned to Cass. "You come with me. Sally Mae would like that; she would know you this time."

"That is a kindness," said Cass. He rose and looked away across the hills. "I'll come another day, I promise."

"No, you won't," said Roger, smiling.

"Ah, well," said Cass. "Love to my good cousin."

The two men shook hands, and Roger Lewellyn walked away in his old green swallowtail coat and plug hat, swinging his cane. He passed through the gate and into the Pontotoc Road, and there the light seemed to absorb him, and in a moment he was gone.

Cass thought how all the roads the armies had traveled must have their visions in this hour of remembering, and perhaps a watchful rider might sense them: quick shadows, figures glimpsed but not really seen, cold patches over bridges, voices heard amid the chatter of birds or under the noise of moving water. A great moth might flutter past the rider's face, come out of the brooding trees and gone again, that quick, and the rider's horse might well grow restless, and he would spur her on toward village or town or cabin and leave the road to the coming night. He would not see then—nor was he meant to see—the lean, gaunted figures striving in the dust under their slanted rifles and cased colors, their long stride bearing each to his own meeting with the Angel of Death in some field or wood beyond. The rider, safe now in a place where lamps would soon be lit, would not see them, but he would know—as he was meant to know—that he had passed through their phantom columns, and later in sleep he would dream, perhaps, of a circle of fires under the black kettle of the sky.

Cass walked slowly down the hill and up another, and in time he came to the Wakefield plot with its own iron fence and planting of cedar trees. Cass's mother had an old-fashioned rounded stone carved with a weeping willow. Janie's stone was in the current ornate style, with a descending dove. Cass had a colored man keep the weeds cut and the periwinkle trimmed in summer, and he painted the fence himself every other fall. He never cleaned the stones, however. It seemed right to let the moss and lichen grow, while the cedars and the rain darkened the stones with the soft patina of time. Often Cass wished that Spanish moss, with its dignity and air of sorrow, grew this far north.

Cass rested his elbows between the iron spikes. Lightning flickered against the darkening sky, and the cedar tops began to rustle in the wind. Inside the fence, a little tabby cat perched on Janie's stone, eyeing a mole she had rooted out, which now squirmed blindly in the brittle grass. As Cass watched, the cat pounced on the mole and batted it into the periwinkle. She crouched, waving her tail, and pounced again, disappearing into the cover. After some rustling of shrubbery, she emerged with the mole in her jaws, dropped it, batted it out of sight again. Cass threw a pine cone and whacked the cat on the head. The cat glared at him, then lifted her tail and stalked off in such a high dudgeon that Cass had to laugh.

The fence was all laden of honeysuckle in late bloom. Cass plucked a blossom, drew out its stem, and sucked the sweet nectar. He did not blame the tabby for wanting to kill the mole; that was only her way. In spite of all he had seen, Cass still believed in the fundamental decency of cats and men. He knew that God believed in it, too, in spite of all *He'd* seen—in spite of all His grieving and all the lies told about Him down the bloody ages. He was God after all, and had made all creatures, and He had taken the noble chance of granting to one of them a will of its own, and in the end, the gift had been worth all the trouble. Maybe the right to choose was the best gift of all and the best proof of love. It was more precious even than life itself, for without the possibility of defeat, the victories would have no meaning.

The cemetery was aglimmer with fireflies, and as he watched them, Cass thought about something Bushrod Carter told once after the Stones River battle: how he had seen the souls of the slain rise like blackbirds toward heaven. Cass had held fast to that image ever since, but now he thought he might let it rest. If Bushrod had lived, if he had come home, if he were standing here now, perhaps he would agree that souls, at the end of day, rose more like fireflies, their lights burning for a little while longer over the tired earth.

Cass flipped up the collar of his frock coat and looked toward the Pontotoc Road. Then he turned southward across the hills, the long way home, while the first drops of rain fell around him and a whippoorwill called from the trees.

About the Author

HOWARD BAHR, a native of Mississippi, teaches English at Motlow State Community College, in Tullahoma, Tennessee. His first novel, *The Black Flower,* was a *New York Times Book Review* Notable Book and received the Harold D. Vursell Memorial Award from the American Academy of Arts and Letters. His second novel, *The Year of Jubilo,* was also a *New York Times* Notable Book. He lives in Fayetteville, Tennessee.